Praise for *Sell*

"An incredibly enjoyable book

"Canny hints for garage-sale su
mysteries for the intrepid heroi

"Harris has carved out a name for herself in the cozy mystery world with her engaging, humorous Sarah Winston mysteries."—*Washington Independent Review of Books*

Praise for *Let's Fake a Deal*

"Who knew organizing garage sales could be a dangerous occupation?"—*Kirkus Reviews*

"I just love Sherry Harris's Garage Sale series. It's provocative, well-written, and always entertaining."—*Suspense Magazine*

Praise for *The Gun Also Rises*

"A roller-coaster of a mystery penned by a real pro. This series just gets better and better. More, please!" —*Suspense Magazine*

"Author Sherry Harris never disappoints with her strong, witty writing voice and her ability to use the surprise effect just when you think you have it all figured out!"—*Chatting About Cozies*

"This series gets better with every book, and *The Gun Also Rises* continues the trend. If you haven't started this series yet, do yourself a favor and buy the first one today."—*Carstairs Considers*

Praise for *I Know What You Bid Last Summer*

"*I Know What You Bid Last Summer* is cleverly plotted, with an engaging cast of characters and a clever premise that made me think twice about my shopping habits. Check it out."—*Suspense Magazine*

"Never one to give up, Sarah continues her hunt for the killer in some unlikely and possibly dangerous places. Fans of Harris will appreciate both the clever mystery and the tips for buying and selling at garage sales."—*Kirkus Reviews*

"Each time a new Sarah Winston Garage Sale Mystery releases, I wonder how amazing author Sherry Harris will top the previous book she wrote for the series. I'm never disappointed, and my hat's off to Ms. Harris, who consistently raises the bar for her readers' entertainment."—*Chatting About Cozies*

Praise for *A Good Day to Buy*

"Sarah's life keeps throwing her new curves as the appearance of her estranged brother shakes up her world. This fast-moving mystery starts off with a bang and keeps the twists and turns coming. Sarah is a likable protagonist who sometimes makes bad decisions based on good intentions. This ups the action and drama as she tries to extricate herself from dangerous situations with some amusing results. Toss in a unique cast of secondary characters, an intriguing mystery, and a hot ex-husband, and you'll find there's never a dull moment in Sarah's bargain-hunting world."—*RT Book Reviews*, 4 Stars

"Harris's fourth is a slam dunk for those who love antiques and garage sales. The knotty mystery has an interesting premise and some surprising twists and turns as well."—*Kirkus Reviews*

"The mystery of the murder in *A Good Day to Buy,* the serious story behind Luke's reappearance, the funny scenes that lighten the drama, the wonderful cast of characters, and Sarah's always superb internal dialogue will keep you turning the pages and have you coming back for book #5."—*Nightstand Book Reviews*

Praise for *All Murders Final!*

"There's a lot going on in this charming mystery, and it all works. The dialogue flows effortlessly, and the plot is filled with numerous twists and turns. Sarah is a resourceful and appealing protagonist, supported by a cast of quirky friends. Well written and executed, this is a definite winner. Bargain-hunting has never been so much fun!"
—*RT Book Reviews,* 4 Stars

"A must-read cozy mystery! Don't wear your socks when you read this story 'cause it's gonna knock 'em off!"—*Chatting About Cozies*

"Just because Sherry Harris's protagonist Sarah Winston lives in a small town, it doesn't mean that her problems are small. . . . Harris fits the puzzle pieces together with a sure hand."—Sheila Connolly, Agatha- and Anthony-nominated author of the Orchard Mysteries

"A thrilling mystery. . . . Brilliantly written, each chapter drew me in deeper and deeper, my anticipation mounting with every turn of the page. By the time I reached the last page, all I could say was . . . wow!"—*Lisa Ks Book Reviews*

Praise for *The Longest Yard Sale*

"I love a complex plot and *The Longest Yard Sale* fills the bill with mysterious fires, a missing painting, thefts from a thrift shop and, of course, murder. Add an intriguing cast of victims, potential villains and sidekicks, an interesting setting, and two eligible men for the sleuth to choose between and you have a sure winner even before you get to the last page and find yourself laughing out loud."
—Kaitlyn Dunnett, author of *The Scottie Barked at Midnight*

"Readers will have a blast following Sarah Winston on her next adventure as she hunts for bargains and bad guys. Sherry Harris's latest is as delightful as the best garage sale find!"—Liz Mugavero, Agatha-nominated author of the Pawsitively Organic Mysteries

"Sherry Harris is a gifted storyteller, with plenty of twists and adventures for her smart and stubborn protagonist."—Beth Kanell, Kingdom Books

"Once again Sherry Harris entwines small-town life with that of the nearby Air Force base, yard sales with romance, art theft with murder. The story is a bargain, and a priceless one!"—Edith Maxwell, Agatha-nominated author of the Local Foods mystery series

Praise for *Tagged for Death*

"*Tagged for Death* is skillfully rendered, with expert characterization and depiction of military life. Best of all Sarah is the type of intelligent, resourceful, and appealing person we would all like to get to know better!"— *Mystery Scene Magazine*

"Full of garage-sale tips, this amusing cozy debut introduces an unusual protagonist who has overcome some recent tribulations and become stronger."—*Library Journal*

"A terrific find! Engaging and entertaining, this clever cozy is a treasure—charmingly crafted and full of surprises."— Hank Phillippi Ryan, Agatha-, Anthony- and Mary Higgins Clark–award-winning author

"Like the treasures Sarah Winston finds at the garage sales she loves, this book is a gem."—Barbara Ross, Agatha-nominated author of the Maine Clambake Mysteries

"It was masterfully done. *Tagged for Death* is a winning debut that will have you turning pages until you reach the final one. I'm already looking forward to Sarah's next bargain with death."—Mark Baker, *Carstairs Considers*

Mysteries by Sherry Harris

The Chloe Winston Sea Glass Saloon Mysteries

FROM BEER TO ETERNITY

A TIME TO SWILL (Available in 2021!)

The Sarah Winston Garage Sale Mysteries

ABSENCE OF ALICE

SELL LOW, SWEET HARRIET

LET'S FAKE A DEAL

THE GUN ALSO RISES

I KNOW WHAT YOU BID LAST SUMMER

A GOOD DAY TO BUY

ALL MURDERS FINAL!

THE LONGEST YARD SALE

and

Agatha-Nominated Best First Novel

TAGGED FOR DEATH

ABSENCE
OF ALICE

A Sarah Winston Garage Sale Mystery

Sherry Harris

KENSINGTON
PUBLISHING CORP.

www.kensingtonbooks.com

KENSINGTON BOOKS are published by

Kensington Publishing Corp.
119 West 40th Street
New York, NY 10018

All Kensington titles, imprints, and distributed lines are available at special quantity discounts for bulk purchases for sales promotion, premiums, fund-raising, educational, or institutional use.

Special book excerpts or customized printings can also be created to fit specific needs. For details, write or phone the office of the Kensington Sales Manager: Attn.: Sales Department. Kensington Publishing Corp., 119 West 40th Street, New York, NY 10018. Phone: 1-800-221-2647.

Kensington and the K logo Reg. U.S. Pat. & TM Off.

First Printing: January 2021
ISBN-13: 978-1-4967-2253-9
ISBN-10: 1-4967-2253-1

ISBN-13: 978-1-4967-2254-6 (eBook)
ISBN-10: 1-4967-2254-X (eBook)

10 9 8 7 6 5 4 3 2 1

Printed in the United States of America

To Bob
Thank you for your love, laughter
and for being my head cheerleader

Chapter One

Alice Krandle was breathing down my neck. Literally. I could feel her warm breath on it and smelled the spearmint gum she always chewed. Alice didn't have a good sense of personal boundaries and stood way too close as I looked at a painting she had of the Old North Bridge in Concord. This is why I loved my job as a garage sale organizer. It never got old working with new people and trying to jolly Alice out of her moods had been fun.

My friend Carol Carson was here to help me price the art. Carol owned the shop Paint and Wine and was a talented artist herself. The paintings were the last things that needed to be priced before the sale tomorrow.

"This painting is an oil, and it looks like it was painted using the alla prima or wet-on-wet technique," Carol said. "That allows the artist to finish a painting in as little as thirty minutes."

It was stunning with its vibrant fall colors.

"I paid five hundred dollars for that. Quite a steal," Alice said. Alice, though in her late seventies, stood straight as a flag pole. She had hair the color of a stainless steel appliance, and skin as wrinkled as a linen skirt.

"I'll be lucky to get two fifty for it at the garage sale," I said. More like one hundred, and even that was pushing it. I had to lower Alice's expectations. The painting was two feet by three feet. The artist was local and had a good reputation in New England. But still, this was a garage sale. I twisted the pink ruby ring on my right hand that I'd bought at an estate sale in January to celebrate my upcoming two-year business anniversary. I loved its gold filigree with tiny diamonds set in the swirls. I'd been proud to be able to buy it for myself. I gave it another twist. This whole sale, and Alice's expectations, was making me nervous.

"I'm sure that you can do better than that." She waved a hand around at the paintings in the room. "I know you said people don't collect things like they used to, but people still love art. This is perfect for a tourist or anyone who loves fall in New England."

She had a point. The sale was tomorrow, and this was two weekends before Patriots' Day—the annual celebration of the start of the Revolutionary War here in Massachusetts—so there were lots of tourists in the area for all of the different events.

I looked at Carol. She was tall, thin, and, could have been the model for artist Barbie. Today she wore a turtleneck sweater belted at her hips, faux leather leggings, and stacked-heeled boots. "Why don't you try three hundred," she suggested.

Because no one would pay that much? People went to garage sales for the bargains and to bargain—it was part of the game. Garage sale attendees carried cash around like they were Brink's guards.

"Make it three twenty-five," Alice said.

I did an inward sigh, but made the tag like Alice wanted. The frame was a nice quality walnut, and frames were expensive. They sometimes brought a good price even when what they held wasn't valuable. I'd keep my fingers crossed. Alice had already turned down a sizeable sum of money from my new competitor, Zoey Whittlesbee. Zoey had wanted to buy the whole lot from her and had offered her cash. *Cash!* Zoey had worked for me briefly over the winter, soaking up all the lessons I'd learned attending and organizing garage sales. I wondered why Zoey had offered Alice so much and where she had gotten the money to offer to pay such a sum. I'd been in business for two years, and now made enough to support myself, but not enough to throw around that kind of money.

Part of what puzzled me about the offer was that people don't collect things like they had in the past. Millennials didn't want old china sets or silver or Hummel or Lladró figurines like their parents did. God forbid if something didn't spark joy. Boomers who were downsizing complained *a lot* about the prices they were getting for their prized possessions. That made me circle back to my original thought. How the heck could Zoey, who had just started her Zoey's Tag Sales business three months ago, offer to pay Alice that much money with no guarantee of making it back?

Alice had explained when she hired me that if someone would offer that much for all of her things, individually they must be worth much more. Unfortunately, it didn't always work that way in the world of garage sales. I'd explained that to her and put it in writing when we signed the contract. Alice said she understood. I just hoped she really did. She might have more confidence in me than I did myself.

We moved on to the next painting. Thank heavens my assistant Harriet Ballou would be helping me the day of the sale. She was a former FBI hostage negotiator, and I'd seen her in action. One time she'd actually gotten more for a piece than the original asking price. And I'd seen her talk the price of a Tiffany bracelet down at the thrift shop until the woman had almost given it to her for free.

An hour and much discussion later, it was time for Carol and me to go. We'd finished pricing the last ten paintings. I'd never had a client hover over me while I priced. It was exhausting, and I was starving. Time to do something about both.

I pulled up to Paint and Wine, or Paint and Whine as I liked to call it, at two forty-five. I called it that because Carol listened to me complain about life when I needed to vent. We had known each other since I was eighteen and had both been military spouses. Our husbands had both been stationed at nearby Fitch Air Force Base. "How did you know the painting Alice had was done using the—what did you call it?—alla prima technique?" I'd read up on the artist, but didn't remember that bit about him.

"I've met the artist a couple of times at events."

"Alice thought you were a genius. So did I for that matter."

Carol laughed and opened her door. "I am one."

"Thanks for your help."

"Anytime. She has some nice pieces. It will be okay."

I nodded, but I wasn't as sure about that.

I picked the absolutely worst time to walk into Di-Napoli's Roast Beef and Pizza. I looked up from my phone just in time to see a stray round of pizza dough flying through the air. It landed on my head, draping like a doughy wedding veil.

"I'm sorry," a deep male voice said. Hint of a Boston accent.

Someone lifted the front of my pizza veil, and I gazed up at a man with deep brown eyes, a boyish charming face, and a look of horror. I blushed like a bride.

"I'm the one who's sorry." I'd ignored the Closed sign hanging on the front door because DiNapoli's was never closed to me. In my defense the door was unlocked. But I'd forgotten that Angelo had decided it wasn't enough for him to cook. He needed to share his talents with the world. Angelo had started giving cooking classes weekday afternoons. Apparently today was pizza dough 101.

Angelo and Rosalie, the owners of DiNapoli's and my "so close we were almost family" friends, rushed to my side, as did the other four attendees. All had caught their pizza dough and deposited the rounds on pizza pans before heading over. I could feel a bit of dough on my cheek. Charming guy held the dough off my face with one hand and reached over and swiped the bit off with the other hand, murmuring another apology. I blushed some more, wondering how I would ever get the dough out of my hair before my date with my boyfriend Seth tonight. Maybe the dough would just blend with my blond hair like chunky highlights.

Rosalie looked at me with her warm brown eyes crinkling in concern. "Are you okay?"

"Everything but my pride is fine." I glanced again at the newcomer, who was still holding the dough off my face.

"Maybe if we all take a side we can just lift the dough off her hair and it wouldn't stick as much," Angelo suggested.

Most of the people moved out of my line of vision, but I could feel them surrounding me.

"On the count of three," Angelo said. "One, two, three. Lift."

The pizza dough came off. Sort of. I patted my head and felt bits of dough. I looked at the charming guy. "Sorry to ruin your crust."

"It was like a UFO sailing across the room. Not your fault. I'm just sorry you had to be the landing pad."

"This is Emil Kowalski. My nephew," Rosalie said.

Now I saw the resemblance. The warm eyes, a smile similar to Rosalie's. But his hair was lighter brown than Rosalie's.

I stuck out a hand. "Hi. I'm Sarah Winston."

"Ah, I've heard a lot about you."

Oh, boy. With all the things that had happened in the past two years of my life, that might not be a good thing. I looked at Angelo. "Sorry to ruin your class."

"He should have locked the door," Rosalie said. "Anyone could have walked in. We were lucky it was you instead of some person who would sue us for damages."

Angelo shrugged. "Let's get back to our class, people."

Everyone went over to the stove behind the counter where customers placed their orders. That's when I noticed the nice aroma of tomatoes, basil, and garlic. I was hungry, which was why I'd come here in the first place. My home away from home.

"Emil's been working in Rome, Italy, for many years," Rosalie said.

That explained why I hadn't met him before. I needed a chart to keep track of all of the DiNapolis' relatives, as Rosalie and Angelo both had lots of siblings and thus lots of nephews and nieces.

"He's very accomplished. International business." She

leaned in a little closer. "He's only a year younger than you *and* single. Plus, he's learning to cook." Rosalie looked over at Angelo with his fringe of hair, nose slightly bigger than it should be, and the start of a paunch. "Nothing sexier than a man who can cook."

I glanced over at Emil just as he looked up and grinned. *Oh, boy*, I thought again. "Rosalie, you know I'm happy with Seth."

Rosalie put her hands out in a little shrug. "Things can change."

"But I hope they don't." Seth was amazing. He had served as interim district attorney after the prior DA had gotten ill and had to resign. Last fall, Seth had won his first election, so he could continue his work as the district attorney for Middlesex County. He was the youngest DA ever elected in our county.

Seth had also been named Massachusetts's Most Eligible Bachelor year after year, including this year, to my chagrin. I had hoped someone would realize he was taken. Off the market. Mine. I got why he kept getting named because who didn't love a smart and handsome man? But what most people didn't know was how he supported me in ways my ex-husband never had, never could.

"You're like family already," Rosalie said.

I pictured a wedding where I married Emil. Rosalie and Angelo smiling happily. The marriage. The inevitable divorce—guess I wasn't over my divorce yet. Rosalie and Angelo barring the doors of DiNapoli's to me when they sided with Emil. It had only been two years since my divorce—less, really, because CJ and my lives had intertwined after we'd split up, and we'd almost gotten back together last spring.

"Are you okay?" Rosalie asked. "You just smiled and then frowned."

"Just picturing the future." One that would never happen.

Rosalie patted my arm. "Let me get you some food."

Thank heavens she dropped the matchmaking routine.

Thirty minutes later my stomach was full of pepperoni stromboli. Rosalie wouldn't let me pay, insisting that it was their fault I now had dried pieces of pizza dough in my hair. I gave up arguing and thanked her before leaving.

I walked home, crossing Great Road, and up one side of the town common. It was a big rectangle of greening grass that proved spring was coming. The towering white Congregational church was at the south side of it, facing DiNapoli's and other businesses like Carol's shop. The sun was warm, and I would soon be celebrating the second anniversary of starting my garage sale business. I was throwing a huge garage sale of my own a week from tomorrow. I was pretty darn excited about it.

Back home in my second-story apartment I stood in front of the mirror using a fine-toothed comb to try to get all of the bits of dried dough out of my hair. They were hard to see in my blond hair, but I wanted to get as much as possible out before I showered. I pictured a cycle of wet and dry dough ruining my day. But once I shampooed and showered, things started to look up. An hour and a half later I fixed a cup of tea and went into my living room and sat down on the couch.

I loved my small apartment with its wide-planked floors that I'd painted white. I'd filled the room with treasures I'd found at garage sales—an old oriental rug, a flat-topped antique trunk I used as a coffee table, a down-filled couch that my mother had made slipcovers for, an end table that someone had made by hand, and of course my grand-mother's oak rocker. My phone rang. The number was unavailable. I hoped it wasn't a telemarketer.

"This is Sarah. How can I help you?" It's how I answered calls with numbers I didn't recognize or that were blocked just in case it was a new client.

"Sarah Winston?" a man said.

He sounded weirdly like the actor Jack Nicholson when he starred in *The Shining*. A scary movie I wished I'd never seen and could never quite get out of my head. The scene when Nicholson said, "Here's Johnny" stuck with me even when I didn't want it to. "That's me."

"I have Stella," he said.

Chapter Two

Stella Wild was my landlady and good friend. I took my phone away from my ear and looked at it like it would show who was on the other end. But all the screen showed was "unavailable" and the different options like mute, keypad, and speaker. Why would he, whoever he was, say something like that? Staring at my phone told me nothing, and I could hear a tinny voice still jabbering away.

"Are you there, Sarah?" he asked when I put my phone back to my ear.

"What do you mean you 'have' Stella?" Little prickles of alarm ran up the back of my neck. "I don't believe you."

"Sure you do. If you want to get Stella back alive, I have three rules. First rule: You can't go to the police, your friend Seth, or Mike 'the Big Cheese' Titone for help. If you do, I'll know. Don't even talk to the police." His voice changed to a sneer when he said, "your friend Seth."

"Who is this?" I was sure Jack Nicholson wouldn't be prank calling me. I couldn't imagine anyone would kidnap Stella. And even if they did, why call me? I didn't have ransom money. This had to be a terrible joke.

I looked out my front window to the Congregational

church on Ellington's town common. No answers there. I could understand how someone might know about my association with the police and with Seth. There were articles in the paper, online too, that anyone could dig up if they searched my name on the Internet. My friendship, if you wanted to call it that, with Mike was not as public. It made me wonder if someone had been watching me.

Mike had done me a favor or two or ten from time to time. He had mob connections, helped Seth out sometimes, and occasionally lived in the apartment next door to me, which he rented full-time from Stella. But Ellington was a small town; probably lots of people knew Mike came out here. He went out running. Any number of people could have seen him here. He had to buy groceries while he was here too. Secrets could be hard to keep in a town like Ellington.

"Rule number two: You have to go about your daily routine like nothing's happened. And act natural."

"Listen, I don't know who you are—"

"Oh, but you do, Sarah."

The words, the intonation, chilled me. The prickles of unease turned into straight-out alarm.

"Rule number three: You'll complete all the tasks I send you while following rules number one and two. And you have a week to do it if you ever want to see Stella again."

The call ended before I could say anything else. I dropped into my grandmother's wooden rocking chair and rubbed my hands over the soft, curved wood arms. Stella was on her way to Los Angeles to perform in *The Phantom of the Opera* for two weeks. This had to be a prank. Someone had a very sick sense of humor.

I dialed Stella's number. It was afternoon in LA, two p.m., and five here in Massachusetts. "Pick up, pick up, pick up," I muttered as I waited for a connection. I looked out the window again. April in Ellington went from winter to spring and back again. Today it was spring with lots of sunshine and little buds starting to peek out on the trees. Wait. Stella would still be on the plane. Her flight wouldn't land for another hour. There was no way she'd answer.

I heard the connection. "Stella?"

"Sarah, I didn't know we'd be talking again so soon."

It was the same male voice. My stomach rolled like I was in a plane with the worst turbulence ever. "Prove to me you have Stella."

"I'd be delighted to. I was a little surprised, and might I add disappointed, that you didn't ask me during our first call. You are usually more on your game than that."

This person thought this was a game? "Right." I kept my voice calm, somehow. "If you have her put her on the phone. I'll ask her a question that only she'd know the answer to." I wanted to add "you sicko" but managed not to.

"S-S-S-Sarah."

It was Stella, but her voice trembled so much that she hardly got my name out. "Stella. What's going on? Where are you?"

"I don't—"

"Ask her the question that will prove to you I have her or this call is over," the man said.

I wasn't sure I needed to ask. The terror in her voice was enough to convince me it was Stella and that something was horribly wrong. But just in case I went ahead. "What did you give me for Christmas last year?"

I heard a muffled sob. I put a fist to my heart and rubbed. "Vintage postcards."

"Of what?" I had to be sure. Probably lots of people knew I liked them.

"Monterey. One was dated 1932."

I'd grown up in Pacific Grove, the town next to Monterey, California. Stella had found and framed three vintage postcards of the area. They were hanging near the door of my apartment. I choked back a sob. "Stella—"

"Stella's tied up, dear. Pun intended. But I have a task for you. Go to 115 West Elm Street. I've left you a present. The door's unlocked. And remember the rules." The call disconnected.

Just after five thirty I pulled my old, white Suburban up to a pleasant-looking Cape-style house that was tucked away from its neighbors on a quiet cul-de-sac. Green roof. White siding. Lots of trees. Of course there would be. There was a For Sale sign stuck in the lawn. A chipper-looking real estate agent smiled at me from the sign. Dark-haired, pretty. Involved with whoever made the call? I didn't recognize her name. Why would she be behind this?

I'd debated whether to come or not. Part of me still hoped this was an elaborate joke. That I'd go into the house and Stella would leap out and say, "Gotcha." But it was hard to imagine that Stella intentionally would scare me. The less hopeful part of me had prepared a little before dashing over here. I had a small can of hairspray in the pocket of my jacket and had stuck a bottle of wine in my purse. They weren't much in the way of weapons. My plan was to use the spray and then whack whoever was here with my purse if I needed to.

I forced myself out of my Suburban and jogged up to

the front door. The door, with its lockbox, was ajar, but I knocked anyway. Waited. Knocked again. I cupped my hands to the sidelight beside the door. Peered in. The house was empty—not a bit of furniture and no art on the walls. Nice wood floors. No rugs. A staircase to the right and a living room to the left. A foot with a black Mary Jane shoe stuck out into the hall from what might be the dining room. I shoved the door open. Raced down the hall.

It was a woman dressed like Alice in Wonderland, complete with a blond wig, blue dress, starched white apron, and white tights. Alice in Wonderland was clearly dead. I closed my eyes for a couple of moments. Forced them open and looked at Alice again. There were no signs of trauma. Her hands were neatly folded across her chest. Her makeup was thick and garish, with bright circles of blush and heavy blue eye shadow. A cell phone lay to one side. It was obvious she'd been arranged.

It wasn't Stella. Thank heavens. But it was someone. I didn't recognize her, and I backed away, leaned against the wall for support. Buzzards filled my head. Wings flapping. *Focus*. The buzzards came back. I grabbed my phone to call the police and remembered the rules. No police.

To hell with that. I had to call the police about someone who was dead. I couldn't stay silent no matter the consequences. *Forgive me, Stella*. I dialed, reported, and hung up. I'd almost cried when the dispatcher had asked if I was in danger. I had said no even though I wasn't sure. I raced around the rest of the house looking for Stella. I didn't go in the creepy-looking basement. I'd seen that movie one too many times and I knew the police would search the house when they arrived.

When I returned to Alice in Wonderland I snapped a picture of her, because the more I looked at her the more she seemed a bit familiar. I wanted the picture to study later when I was calmer. The cell phone placed near her started ringing. It looked like Stella's phone with its *The Phantom of the Opera* case. My phone buzzed with a text message.

Pick up, Sarah. The passcode is 222212.

I grabbed the phone even though it was evidence. "What?"

"You broke my rules."

How could he know already? I hadn't even heard sirens yet. Was a dispatcher doing this? Maybe not. Lots of people had police scanner apps. It could be anyone monitoring them.

"Like with any game, when you break a rule, there are consequences. This is a major penalty. I dock you twelve hours. You now have six days and twelve hours to find Stella. To save Stella."

I choked back what I wanted to say. Made a muffled sound instead.

The caller laughed. "This is hard, isn't it, Sarah? But then, you make life hard. Keep the phone. Don't tell the police you have it. You'll use the phone to convince Stella's friends she's okay out in Los Angeles. Just busy preparing for the play. Especially Awesome. He'll be the tricky one."

Awesome. My nickname for Nathan Bossum. Stella's fiancé who was a cop.

"Good luck, Sarah."

"Who is she?" I asked, sickened to think she might be dead because of me. No. Not because of me. Because of him.

"How can you not know?"

I looked at the body again. I didn't know her.

"It's Alice in Wonderland, silly."

Chapter Three

Awesome stood beside me looking down at Alice in Wonderland. Of course it was Awesome. Did the sicko who was doing this know that Awesome would be on duty when he'd arranged this? Or was it just serendipity? If you could call it that. A slew of technicians and police milled around the scene. Awesome had tried to pull me away from Alice in Wonderland, but I'd refused to move, using the edge of hysteria coursing through me to my advantage.

I hadn't answered any of his many questions. How could I? And a debate in my head kept going round and round. Tell him about the call. The rules. Telling him might mean Stella ended up dead. But keeping the secret might mean she ended up dead too. Which was worse? Which was right? Maybe if I figured out who Alice in Wonderland was or why the victim was dressed like that, it would give me a clue as to who had Stella. The kidnapper thought this was a game. Maybe I should play along like it was one.

I studied Alice in Wonderland again, trying to commit every detail to memory even though I'd snapped the picture earlier. The blond wig was slightly askew, and brown hair peaked out underneath. Her eyes were closed. Cheeks and lips heavily rouged against the death pallor. The Alice in Wonderland costume looked expensive, not like some cheap rip-off available anywhere. Maybe that would be a lead. Her nails were painted a bright red. No jewelry. White tights. Black Mary Janes, brand new with no dirt or wear on them. She could be anywhere from twenty to fifty. It was hard to tell.

I turned abruptly and headed out of the house, breathing in the fresh spring air. Shadows were growing longer as the sun traveled west. Not only the actual shadows, but also the ones around my heart. Awesome had followed and stood beside me, tall, lean. He looked like someone you wouldn't want to meet on a lonely street at midnight. His hair was almost military short. Skin slightly tanned from a trip to Florida he'd taken recently with Stella.

"Do you know her?" he asked.

I shook my head. "No. At least I don't think I do."

"What's that supposed to mean?"

"Give me a break," I snapped. "She's heavily made up. In a costume. Dead." My voice shook. As did the rest of me. The air had cooled significantly since I'd arrived.

"Let's go sit in my car." Awesome gestured to a police car at the curb.

"No. The fresh air feels good." It was a lie. But I couldn't be in the intimacy of the police car with him face-to-face, just the two of us. Not until I knew for sure what to do. And how the caller knew I'd contacted the police. That I had connections with the police, Seth, and Mike.

Awesome put his hands up. "Okay."

"I'm sorry. It's disturbing." If only he knew. "Where's Pellner?"

Scott Pellner was another police officer here in Ellington. We'd met when my ex-husband was the town police chief. After a rocky start and some shared secrets, we'd come to trust each other. I'd rather talk to Pellner or anyone else. A state police car pulled into the cul-de-sac. Dreams do come true. Only three towns in Massachusetts had their own homicide divisions—Boston, Worcester, and Lowell. All the rest depended on the state police to run murder investigations alongside the local police.

Lying to someone I didn't know would be much easier than lying to Awesome. We watched as a man and a woman climbed out of the car, slammed their doors, and approached us.

Awesome sighed. "Rodriquez is a jerk."

Awesome had been a homicide detective in New York City. He could easily run the investigation himself. He'd left the NYPD for what he thought would be a less stressful job here in Ellington just over a year ago. That led to another thought. Where was Seth? As DA he usually came to crime scenes. A gray sedan pulled into the cul-de-sac, but it was two assistant DAs not Seth. Little strands of worry plucked at my heart. The cul-de-sac was now full of cars and vans. Lights from a couple of the police cars flashed blue round and round, painting the house blue then white, blue then white. Just like Alice's dress. I really had gone down a rabbit hole this time.

Chapter Four

"How did you happen to be here?" Trooper Leslie Kilgard asked.

Awesome was wrong. He might think Rodriquez was a jerk, but my money was on Trooper Kilgard. Even though up to this point all the questions had been routine, she'd just hit the one I was most afraid of. The one I'd been grappling with since I'd called 911.

I couldn't say a client wanted to meet with me and that I'd gotten the address wrong because they would want either a record of my phone calls or texts to prove it. Or heaven forbid, to talk to the client. I couldn't have someone poking around in my phone with Stella kidnapped. *No cops.* But Trooper Kilgard had a way of making every question sound like an accusation, starting with when she'd asked for my name and address a couple of minutes ago.

Her black hair was pulled back in such a tight bun that it made my scalp tingle just looking at it. Her features were delicate. Her shoulders broad. Her skin light brown to my pale peach. While my eyes were deep blue and often called warm, her eyes chilled me. Brown. Boring into me, yet reflecting nothing back. She'd make a good psychopath. I shrugged. Maybe she was one. Just because you were in law enforcement didn't mean you couldn't be a psychopath too.

"Ma'am? Why were you here?" Rodriquez with his clear brown eyes, his firm jaw, and his crew cut was more comforting. If he wasn't prior military, he looked like he was, and that was a world I understood.

"Sorry. I've been thinking of buying a house." It was the best I could do. I glanced at Awesome. His eyebrows lifted slightly. A sure sign of surprise in his otherwise serious face. It wasn't a total lie. I'd like to buy a house. I just couldn't afford one in this area. And I didn't want to leave the town common, DiNapoli's, or Stella. *Stella!* "I was driving around checking out possibilities. I stopped to pick up a flyer and noticed the door was ajar." That sounded good. If only my voice weren't shaky. I continued to hope everyone would think it was in reaction to finding Alice in Wonderland.

"I thought maybe the realtor was here, so I opened the door to call out and saw the shoe. Then the b-b-body." Reliving the fear that it had been Stella was horrible. Made even worse with Awesome standing next to me. I was sorry someone was dead, but relieved it wasn't Stella.

Everyone seemed to accept that explanation. I answered more questions, exchanged information, and was told I could leave. The troopers walked off, leaving me alone with Awesome again.

"How did they get into the house?" I asked Awesome.

"They might have picked the lock. There are no signs of forced entry."

"Or had the key. Who owns this house? How many

realtors know the code?" That was a long list of suspects someone would be following up on.

"We don't know yet. We're trying to track down the realtor."

Kind of surprising the realtor wasn't immediately available. The realtors I knew were always by their phones.

"Do you want me to drive you home, Sarah?" Awesome asked.

"No." It came out way more like a yelp than I wanted it to. "Thank you. I need my car."

"I could have someone drive it over."

I patted his arm. A little harder than I intended too. *Be careful, Sarah.* "You've got plenty to do here. This is more important." I couldn't believe I'd managed to sound somewhat calm because inside I was a shaky mess. Nothing since the phone call about Stella had gone right.

"No one's at your apartment building, are they? The Callahans aren't back from Florida. Stella's in LA, and Mike isn't living there, is he?"

Mike used the apartment from time to time when he needed to disappear from Boston for a few days. He was a bit of an enigma with one foot in the world of the mob and one foot trying to fight them. It seemed like he'd been out here more often of late. Stella—*Stella*—thought it was because he was interested in me, but Mike knew I was in a relationship with Seth. I'd actually been worried for Mike with all his appearances. Something was going on with him, and it probably wasn't good.

"No. Mike's not there. But Seth is coming over. He'll probably be there when I get home. Thank you though."

I turned and almost ran to my Suburban. I started it with a shaky hand. Flipped on the seat warmer to high. Looked back at Awesome who stood hands on hips looking at me. At least that was what it looked like he was doing in the darkening evening. I waved, hoping to reassure him, and snaked my way through all of the vehicles in the cul-de-sac.

The police had set up a barricade at the end of the cul-de-sac that they moved to let me out. I saw a dark-haired woman charging toward them who looked like the woman pictured on the For Sale sign. I slammed on my brakes and rolled down my window. "Excuse me. Are you the realtor who has the house listed back there?" I jerked my thumb toward the house.

She glanced at me, then at the police, and then focused back on me. "Yes. Do you know what's going on?"

I shook my head. I knew there was a dead woman in the house, but I certainly didn't know what was going on. "I was driving around looking at houses that are on the market when I came upon all of this. Is the house okay? Still available?"

"Yes. Of course."

"Do the Saffaros own it?" The Saffaros were my parents' next-door neighbors in California. I was just hoping if I said the wrong name, she'd provide the right one.

"No. It's the Ghannams' house. June and Yousef, but they've already moved to Arizona." She kept looking from me to the police. "Listen I've got to go find out what's going on. If you're interested in a house, here's my card."

I took her card, happy to have the name of the home-owners and her name as well. "Thanks." I watched her walk off. She didn't give me a backward glance as she hurried toward the police. I had found out two things during our brief conversation. The realtor didn't have any idea who I was. She gave no sign of recognizing me.

Didn't act nervous. I didn't think she had anything to do with Stella's kidnapping or what had happened to Alice in Wonderland. And I had the names of the owners. I'd look them up when I got home. Home. I was grateful to be heading home. To be heading to Seth.

My building was dark. Seth's car was nowhere to be seen. I'd hoped he would already be here. Sitting on the porch waiting for me so I could throw myself in his strong arms. The building, an old wood house with a wide, covered porch, had been converted into four apartments—two up and two down.

I ran up the steps, crossed the porch, entered, and flipped the foyer light on. Stella's apartment was to the right, and the absentee Callahans' on the left. I stood for a moment listening. For what I wasn't sure, but all the creaks and complaints the old house made sounded like footsteps and made me jumpy.

I locked the front door behind me. Something I rarely did. But as Awesome had pointed out, I was alone here. I checked the door to the basement. It was closed. I grabbed a chair from the foyer and wedged it under the door.

Before I headed upstairs I decided to search Stella's apartment. I had her keys, so I let myself in. It was too quiet with her and her cat Tux gone. Tux was with Stella's aunt. I'd volunteered to take care of him, but Stella was going to be gone for two weeks. She knew I was allergic to him and didn't want me to have a reaction.

I flipped on the overhead lights but left the door wide-open. Just in case her kidnapper was here waiting for me. Maybe this was a trap. I shook my head. I was losing it. Why would a kidnapper sit here just hoping I'd walk in at some point? Nevertheless, I scanned the living area, which was open to her kitchen unlike mine. I crossed the space, threw open the door to the bathroom, empty, the linen closet, no one hiding in there, and finally her bedroom.

It looked as it always did, only a bit neater. A closed purple suitcase sat on top of the bed. I lifted it. Heavy, probably packed with the clothes Stella was supposed to take with her. Looking at it finally made all that had happened in the last few hours hit home. It also made me realize I not only had to keep Awesome thinking everything was okay, but the director in Los Angeles would wonder what happened when Stella didn't show up. What could I say that would buy her a few days? I finally ended up texting that Stella had the flu and had rescheduled her flight for a few days from now. I hoped it bought her the leeway she needed.

After I hit send I resumed my search. I flung open the closet, only clothes and shoes, and looked under the bed, no dust bunnies or monsters. I sat on her bed next to her suitcase for a moment before I opened it, afraid of what I'd find. I unzipped the zippers slowly. Threw back the top and stared down.

Clothes. Neatly packed. I dug through the suitcase on the off chance some clue would be in here. Shoes, cosmetics, a blow dryer. Nothing unusual. I closed it, zipped it back up, and stuck it in the closet. Just in case Awesome stopped by for some reason. Nothing would say "something is horribly wrong" like finding Stella's packed suitcase out on her bed.

Then I started yanking open drawers and going through them. No journal. No threatening letters. No indication that she wasn't where she was supposed to be. It made sense. If someone had threatened her, she would have told Awesome. Unless she had some reason not to.

I continued searching the apartment, but found nothing that made me think "aha." It was disappointing, maddening. How was I going to figure this out? After locking back up, I dragged myself up the stairs to my apartment. There I turned on every light. I flopped into my grandmother's rocking chair and took out the two phones I now had. No messages or calls on either of them for me.

But Awesome had sent a text to Stella. **Miss you already, babe.** I scrolled through their past messages. That was a surprise. Stella wrote words out instead of using text shorthand like "u" or "i." For a moment I pondered not following Stella's normal style as a hint to Awesome. But if I did that it might put Stella in more jeopardy. I typed out an answer. **Miss you too. Checking in to my room. Later.**

I stared down at Stella's phone. Went through the settings. I turned off all the location tracking ones. Next, I took out my own phone and did the same. Then I called Seth. He didn't pick up and prickles of nerves shook me. I dialed again. This time he answered. Relief. "Where are you?" I asked.

"I'm not going to make it tonight." His normally strong voice sounded hesitant. "I'm sorry. I'm tied up." The call disconnected.

Chapter Five

I stared down at my phone. That wasn't like Seth. Even when he was busy, he'd take a few minutes to talk. To tell me he loved me. I had no doubt he knew by now that I'd found a body. Another one. He would have been contacted right away. First, he didn't show up at the crime scene. Now he didn't ask me about it. Or even ask how I was. Seth was a mover of mountains when I was in trouble. Me finding a body was trouble. *Tied up*. Had he ever said that to me before when he was in a meeting? Never. *Oh, no*.

Before I realized what I was doing, I was speeding down Great Road, east to Bedford where Seth lived. I had to make sure whoever had Stella didn't have Seth too. I could barely breathe. I cranked a left into the neighborhood of small Cape-style houses where Seth lived. A native of this area would say they banged a left. I sped down the block. The house was dark as I parked across the street and down one house.

I managed to ease out of the car. Close the door quietly. I crept up his driveway, took my key out, got it in the door on the first try, and unlocked it. The first floor was dark, but light spilled into the hall from the open basement door.

I barreled toward it. A man—huge, bald, angry-looking—stepped into the hall from the living room. I whacked him in the stomach with my purse. He doubled over and dropped to his knees. I paused, astounded, and then remembered the wine bottle I'd shoved in there earlier.

I skirted around him. Shouted for Seth. Almost flung myself down the stairs. Another huge, thick-haired man started up. I swung my purse again. Caught his ear, and he stumbled back. I flew down the last few steps. Turned to the right. Seth stood there. Not tied up. The Red Sox game was on. Pizza boxes were scattered on the coffee table. I hurled myself into Seth's arms. He grasped me to him. I realized he was shaking a little.

Footsteps thundered down the stairs. I turned in Seth's arms. Kept him behind me. The man who I'd whacked in the stomach burst into the room. A gun out. *A gun.* The other man joined him with a gun of his own.

"It's okay," Seth said. "This is Sarah."

The men hesitated, then holstered their guns.

"Just give us a moment," Seth said.

They looked at each other, and some message passed between them. They left the room. One holding his stomach, the other his ear.

I turned back to Seth. He wore a soft gray, long-sleeved Henley shirt that hugged his broad shoulders. Even in a casual shirt and jeans he looked knee-weakening handsome. The first time I'd laid eyes on him had been in a bar in Lowell, a town thirty minutes north of here, over two years ago. He was meant to be my fling after my divorce. A one-night stand. But he'd called and persisted, and here we were.

"You aren't tied up." The buzzards were back in my head. Flapping ferociously, darkening my vision. I brushed by him, sat on the couch, and put my head between my knees. I wanted to throw up, but not in front of Seth. He sat next to me and rubbed my back. I wanted to think that he'd blown me off for pizza and the game with the guys. But first, he'd never do that to me, especially knowing I'd just found a murder victim, and second, by now I knew a lot of his friends. These two weren't friends, and then of course there were their guns.

Seth must be in some kind of danger. I lifted my head, grabbed Seth's face, and kissed him. I pulled back, took in his mussed wavy dark hair and dark brown eyes. "I love you."

"I love you. I'm sorry I scared you." He leaned his forehead against mine. "You stood in front of me with two men pointing guns at you."

The thought of that combined with whacking them both had me dropping my head back between my legs. "What is going on?" I sat back up.

Seth hesitated. Glanced at the stairs. "I wasn't going to tell you. Wasn't supposed to tell anyone."

Seth and I had always had a hands-off policy. We didn't boss each other around. Didn't give each other honey-do lists. Seth was exceedingly patient with the situations I'd found myself in since we'd met. It was why I loved him. He didn't want to change me. He respected me and the decisions I made. My ex hadn't always done that.

"You have to tell me." Ironic that I was demanding he tell me what was going on when I wasn't going to tell him a thing about Stella.

"Someone tried to kidnap me this morning."

I clapped a hand to my mouth. "What? When? Where?"

"Six thirty. You know how I always stop at the Dunkin' Donuts in Bedford before I go to work." He looked down at his hands for a moment. "Stupid of me to always keep the same routine."

I took his hands. His warm, mine freezing.

"I came out. A black panel van was parked next to me. The door slid open, and this masked figure tried to get me into it. I fought and broke free. The van went tearing off."

Tears dripped down on our hands. Seth released mine and gently wiped my cheeks. "It's okay. I'm here."

Stella had scheduled a ride share to pick her up at eight this morning to take her to the airport. If only she'd have let me take her like I'd offered to. Maybe she'd be safe. But the kidnapper had had plenty of time to get to her if kidnapping Seth didn't work out. Maybe the ride share was another lead I could track down. Someone was obviously very, very upset with me. Why?

"How are you going to stay safe?" I asked. Just because the sicko didn't succeed the first time didn't mean he wouldn't try again.

"I have the guards. I'll lay low."

"If I can get by those guards, anyone can."

Seth smiled. "You were a force." Then he frowned. "What caused you to rush over here like that?"

"Something in your voice. How abrupt you were." I shook my head. "It wasn't like you, and it scared me."

"I'm sorry. Those two"—Seth pointed to the ceiling—"will never live this down. I'm sorry I couldn't be at the crime scene." He paused, wrinkled his brow. "What were you doing at that house?"

Ugh. I'd told Awesome and the troopers I was thinking of buying a house. I didn't want to lie about that to Seth. He'd probably be upset if he thought I was planning to buy my own house, and he'd had enough upsetting for one day.

"It was for sale, and I saw the door was ajar. Something seemed off." That was all true.

Seth nodded. "How are you doing?"

I was grateful he didn't press me on the matter. "I don't know." I did. I was a hamster on a wheel, racing in circles, going nowhere. "Do you have any idea who tried to kidnap you?" Maybe it would help me find Stella.

"No. There haven't been any threats lately."

I hated that there were ever threats, but I guess it came with the territory.

"Of course, we're looking through old cases. Checking who's out of prison who might have a connection to me."

That was good because they might find the kidnapper before I ever could. It sounded like the kidnapper had made a mistake, and now the DA's office and probably the police were on his trail. I cuddled into Seth, and he threw his arm around me, drawing me closer.

"Stay," he said, kissing the top of my head.

I thought of Stella. If her captor called me in the middle of the night to do some task, it would be hard to explain to Seth why I was leaving. "I can't." I looked at the TV instead of Seth. "It would be too awkward with the guards here." That wasn't a lie—at least not much of one. I stood. "Be safe."

Seth walked me to the door past the sheepish guards. He kissed me like they weren't there, and then one walked me to my Suburban. He only stepped back when I started the car and locked the doors.

I had started my drive home when my phone rang.

"Ah, Sarah," the kidnapper said. "You've had a busy day. Where'd you take off to in such a hurry?"

That question gave me more information. Every little bit would help me find Stella. He might have some surveillance in place at my house, but he didn't have any kind of tracking device on Stella's phone, my phone, or my car. Because if he did he'd know exactly where I'd been. Unless this was some kind of test. Might as well find out.

"I needed ice cream. I'm going to Bedford Farms." Actually, I did need something in my stomach. I drove toward Bedford Farms Ice Cream. They had the best ice cream on the planet. I hadn't eaten in hours, and nothing else sounded good. I'm not sure even ice cream sounded good. But I couldn't help Stella if I fell apart.

"Oh, they have the best ice cream. I like the Green Monster."

"What do you want? Because I'm sure you didn't call to talk about Bedford Farms."

"Nothing. Just wanted to wish you sweet dreams."

I hung up before he got a chance to. Somehow it felt like a small victory. I'd suspected since the first call someone local was doing this, and the intimate knowledge of Bedford Farms ice cream flavors proved it to me. I turned into the parking lot of Bedford Farms. It wasn't crowded tonight, but I caught them just before they closed. I walked up to the window to order a small cup of Almond Joy. Minutes later I was back in my Suburban, motor running with the heated seats and heater on high. My cup held two softball-sized scoops of ice cream. Their idea of small and mine were vastly different.

As I spooned in the ice cream I thought about seeing Seth. How the guy calling me didn't know that. After I finished I drove home and studied the outside of the house for cameras. I spotted one trained on the front door attached to the roof of the porch. I dragged one of the wicker chairs I'd bought for Stella under it. Climbed on and ripped the camera down. For good measure I stomped on it when

I got off the chair. The crunch was the most satisfying thing that had happened to me all day.

After going through my routine of unlocking and re-locking the front door, listening in the foyer, and checking to make sure the chair was still wedged under the basement door, I headed up to my apartment. I'd left every light on when I'd dashed over to Seth's house.

I was filled with a righteous anger. Whoever was doing this had picked a fight with the wrong person, and if he expected me to be cowed, to do nothing, he had something to learn.

But then my anger faded back to fear. Had Alice in Wonderland been killed because of me? Some poor woman just going through her life and had it snatched away because someone wanted to hurt me? Because, as he said, I "made life hard."

My phone buzzed with a text.

Broken camera, deduct four hours.

That meant sixteen less hours to find Stella. "Screw you," I said. I didn't bother answering. Instead I looked up June and Yousef Ghannam. They stared out at me with perfect smiles, which wasn't too surprising because Yousef was a dentist and June was a dental hygienist. He wasn't my dentist and as far as I knew I'd never met them, although I guess they could have come to a garage sale I'd run. I found pictures of Yousef's retirement party and of the Ghannams standing in front of a large stucco home with cacti in the yard. They seemed unlikely candidates for people who were behind Stella's kidnapping.

Stella's phone buzzed. Awesome. **How is your room?** 😵

Nothing fancy but close to the theater. I replied for her. I remembered her telling me that before she left. She was happy that she'd found a place close enough to walk back and forth to the theater. Stella didn't want to have to deal with the traffic in Los Angeles.

Texting with Awesome made my stomach churn. If I got Stella back, no when I got Stella back, this would be the part that was hardest to explain.

Meeting the rest of the cast in a few minutes.
Love you.
Please forgive me, Awesome.

Love you too. ♣

I could have left it at that, but maybe he'd found something out about Alice in Wonderland. Something he would share with Stella. I fought back the guilt I felt for lying again. This was for Stella I reminded myself. I typed in: **How was your day?**

I waited, watching the little dots as he typed. He must be typing a lot because it was taking a while. Then the text popped up.

The usual.

The usual? Really, Awesome. A murder wasn't the usual in Ellington.

I tossed the phone aside. Turned on the local news. Nothing yet about Alice in Wonderland or a Jane Doe. My phone buzzed again. Another text.

Well done with Awesome. You gain four
hours back.

Six days and twelve hours to find Stella. If he knew

what I'd texted to Awesome, he must have downloaded some kind of app on Stella's phone. I did a quick check of Stella's apps. I didn't see anything unusual, but I'd read that apps like this could be running in the background. That was also good to know. I decided to play along. It was better to let him think I was freaked out, malleable.

Thank you.

You're fun to play with, Sarah.

I just want Stella back.

I'm sure you do. Good night. The game begins again in the morning. And I have a surprise for you!

What did he mean by that?

Chapter Six

Sounds of people moving around in the apartment next door had me leaping out of bed Saturday morning. A quick glance at the clock showed that it was just after six. I had six more days to find Stella. I was grateful I'd managed to get a few hours of sleep.

I shoved my arms in my fluffy, purple robe, flew out of my apartment, down the short hall, and burst through the door of the other apartment. Three men twirled around as they pulled out guns and pointed them at me. More men. More guns.

"Sarah, you scared the bejesus out of me."

It was Mike "the Big Cheese" Titone and his two brothers, Francesco and Diego. They all shoved their guns into the back of their pants. I did a round of hugs after the guns were put away. I'd gotten to know all of them over the past two years. Despite their tough exteriors they had always been kind to me. But their being here could make things more difficult for me. When Mike was in residence, someone was always sitting outside his apartment door, which meant someone would know if I left in the middle of the night. That might raise suspicions. Make them ask questions I didn't want to answer. This must be the "morning surprise" the kidnapper had promised me.

Another problem was that I'm not good at hiding things from people. Most of my emotions played across my face, and to survive in the mob one had to have a keen sense of human nature. Mike might realize something was up. On the other hand, Mike's presence also offered me a bit of protection. They wouldn't let anyone by without checking him or her out. I realized now how scared I was that the kidnapper was just going to get tired of the game, show up, and kill me. I'd buried that thought behind my worries for Stella.

"What are you doing here?" I asked. Usually Mike only stayed here when there was someone after him in Boston.

The brothers glanced at one another. They all had the same ice-blue eyes, but Mike's were always the most difficult to read. He was a runner, thin, dark-haired, and possibly dangerous. Francesco was the tallest and broadest. He had a thick, Tom Selleck-like mustache. Diego was a couple of inches taller than Mike and had a little more bulk to him. Mike had told me once that they were all named after different uncles. Mike's full name was Michelangelo, but I was pretty sure he'd kill anyone who called him that. I knew that Mike was the oldest because he always seemed to be in charge. But I didn't know about the place of the other two in the family.

"There was a threat against me, so getting out of town for a few days seemed wise. We've taken the usual precautions. No one in Boston should know I'm here."

The usual precautions meant someone drove their phones someplace. That way people would think they were in Miami or Atlantic City or Trenton, anyplace but Ellington. Ellington wasn't the kind of town where mobsters hung out.

"Sorry I startled you." I turned to go, but remembered I was supposed to be acting normal, even though I felt anything but normal. "Other than being forced out here, what's up? How's the cheese business?" Mike had a beloved cheese shop, Il Formagio, in the North End, the Italian section of Boston. He also had a huge warehouse full of all kinds of massive cheese wheels. As far as I knew the business was legitimate and not some cover for money laundering or other mob-type activities.

"It's gouda," Francesco said. The rest of us groaned.

"Now you can see why my brothers never have girlfriends. They're just so cheesy," Mike said. That brought another round of groans. Mike put a hand on Diego's shoulder. "Seriously, Diego just broke up with someone. He has terrible taste in women. You have any single friends?"

This morning just kept getting stranger. Diego blushed. Blushed! Quite a sight on a supposed tough guy.

"See if I ever confide in you again," Diego said.

"What about me?" Francesco piped up. "I could use someone to cook, clean, and darn my socks."

My eyes narrowed—thus my problem with not showing my emotions.

"I'm kidding, Sarah. I only want someone to clean. I'm a good cook." He put his hands out palms forward. "I'm kidding, really."

"Most of my friends are married, but I'll think about it." Like I'd fix a friend up with a guy who might be on the right side of good, but also lived on the outskirts of the mob world. "I have to get going."

"What about you? What are you up to, Sarah?" Diego asked.

"I'm doing a garage sale for a client this morning. If you get bored, come on over. She's got a lot of knickknacks. And actually some nice paintings." I rattled off the address for them. I smiled at the thought of the three of them purchasing Hummel or Lladró figurines. I waved my hand and walked back toward my apartment, wondering how having them here would affect my effort to find Stella. To save Stella.

"Sarah," Mike called.

I stopped at the door to my apartment. Waited until Mike walked over to me.

"Are you okay? You seem off. And the front door was locked this morning. That was a first."

Ugh. This is why Mike's being here was problematic. "I lock the door when I'm the only one here." That sounded good. "I'm fine. Just tired. Busy at work, which is a good thing." I pasted on a smile. "Any news on Jimmy?" Jimmy was a computer genius who had helped Mike in the past and was the reason Mike had lived here in January. I'd had a run-in with Jimmy during that time. Then Jimmy had been pulled out of Boston Harbor—dead. I'd thought Mike had something to do with it, even though he denied it. When I'd confronted Mike about it last January, he had said he'd tell me if he found out who'd killed Jimmy.

"Nothing. I've got guys working on it, but everything's come up a dead end."

"Yeah, especially a dead end for Jimmy. Are you being honest with me?"

Mike nodded and walked back to his apartment, but at his door he turned and gave me a long, worried look.

* * *

I made coffee, showered, and checked the news for information on Alice in Wonderland. The only coverage was that an unidentified woman had been found dead in an empty house in Ellington. No means, motive, or opportunity. I guess I knew the motive—someone was trying to get to me for some purpose. And I was probably obstructing justice by not telling the police what I did know. I guessed I should be grateful there was no mention that the woman had been found by Sarah Winston, professional dead-body magnet. It's not a title I enjoyed holding.

I had to focus on finding Stella because the weight of the thought of someone else getting killed because of me was almost too much to bear—not even counting my need to save my friend. If I could find Stella, it would make the madman stop. That's what I had to do. I'd decided while I was in the shower that I would give myself three days to find her. By the end of three days, on Monday, maybe I'd know who I could confide in without Stella getting hurt or killed. I was going to have to go to someone—probably Seth or Pellner. I knew I couldn't go to Awesome because he might kill me on the spot for not telling him sooner.

My phone buzzed with another text. How did you like your morning surprise?

If you're talking about Mike's arrival, it was mean.

I texted back. Let him think I was freaked out.

If a game is easy to win, it really isn't fun.

This isn't a game. I shot back. It's a crime.

I have a lot in store for you today.

What did that mean? I didn't respond. Despair, like a bony hand, clutched my throat. I'd been in a lot of tough situations. But nothing like this where I was so alone. I didn't know how to move forward. There'd been days after my divorce when I'd experienced emotions similar to this. Then I'd put one foot in front of the other—kept moving forward. That's what I had to do today.

I drove around putting up signs to help people find Alice Krandle's house. I hammered them in with more vigor than usual. Some I taped to street signs or telephone poles. The signs were simple because if there was too much information on them people couldn't read them as they drove down the street. Some had the words *garage sale* and the address. Some were only an arrow pointing. They were all a fluorescent lime green so they stood out. After the sale was over I would drive back around and take them all down.

As I drove I looked for places that a kidnapper might stash a hostage. I had noticed a couple of empty storefronts on side streets. One used to be a coffee shop and one a beauty parlor. The kidnapper had said he had "a lot in store for me today." Was that a hint? I'd have to check them out later. But the fact was, Stella could be anywhere, including private houses with basements and attics to hide someone in.

I'd have to figure out some other way to find Stella. Even after a long night of thinking of possibilities, I had no idea who would kidnap Stella or who would do this to me. The hard part was putting all that aside for now to focus on the sale. I worried about what I'd do if the kidnapper called demanding I do some task in the middle of the sale. Acting normal didn't include abandoning a client. *Deep breaths.* Worrying about things I had no control over was becoming a hobby for me.

Harriet's bright red Porsche was parked in front of Alice's house by the time I pulled up. Alice lived in a newer development on the west side of Ellington called Patriots Ridge. The houses were big, and most cost over a million dollars. Alice's house was a beige brick with a covered porch. A wide flagstone path wound from the driveway to the front door. Bushes were neatly trimmed. The sky was a pale blue with some thin, high clouds. Winds were gusting.

I'd met Harriet last winter when I'd hired her to help me with a sale. Harriet had been staying with a niece who lived next door to Carol and had been recovering from some medical issues. Harriet had been driving her niece crazy by reorganizing things around her house, so Harriet came to help me. When her niece had taken a turn for the worse, Harriet had stayed on and continued to help me with garage sales as needed.

A handful of people had already lined up outside of Alice's door, and the sale didn't open for another thirty minutes. Early birds. The good thing was that, unlike with an outside garage sale, they couldn't start poking around. However, it also let me know people had seen the ads I'd put online and in the surrounding local papers. I'd mentioned antiques, and that was what usually drew the early birds.

There were only three of us working this sale—Harriet, Alice, and me. Alice was going to be at the back door to make sure no one left that way. I would be by the front, checking people out, and Harriet was going to float. I knew she would also help answer questions and negotiate prices with the attendees.

This was only the second time I'd done a sale inside, and I was a little worried about the small staff, but that was something Alice had insisted on to save money. I'd found out early on that when Alice wanted something, it was done her way. The sale was going to run from nine to three thirty.

Harriet climbed out of her car once I'd parked behind her. She was dressed in a yellow batik-print tent dress over leggings on her long legs. The dress looked vintage, and Harriet carried the style off well. Short boots finished off the look. Her brown hair was streaked with gray.

I nodded hello to the people on the porch.

"Can't you let us in already," a man asked. He tapped a foot, twitchy and impatient looking.

"Thirty minutes. It will be worth your wait," I said as I breezed by.

Alice looked harried when we went in.

"There are people outside on my porch," she said. "They've been knocking and ringing the bell."

"I warned you this might happen," I said. "It will be all right. I've done this a time or two." I could have kicked myself for sounding short. Stella's kidnapping meant I was stressed beyond anything I'd experienced before. But I had to focus. If I projected confidence, maybe Alice would calm down. We'd blocked off access to the attic and the basement where the things Alice was keeping were stored. My back started to hurt just thinking about all that moving of furniture. Alice had paid in advance and extra for that service. Harriet and I had managed most of it ourselves with an assist from my brother as needed.

"Just remember, your job is to stay by the back door and make sure no one sneaks out that way," I said. My hope was that by assigning her a duty it would keep her from running around bothering people. I could easily see her protesting as we bargained over prices.

"Got it." Alice bobbed her head up and down.

Chapter Seven

We were only an hour into the sale when, out of desperation, I texted my friend Eleanor for backup. Alice was breathing down everyone's necks and wouldn't stay by the back door. I'd seen two people set down things they looked like they were going to buy and leave after encountering Alice. At this rate, I wouldn't come close to the sum of money Zoey had offered her.

Eleanor bustled in twenty minutes later. She was a part-time school nurse at Ellington High School and also managed the Fitch Air Force Base thrift shop. Both meant she dealt with a lot of uncooperative people. Her bright brown eyes and smooth complexion hid a spine of steel.

"Why don't you have any signs up?" Eleanor asked.

I raised my eyebrows. "I put up lots of signs on my way over here."

"There aren't any now. Fortunately, I had the address."

"Who would take down my signs?" It was a rhetorical question. I was very careful about where I placed my signs to make sure they weren't on private property and fell within Ellington's codes.

"Zoey?" Eleanor said. "She wants to be the only garage sale organizer in town."

"I know she does." Zoey had undermined me at every chance she'd gotten for reasons I didn't understand. I didn't mind the competition—at least not too much. It was the way she'd gone about it. The very first ad she'd put in the paper had more or less accused me of stealing from my customers. I didn't like that one bit. "But I can't imagine her doing something like that."

"Do you want to go put some more up?"

"I don't have time. I'd have to leave to make more signs and then spend the time putting them out. We have a good crowd. It will hinder a few people, but hopefully not many."

Alice walked up just then. "Is there a problem?"

"Not at all." I hoped not anyway. I introduced Eleanor to Alice.

"I told you I didn't want to pay for an extra person," Alice said.

"I'm a volunteer," Eleanor said. "Free labor because I love a good garage sale." She soon had Alice by the arm and led her back to the kitchen where the back door was. I waved a thank-you as Eleanor winked at me over her shoulder. If she wouldn't let me pay her by the hour, I'd take her out to dinner sometime.

Three hours later things were going well. Being busy kept my anxiety about Stella down to a minor buzz. Although I'd had to send a text to Awesome just to keep up the pretense of all being well with Stella. We'd sold a lot of the big antique pieces like an armoire, a bookcase, and a desk that could be hard to sell. Even better, the people had paid the full asking price. Harriet had been working with them. I chalked that up to her special skills as a negotiator.

"I like that painting," I heard a man say to his wife.

They were looking at the painting of the Old North Bridge. Harriet walked over to them.

"Are you familiar with the artist?" she asked.

The couple shook their heads.

"He's very well-known in this area." She glanced around and leaned in as if she didn't want anyone else to hear, which immediately drew the attention of everyone in her vicinity. "He's known as the Bob Ross of New England."

That drew "ooohhhs" from the group surrounding her. The couple who'd first looked at the painting realized they weren't alone and stiffened. I pressed my lips together so I didn't laugh out loud. I ended up emitting a choking sound. Bob Ross had had a painting show called *The Joy of Painting* on PBS for eleven years in the eighties and nineties. He'd painted something like thirty thousand paintings and over one thousand of them on his television show. While Bob Ross had died in 1995, he'd reemerged in popularity. The *New York Times* had recently published an article wondering where Ross's paintings were.

The local artist Harriet was referring to had a painting show on a local-access station with a small following. I'd looked him up before Carol and I had priced his painting. He was prolific, but since he was still alive and still painting hundreds of pictures a year, the price of his paintings had actually gone down since Alice had bought hers.

The original couple looked at Harriet. "We'll take it," the wife said.

"I'll top that price by fifty dollars," someone else said.

"That's not fair," the wife from the first couple said.

"I'll pay one hundred more," a third person offered.

Soon Harriet was running a little auction for the painting. The price went up to seven hundred—two hundred more than Alice had originally paid. I couldn't believe it. But it didn't stop with that painting. A group was following Harriet around and bidding up the price on every piece she held up and described. I could barely contain my glee. I didn't know how Harriet kept a straight face. I only hoped I didn't get an angry call after someone went home and checked prices of the local artist's paintings. With any luck for the buyer the artist would quit painting, and then the price might actually go up.

By the end of the sale we'd topped Zoey's offer to Alice by two thousand dollars. I couldn't believe it. It was one of my most successful sales ever. I had Harriet and Eleanor to thank for it. Harriet because of her negotiating skills and Eleanor for keeping Alice out of the way.

"I told you, you could do it," Alice said. "Thank you."

"You did, Alice. I'm happy for you."

As we left Alice's house, I'd offered to buy Harriet and Eleanor a very late lunch or maybe it was an early dinner after we finished at four twenty for the day, but they both had other things to do. I walked to my car and spotted one parked across the street. It had one of those magnetic signs on the door. This one read: Zoey's Tag Sales. Zoey sat behind the wheel. She was a petite woman who had a tanning booth tan that didn't suit her—wouldn't suit anyone. When she saw me, she started her car, waved her middle finger at me, and took off. I stared after her. What was her problem?

I still hadn't figured it out by the time I got to DiNapoli's. They were doing a brisk business even though it was four forty-five on Saturday. There were no cooking classes on the weekend, and this was why. I waited in line, trying to decide what to order. My worries about Stella came storming back. During the sale my fears had gone to a gnawing anxiety, but now it took over like a roaring beast as I pictured her alone and scared.

"Hey, lady, you going to order or get out of the way?" the man behind me asked.

"Sorry." I looked up, and Rosalie watched me with crinkles around her eyes.

"We have a special for anyone who's found a dead body in the past two days," Rosalie said. "Fifty percent off."

I had to smile. Rosalie was always coming up with unique ways to give me a discount. But I guess the word was out that I had found Alice in Wonderland.

"What can I get you?" Rosalie asked.

"A Greek salad, please," I said. Their Greek salads were amazing, with loads of Kalamata olives, feta cheese, tomatoes, cucumbers, just the right amount of onions, and their fabulous house vinaigrette. It was a heaping pile of goodness with a thin layer of lettuce on the bottom. Unlike most Greek salads, where there would only be a couple of olives hidden in the lettuce. "And a coffee please."

"How are you? Why didn't you tell us you'd found another body?"

"I've been busy. Just done with a great garage sale." I worked on smiling.

Rosalie frowned at me.

"Really. I'm fine." There wasn't much conviction in my voice. Fortunately, the line behind me was long enough that she didn't have time to grill me.

I found a table and sat checking my phone for messages until my food was delivered. It was a huge Greek salad but there was also a serving of chicken and broccoli in a creamy sauce topped with shaved Parmesan cheese. Steam

still rose from the pasta. I looked at the kitchen to see
Angelo watching me. I blew him a kiss and took a big bite
of the pasta. He smiled and went back to work.

I ate a few bites as I tried to figure out what to do about
finding Stella. I wondered if there was any news about
who Alice in Wonderland really was. I searched my phone
and found a few articles. None of them gave the name of
the victim or mentioned that she had been dressed like
Alice in Wonderland. I wondered how long the police
could keep that a secret. One article mentioned that I'd
found the body. If Rosalie knew it was all over town.

"You're hurting my feelings."

Chapter Eight

I jerked my head up to find Angelo standing across the table from me. I'd hardly eaten anything, which I knew would offend Angelo. Rule number one at DiNapoli's was eat all your food. Rule number two was don't leave food behind if you don't finish. Angelo considered that a personal insult. "I'm sorry. I got distracted." That worried me, because with a kidnapper on the loose I couldn't afford to not pay attention to what was going on around me.

"Don't get me started on phones at meal time," Angelo said. He pulled out a chair and sat across from me.

I didn't want to. I'd heard him talk at length about phones and food before. "The Greek salad is delicious. Best one I've ever had."

Angelo smiled.

"And this vinaigrette is the best. I've told you before—you need to bottle it. That way I could have it whenever I want."

"I'll go put some aside for you," Angelo said.

Whew. I had managed to get him off the phone topic. As much as I loved him, he could go off on a topic like no one I'd ever known. Of course with a name that meant "messenger of God," Angelo believed it was his duty to share his messages. Frankly, I don't think most of the messages Angelo shared came from God. He had strong opinions on how the world should be run. If not the world, at least Ellington. It made me smile.

"There. I like that smile. You've been preoccupied since you came in, and I'm worried about you."

"I have a secret. It's weighing on me." I clapped my hands to my mouth. I hadn't meant to say that. "Don't tell anyone."

"I won't. It's a secret, right?" He smiled.

"Yes. And it would be awful if anyone knew I had mentioned it." I thought of Stella, of the dire consequences for her. The kidnapper hadn't mentioned Angelo, but I'm sure he wouldn't want Angelo to know. As much as I loved Angelo, secrets weren't his forte.

"Did I ever tell you about the time I picked my mother up at the airport after she had been home to Italy for a visit?"

"I don't think so." We stared at each other for a few moments. *Ah.* I ate some of the pasta. Angelo wasn't going to talk if I wasn't going to eat.

He smiled and nodded. "I waited for her inside the airport. She burst out of security like someone was chasing her, which worried me. What had my mama done now?" Angelo leaned forward. "'Come on,' she yelled as she charged by me. I couldn't imagine what she was up to. Fortunately no one was chasing after her. But then again, I didn't wait long to find out if someone was gonna come." He shook his head. "'Mama, don't you want to take your coat off? It's ninety degrees out.' That's what I asked her."

He looked at me. "She was wearing a black wool winter coat. It dragged on the floor. She shook her head and charged out of the airport. I knew Mama was up to something. She wouldn't even take it off as we walked to the car. Not even in the car. When we got to her house, she finally took the coat off. Figs."

"Figs?" I asked.

"She had figs up her sleeves, in her pockets, tucked in the hem."

I laughed. "How did she get through security in Italy?"

"Probably bribed someone." Angelo shook his head again.

"What about when she got here and had to go through customs?"

"It's not like you go through scanners on the way back into the US. And my mama does a great helpless old lady act when she needs to."

I laughed. "Why did she have figs?"

"Because she wanted me to taste the best figs in the world. The ones my great uncle grew." He pushed back his chair. "I have to get back to work. I'll get the vinaigrette for you and wrap that if you aren't going to finish."

I handed him my plate. "Thank you, Angelo, for the food and the story."

Angelo went to the kitchen, and I stared after him. Usually his stories had some point, but I wasn't getting this one. He brought the wrapped food and the vinaigrette over to me in a bag.

"I'm not sure I understand the point of your story," I said as I stood up and took the bag.

"Mama had a secret, but it was for a good reason. Sometimes you keep a secret, but it's for a good reason."

I hugged Angelo. "Thank you." I left with a bit of spring in my step. But by the time I got home and walked past Stella's empty apartment, I again pondered the magnitude of my secret. Second-guessed what I was doing. Francesco was sitting outside the door to Mike's apartment. I gave him a quick wave and hustled inside my apartment. Time to think about next steps.

Empty buildings are fascinating, aren't they, Sarah?

Another freaking text after a mostly quiet day. Well, if you counted finding out Mike was living next door as quiet. Was the kidnapper giving me a hint? Did he know I'd driven by a couple of empty buildings as I put signs up this morning? If he did, it meant he was following me, which was scary. No matter. I had to go check out the buildings I'd passed on the way to Alice's house. If I combined this text with the earlier one saying he had something "in store" for me, it was my only possible move. Thank heavens there weren't many to check.

I shoved my leftovers and the vinaigrette in the refrigerator and hurried out the door, waving to Francesco again—*act natural,* the kidnapper had said

"Busy day?" Francesco asked.

"Yes. And it's not over yet." I didn't linger, but hurried down the steps and out to the parking lot to my car. I drove over to one of the empty storefronts I'd seen earlier in the day. This was a longshot, but sitting at home in the quiet seemed worse. At least it was still light out since the sun didn't set until around seven thirty this time of year.

I reached the first empty storefront, but didn't stop. Instead I drove around the block and then down the alley behind it. If anyone was following me, I didn't spot him or her. I finally pulled into the parking lot in front of the store. The store was at the end of a strip mall that housed a nail salon—now closed—a laundromat and a barbershop. It was a one-story building. Nothing suspicious anywhere. A For Rent sign hung in the window with a number to call. No signs saying: This Is Where Stella Is. I sighed. It would be an unlikely place to keep someone with customers going in and out of the other businesses.

I parked in front of the store, got out, and peered in the window. Empty, dusty, cobweb filled. I noticed something on the floor, but it was hard to make out what it was in the dark store. I turned the flashlight on my phone on and shined it in the store. I gasped. It was a roll of duct tape. I backed away, got back in my car, and started it. Instead of taking off, I sat there. It had to be a coincidence.

After convincing myself of that, I drove to the next vacant store I'd seen and went through the same routine of driving around the block. Again nothing. What did my grandmother used to call doing this? A fool's errand. I was the fool. This building was two stories, wood framed with a wooden door set between two bay windows. It was pretty although somewhat run-down. Nothing a fresh coat of paint, some potted plants, and a good window washing wouldn't fix.

I got out of the car and turned in a circle. No one else seemed to be around. There was a For Rent sign in this window, too. The realtor renting the store was the same one who had the listing for the Ghannams' house. That might be significant. Once again I looked through the windows. This space was cleaner than the last one. A metal folding chair lay on its side in a back corner. The kind of chair people were always duct-taped to in movies. My phone rang.

"Hello?" I tried to answer with confidence, hoping this was someone other than the kidnapper, but I heard the question mark in my voice.

"Sarah! I left a present for you in the store. Go on in."

I looked around for a camera, but didn't spot one. There must be one here someplace, but it was the least of my worries.

"I knew you wouldn't just sit around waiting for me to tell you where Stella is. But you know what they say about curiosity."

I didn't want to go into that store. I didn't want to end up on the nightly news. But I didn't want Stella to either. I turned another full circle. Where was he? But I didn't see any curtains twitching, anyone walking or even driving by.

"Go on. Go in. I'll give you a reward."

"I'm not breaking and entering."

"It's only entering, dear Sarah. I did the breaking part for you."

I studied the front door. "I don't see any signs of breaking."

"Of course you don't. I have mad skills with a lock-pick."

He was mad all right. I steeled myself. If it meant some clue or more time to help me find Stella, I'd do it.

"I'll stay on the line with you."

"That's such a comfort." I tried the doorknob, and unfortunately it easily turned in my hand. I stepped inside the building, found a light switch, but nothing happened when I flipped it on. I used the flashlight on my phone and flashed the light around the room, but didn't spot anything other than the chair. I approached it. I could see traces of duct tape around the front legs of the chair. A small piece clung like a tiny flag. Had Stella been here? Taped to this chair. I wanted to punch something. I walked around it. Something was duct-taped on the back. I leaned closer. A small Alice in Wonderland doll.

Chapter Nine

I almost dropped my phone.

"Do you like it, Sarah?"

"Lovely. What's the deal with Alice in Wonderland?" My voice shook more than I'd like it to again.

"It's such a great adventure story, and now you're on an adventure too. We'll see if you come out of this larger or smaller or if you'll disappear like the Cheshire Cat," the kidnapper said. "Take it with you."

This was no adventure. "I wouldn't dream of leaving it behind. I'll add it to my doll collection." I didn't have a doll collection. While I'd loved them as a kid, as an adult I found them all a bit creepy with the ever-present smiles and fake, staring eyes. Eyes that weren't that different from Trooper Kilgard's.

"Have a good evening. We'll talk soon. Oh, and you just won an hour back." He hung up.

Wow, a whole extra hour. How generous. But if that hour made the difference between finding Stella and not finding her, I'd take it. I picked up the chair. I was taking the whole thing. It might have evidence on it, and in two days I was going to quit playing these games and get help.

* * *

I drove home and saw the lights were on in Mike's apartment. While in some ways having him next door complicated things, in others it was nice to have someone else around. Several someone elses. I carried the chair up the stairs with me, being careful to keep the Alice in Wonderland doll out of sight against my body. Mike's brother Diego sat outside the door hunched over a Sudoku puzzle book and with a pen in his hand.

"Hi," I said, holding up the chair awkwardly, keeping the doll hidden. "I've been out doing a little curbside shopping. You never know what you're going to find." I hoped I sounded cheery and breezy. Just another typical day in the life of Sarah Winston.

Diego looked up and shrugged. "I prefer new stuff."

"Lots of people do. Any word on who's after Mike?"

"Nothing yet. We've got some leads, but nothing's panned out yet." He looked back down at his Sudoku.

I guess our conversation was over, but I was relieved and hurried back to my apartment. I wanted to get the chair in and examine the doll. I freed the doll from the chair and stashed the chair in the storage area off my living room. I sat down with the doll. She was cloth, about six inches tall with a face that was painted on. The fabric used for her arms, legs, and face had yellowed. I squished her, trying to feel if there might be something inside her. I didn't feel anything, but I found some scissors and cut the back open.

I took out all her stuffing, which didn't amount to much given her size. No cameras. No recorders. No drugs. No clues. Just something the kidnapper wanted to scare me with. He'd done a fine job. Because I was me, I looked up dolls like her online. Was she valuable? Collectible? Had

I just destroyed something priceless? Was there some kind of message that would lead me to where Stella was or help me figure out who the dead Alice in Wonderland was?

Ten minutes later I knew there were all kinds of soft-bodied Alice in Wonderland dolls for sale. They ranged from Madame Alexander collectibles to a topsy-turvy doll that was three dolls in one depending on which way you flipped it around. But none of them matched the one I had. First, they were all bigger, and second, they all looked newer than this one. Nothing to help me out.

I thought about the story of Alice in Wonderland as I put the shredded doll into a plastic bag. I needed to save it just like the chair in case there was some evidence on it. At the beginning of the tale Alice drinks and eats things that make her big and small. Now I'd encountered a big and small Alice in Wonderland myself. Did that mean anything? I pondered for a moment. Not anything that I could easily figure out.

I busied myself with pricing things for my garage sale because I couldn't stand the thought of sitting around doing nothing and I was out of ideas of what to do. Until Stella had been kidnapped I'd been excited to celebrate my business anniversary. Two years ago Carol had asked me to organize a garage sale for her. During her garage sale a woman had commented to Carol how well organized the sale was and how she'd like to have one but didn't have time. Carol had told the woman I ran a business organizing them, and thus my business was born.

My anniversary sale included an eclectic mix of things. Some leftover from when I'd been married—things I didn't have room for now. A small bit of it was from garage sales

I'd run where people had asked me to take what was left behind because they just didn't want it in their houses. Usually, I took all of that stuff to the thrift shop on Fitch Air Force Base. And some of the other things in the sale I'd found abandoned on people's curbs. Half of it was perfectly good or could be with a little work.

What I'd tried to avoid was small figurines that took up lots of room, time to price, and earned very little money. Unless they had some kind of unusual value like the hand-blown glass vase signed by the artist that I was holding. It was bright yellow, with a rim of bright blue. I'd found it at a thrift shop for fifty cents. The colors were what had attracted me, but when I'd turned it over, I'd realized it was handblown and signed.

I'd brought it home, researched the name, and found out it was by a well-known glass artist in Seattle and worth way more than fifty cents. About forty-five minutes into pricing things, my phone rang.

I dreaded answering, but knew I had too. "Hello." This time I made sure there was no question mark in my voice.

"Sarah, I really think you should go see Seth. He's going to feel neglected if you don't spend any time with him. He's a good-looking man. I'm sure there are plenty of women out there who'd be happy to keep him, well, happy."

I hoped that someday this jerk was going to suffer for what he was doing. Going to see Seth was a problem. After Alice's garage sale I'd sent Seth a text saying I was tired from the garage sale and that I wouldn't see him today. Spending time with him would be almost impossible. The secret I was keeping felt like a canyon between us. But I did miss him, and maybe seeing him would help me sort out some of my feelings about what was going on.

After sending him a text—I didn't want to surprise his guards this time—I drove over. Soon we were tucked on his couch in the basement watching TV. The Celtics were playing a close game. I could snuggle Seth without having to talk a lot.

"Hey," Seth said, gently stroking my blond hair out of my face.

I blinked a couple of times. I'd fallen asleep on his shoulder. "Hey," I said. I looked at the TV, but it was off. "Who won?"

"The Celtics. It was over an hour ago."

"You let me sleep on you that long? I'm sorry."

"You can sleep on me anytime you want. In fact, why don't you just stay? It's after eleven."

"I want to. I just . . . can't." I couldn't think of a good excuse when I was still only half awake.

"Is it the guards?"

"Yes. It is." He had thrown me a bone without even knowing it. Talk about guilt. I pulled away from him. "Have the police made any progress on who tried to kidnap you?"

"The van was stolen. They had gotten a picture of the plates from a security camera. And the van was pulled out of Cambridge Reservoir this morning. They'll go over it for evidence, but it's not likely they'll find anything."

Cambridge Reservoir was five miles south of here, just off the 95. "Maybe they'll find something."

Please let the kidnapper have left his wallet in the van by accident. "I hope things are back to normal in the next couple of days." They had to be, or I'd go mad.

Seth pulled me in for a kiss. "Me too. I miss you."

"I miss you too." I didn't want to let him go, but I did.

On the drive home I again started thinking about why me. Not in a whiny "poor me" way, but in a "who the heck would want to do this to me" way. If I could figure that out, maybe I would be able to find Stella and end this. It was hard to imagine anyone hating me this much. I understood that not everyone liked me, but this was way beyond a mild personality conflict.

I parked, went up the stairs, waved at Francesco, and let myself into my apartment. After washing my face, brushing my teeth, and putting my jammies on, I did a search for costume shops in the area. There was one in Chelmsford which was a couple of towns north of Ellington. It was a long shot, but one of the few tenuous connections to the dead woman I had. I would check it out tomorrow.

I made a list of people who I knew didn't like me. Ones who would be happier if I left town. Seth's mom topped my list. At first, she had thought I was keeping him from the woman she'd picked out as his future wife when he was a toddler. *A toddler!* Who does that? Fortunately, that woman was now happily engaged to someone else. However, Seth's mom still didn't like me because she blamed me for holding his political career back. She pictured him as a governor, senator, or maybe even president. Even though Seth had insisted to me and to her that he wasn't interested, she still resented me. She would never dirty her hands doing this, but she had enough money to pay someone to do it. Seth's parents were both trust fund babies. They owned multiple homes and ran with an elite crowd. I shook my head. This was nuts.

Was the old girlfriend really happily engaged? She seemed to turn up at Seth's house a lot needing advice on all manner of things from birthday gifts to engagement gifts for her fiancé. I knew Seth wasn't interested, but that didn't mean the engagement wasn't some kind of ploy. And Seth had dated a lot of women in the past—ones I didn't know. Could one of them be the perpetrator?

Then there was Zoey. It was hard to believe she'd been hanging around outside of Alice's garage sale. That she'd moved signs to try to ruin my sale. Thank heavens for the ads I'd put online and for people using map apps.

I sent another quick text to Awesome as I'd done throughout the day. Then focused back on the kidnapper. I couldn't imagine that anyone I knew would go so far as to kidnap Stella. I'd had a stalker and had helped solve a couple of murders, but could any of those people pull this off from jail? And it seemed like they'd have to have an accomplice who was making the calls and sending the texts. Who was crazy enough to help someone do that?

Chapter Ten

At eight Sunday morning I dragged myself out of bed after a terrible night's sleep. I had two more days to find Stella before I told someone about her kidnapping. But at nine I had to be at a client's house to price things for a garage sale on the Thursday a week and a half from now. According to my client Thursday was the new Saturday in the world of garage sales. I figured it didn't hurt to try. But how was I going to do both—find Stella and price things? My stomach hurt just at the thought of it. And who knew when Stella's kidnapper would contact me again, telling me to be someplace or do something. I didn't know if I could take finding another body.

I hadn't come up with any answers during the night about who had kidnapped Stella. Thankfully, Harriet was meeting me at my client's house to help price. *Harriet!* I had been so stunned and shocked and busy yesterday, I hadn't even thought about asking Harriet for help. It's possible that Stella's kidnapper didn't know about my friendship with Harriet or her background as an FBI hostage nego-tiator. She'd never been to my apartment and although we enjoyed each other's company, we didn't hang out together.

Talking to Harriet might just be a chance I'd have to take. Maybe Harriet *could* help me find Stella, but I'd have to find a way to convince her to keep it a secret. Not telling anyone official probably wouldn't sit well with Harriet and convincing her would be complicated. Maybe even impossible. I was driving myself crazy with all of the second guessing. I'd just have to see what I felt like when I saw her.

My client lived near the center of Ellington in a neat colonial house that dated back to the 1700s. White paint sparkled, green shutters shined. Windows were polished. It was a stark contrast to the rambling Victorian next door where paint peeled, the porch sagged, and bushes could do with a good trim.

I rang the bell, and John McQuade answered the door. He was petite, well groomed, fastidious. John had told me, when I'd been here before to assess what he wanted to sell and sign contracts, that the man next door was driving him crazy because of his sloppy house and noisy dog. John and his husband had decided to downsize and move into Boston.

After we greeted each other John said, "Like I told you earlier, my husband and I are going out of town for a week. Here are the keys. Text me if you have any questions about something we are selling."

"Will do." John left a few minutes later. This was the cleanest house I'd ever worked in. Everything had its place, and it was in it. I priced as I anxiously awaited Harriet's arrival, tussling with what to tell her. I knew I was in over my head trying to find Stella's kidnapper, and even John's stunning collection of tramp art couldn't distract me this morning.

I'd recently read *Tramp Art: An Itinerant's Folk Art* by Helaine Fendelman to brush up on the history and so I'd have a better idea of how to price things. I loved tramp art—a form of folk art that wasn't necessarily made by tramps or hobos. It was mostly created from the 1870s to the 1940s out of cigar boxes or shipping crates. Anyone with a pocketknife could make something. Most of it was whittled into layers with notched edges. Some were simple frames; others elaborate boxes, tables, or more rare large pieces like dressers, of which John had a few.

Harriet showed up thirty minutes later, wearing a black leather jacket, black skinny jeans, and motorcycle boots. No one would ever guess she was in her sixties. She looked like a biker today, but drove her sporty Porsche. She'd barely shimmied out of her jacket before I started talking. I had to do it now or I might lose my nerve.

"Harriet, I need your help with something. You have to promise me you won't tell anyone or talk to anyone without my permission." I paused. "I know it's a lot to ask, and I wouldn't do it if I wasn't forced to."

"Forced to?" I nodded. Harriet tilted her head for a moment, assessing me. "Did you kill someone?"

"No."

"Have you committed a crime?"

"A case could possibly be made that I've obstructed justice." I'd thought about that a lot last night. Holding back information about why I had really been at the house where Alice in Wonderland was found. The information about Stella.

Harriet fisted her right hand and tapped it against her thigh. "Was it for a good reason?"

This was a good sign. She hadn't said no or walked out or covered her ears. "Yes."

Harriet gestured to two wingback chairs upholstered in pink velvet. I sat on the edge of mine. She settled into hers, stretched out her long legs, and crossed her feet at the ankles. "I know you well enough to know you wouldn't ask me to do this if it wasn't something really important." She sat up a little straighter. "I agree to your terms."

The story poured out of me with tears and pats on my knee from Harriet. I was a teapot that had boiled over. Once the pressure was released, I slumped in my chair, exhausted.

"They tried to kidnap Seth first?" Harriet asked.

The thought still made me ill and angry. "Yes."

"And Awesome doesn't know about anything that's going on with the calls and texts."

I shook my head. "I'm awful, aren't I? But I can't break the rules without sacrificing Stella."

"You're positive he has her?"

"Yes." I'd left out the part about verifying it was Stella by asking her what she had given me for Christmas in my first telling.

Harriet looked up at the ceiling for a moment. "Have you thought about motives? Why you? Why someone would do this to you?"

"I have, but I don't have any idea who or why. It's ridiculous to think that any of the people I have thought of would pull off something like this." I ran through my few suspects with Harriet.

"Have you thought about the repercussions to your

personal relationships with Seth, Awesome, and Mike when the truth comes out? Is it worth the possible cost?"

"Yes." Over and over again. "It's Stella's life we are talking about. I have two more days to find her. I made a deal with myself. If I haven't made any progress by then, I'll tell someone in law enforcement." I paused. "I'm just not sure who."

"Okay. Although I really think you should reconsider and tell the authorities now. That said, how can I help?"

Chapter Eleven

As we priced things, we talked about possibilities of who might be behind this.

"It must be someone local," I said.

"I agree. Someone from your past wouldn't know about Mike helping you out. Unless they've been planning this and watching you for a long time."

That wasn't a cheering thought. "It could be a person with connections to the police or to someone close to the police if they'd find out if I talked to a cop."

Harriet nodded. "Maybe someone who works at the police station. Do you want to send a text message to someone at the EPD? Find out if the person really knows what's going on or if he is just relying on secondhand information?"

"It's too soon. I don't want to risk it. You should have heard"—I stopped and took a shaky breath—"Stella's voice. She was terrified."

Harriet leaned forward. "You're sure she's not in on it?"

That thought had never crossed my mind. I let it sink in and then shook my head. Stella wouldn't do that. "Yes. What would she have to gain? They haven't asked for a ransom. Stella has no reason to make me suffer like this, and she'd never be involved in that poor woman's murder." I set aside the frame I'd just priced. It was cedar with leaves carved into it. My phone buzzed.

There's an auction in Acton in thirty minutes. Bid on lot five. There's a pocket watch I want. Other people may want it too. Don't disappoint me. The kidnapper sent a link to the auction site.

I showed Harriet the message. "I've got to get going. I'll just make it with traffic and trying to find a place to park."

"I'll stay here and price. Call me when you're done, and we can regroup."

I nodded. "I will."

"Go," Harriet said. She made a shooing motion with her hands. I grabbed my purse and hustled out the door.

The auction was being held in a one-story warehouse. I'd managed to find a parking spot, race in, and sign up for a buyer number. They handed me a paddle with the number seventy-two on it. Fluorescent lights hung down from rafters. The floor was concrete, the crowd thick. That could hurt my chances of winning lot five. I edged my way closer to the auctioneer. She stood on a raised platform. This wasn't Sotheby's, and there weren't any chairs set out. People stood in clumps around the auctioneer. She had big hair, dyed red, blue eye shadow, and had just finished selling lot two. Thank heavens I'd made it on time. I didn't want to think about what would happen to Stella if I hadn't.

The auctioneer moved on to lot three. It was two dining

room chairs, mahogany with roses carved in the top. She spoke so fast as she described them that I almost couldn't understand her. I thought again about the kidnapper's telling me to act natural. I raised my number and bid ten dollars. The woman next to me moved away slightly. What was that about? Someone bid fifteen. I raised my bid to twenty, heard a gasp, and realized only two of us were bidding. Everyone else seemed to be staring dumbstruck at me. I'd yet to glimpse who I was bidding against. Whoever it was must be in the crowd behind me. And instead of raising their number, they must be nodding their head or making some other kind of indication, because I hadn't spotted them the couple of times I'd glanced back. Seasoned buyers often did that.

I wouldn't go higher than twenty. I could sell the chairs for twenty each at my garage sale and had set my top price at twenty when I'd first spotted them. The other bidder raised to twenty-five. I shook my head when the auctioneer looked at me.

"Sold to number thirteen for twenty-five dollars." The auctioneer smacked her gavel down. She gave me a slight frown, which made me wonder what the heck Stella's kidnapper had tossed me in the middle of.

A helper brought the auctioneer a vintage tabletop shaving mirror with milk glass bowls in holders and the original brush. He placed it on a table next to her.

"Look at this beauty," the auctioneer said. "She's from the early 1900s. Chrome with a cast-iron base. There's no way you could knock this thing over. There are even clips to hold your razor. As practical today as it was when it was made."

I loved the lines and didn't have anything like it for my garage sale, or maybe I could give it to Seth as a gift. It would be perfect in his bathroom with its old-fashioned tub and fixtures. The bidding started at ten dollars. Several paddles shot up. It went to fifteen, and the same paddles shot up. At twenty I thought it was mine because no other paddles went up. A woman sidled over to me.

"What do you think you're doing?" she whispered. She wasn't looking at me when she said it.

The price jumped to twenty-five. Darn, I wasn't the only one still bidding after all. I was getting a little annoyed. I bid again. "I'm bidding," I said to the woman, following her lead and whispering without looking at her. "Isn't that why we're here?"

"No one bids against Elmer Norman," she said.

Elmer Norman was a New England curmudgeon through and through and lived in Ellington. I'd managed to avoid interactions with him for the most part. But I'd heard stories of people crossing the street, walking out of stores leaving half-filled grocery baskets, and ducking behind trees to avoid him. He was a nasty piece of work who thrived on intimidating people. Just my luck. I glanced around again. Didn't spot him, but I knew he was short, so he must be in the middle of the crowd behind me.

I quit bidding on the shaving stand. He could win this round, but the next one had to be mine. I just hope he appreciated the gesture. Not that it sounded like he would from what I'd heard.

"Smart move," the woman whispered.

A helper brought out a box and tipped it toward the auctioneer. She peered in. "This is lot five. We have assorted frames, a beautiful pocket watch, a vintage alarm clock, and two small samplers. Bidding starts at five dollars."

Bidding zoomed up to fifty quickly. Then almost everyone dropped out. Elmer must have jumped in. But this time I didn't give up, and neither did someone else.

The lady who had spoken to me before glanced at me. "Elmer collects old clocks and pocket watches. You don't want to make him angry."

She was right. I didn't, but I had no choice. I thought about the text message that said I wouldn't be the only one who wanted the watch. Before I knew it, I was bidding two hundred dollars for something that couldn't possibly be worth it. And I hoped I'd brought a credit card with me because I didn't have enough cash on me to buy this.

"Why does the auction house put up with Elmer's behavior?" I asked the woman next to me. "Doesn't it hurt their bottom line when he shows up?"

"He doesn't always jump in right away, so they do okay. Plus, he doesn't show up all that often."

Just my luck Elmer was here today of all days. My stomach felt queasy at three hundred and rising. I heard some noise in the back of the room, cursing. The auctioneer stopped, and I turned to see what she was staring at. The crowd stood aside and I could see Elmer's back, brown corduroy coat, beanie pulled low. He was leaving, knocking people out of his way as he went.

The woman who'd whispered to me before turned to me. "That's a first. I've never seen Elmer leave without something he wanted." She spoke in a regular voice this time. Her brow wrinkled. "Is this your first auction? The stuff in that box can't possibly be worth three hundred dollars."

"I want it." I was saved from having to say more when the auctioneer started back up. I had been hoping that, now that Elmer was gone, I'd have the lot to myself, but someone else was still bidding too. I didn't have time to look given how fast the auction was going. Finally, at four hundred dollars I won, if one could call it that.

The people attending the auction stared at me as I headed over to pay and collect lot five. Their expressions ran the gamut from dropped jaws to raised eyebrows to quizzical frowns. Fortunately, I didn't recognize anyone. Even though I didn't, this story would probably spread through town and back to Ellington before people sat down for their dinners. I hoped my success would earn me more hours to find Stella.

After I paid, I carried my box of prizes to my Suburban, got in, and looked through the box. I took out the pocket watch and opened it to see if it would give any clues as to why someone would want me to buy this particular lot. It didn't look like anything special. No engraving. No cryptic notes tucked in it. No notes to me written on it. No clue as to why in the world someone would want me to buy this stuff unless it was just to jerk me around.

The round alarm clock looked like it was from the fifties with its two big bells on top. At least it worked with its little *tick, tick, tick.* I was getting angrier as nothing panned out. No clues. No answers. The small samplers were cute, and I could sell them at my garage sale. With any luck I'd recoup twenty bucks of the four hundred I'd just spent. The frames were cheap drugstore frames. I could add them to the box of stuff that would be free. After I inspected each item, I placed them on the passenger seat.

I turned over the cardboard box that everything had come in. It was ordinary. A grocery store box that had once held dairy products. What a waste of time and money. I gripped the steering wheel until my knuckles were white.

I wished my fingers were wrapped around the neck of whoever was doing this. Then I relaxed my grip. It wouldn't do Stella or poor dead Alice in Wonderland any good if I couldn't stay calm and focus.

I fired up the Suburban to head back to John's house. As I pulled out of the auction house parking lot, a dark sedan with heavily tinted windows pulled out too. I was too on edge to think anything was a coincidence. I kept glancing back as I drove toward Ellington down the 2A past Concord. The sedan kept at least one car between us. I couldn't see their license plate, and I really wanted to. Maybe this was the person who had Stella. It made sense that he'd be at the auction to make sure I'd done his bidding.

I swerved off onto the narrow shoulder of the road and stopped.

Chapter Twelve

The car was forced to go by me. I swerved back onto the road right behind it to the honks of my fellow drivers. I waved an apology. This wasn't my normal driving style. The black sedan sped up, and I followed. I got close enough to memorize their license plate. Rhode Island plates. *Gotcha*. Finally, I was one step ahead of this guy.

They passed a truck on a dangerous curve and sped off, not that I cared. I had what I wanted, but now what? Asking Awesome or Pellner to track the plate for me would cause too many questions. If Harriet could get someone to do it, she'd have to answer the same questions. Since I had no answers, I turned around and went back to the auction house. Maybe I could find out who had owned the things in lot five. Maybe that would be a clue as to who was behind all of this.

The auction was still in full swing when I returned. People were bidding enthusiastically on a flat screen TV. Quite a different atmosphere from when Elmer was here. Why did the people at the auction let him intimidate them? I saw a sign for an office, made for it, and knocked. No one answered, which wasn't too surprising since the auction was ongoing. I tried the doorknob, but it was locked. Would I have gone in? Probably, if it meant discovering a way to find Stella. I almost didn't recognize who I'd become since I'd gotten that first phone call.

I walked back over to the sign-in table for a bidding number. One woman remained at the table. "Hi, I wanted to find the original owner of lot five. I bought it about a half hour ago."

The woman looked annoyed. "You'll have to talk to the auction house owner. He's over at the checkout. Big guy. Plaid shirt, Handlebar mustache." She put her head back down to some paperwork she was shuffling.

I crossed the back of the room as the auctioneer said that a beautiful antique Victorian desk was their last item of the day. The auctioneer described the desk as walnut with a black lacquer finish and leather top. Under other circumstances I would have loved to take a look and possibly place a bid. But I needed to get this taken care of and move on before the rush of people headed over here to check out.

It was easy to spot the owner. He looked exactly as the woman had described him. "Excuse me," I said when I arrived at the table he stood behind.

"Yes, ma'am, how can I help you?"

"I need to know who owned the items in lot five that I purchased about a half hour ago."

"You do, do you?"

I gave him my most earnest, wide-eyed expression. "Yes."

"No can do."

So much for wide-eyed earnest expressions. "It's important." I hated the pleading tone in my voice. But I'd get down on my knees and beg if I had to.

"I'm sure it is, but we don't share private information about our sellers with our buyers."

"What about letting me take a look at video from your security cameras to see who brought the box in? I wouldn't have their personal information that way."

"I have to give you points for persistence," he said.

That was a good sign.

"But no. No way. Not a chance in—"

"I get it. It's a no," I said. I heard the auctioneer say "sold," and the crowd moved in our direction. As I walked by the registration table, the woman motioned me over. "Here's a list of who put what into the auction. I'm going to be over at the other end of the table packing up."

As soon as she moved off, I grabbed the list. Lot five had been put in the auction by Lew Carrol, and the address was mine. Lewis Carroll wrote the Alice in Wonderland books. This was no help at all, just more taunting by the kidnapper. Another wave of burning anger went through me. I was going to have a stroke before I found Stella. After a couple of deep breaths, I put the paper back down.

"Thank you," I said to the woman.

"For what?" she said with a wink.

"What made you decide to help me?" I asked.

"I've seen a lot of desperate people in my day and you top all of them," she said. "Good luck with whatever you're dealing with."

"Thank you again." I headed back out to my car. There was nothing else I could do right now—or was there?

I sat in the parking lot staring at my phone. I hadn't

heard anything from Stella's kidnapper since I'd been to the auction. That unnerved me a bit. I'd expected instructions on what to do with the pocket watch or a text saying I'd gotten two additional hours for my win. But nothing. Of course, he might dock me for my trick of pulling off on the side of the road.

It wasn't the only reason I stared at my phone. I'd come up with an idea of how to trace the license plate number, but I wasn't sure I could go through with it.

I made myself punch in the number, gripped the phone so hard I expected it to explode in my hand. Prepared myself to hear the voice on the other end.

"Sarah?"

"CJ." My ex-husband. His voice was as familiar as an old blanket.

"Are you okay?"

Not by a long shot. "Yes." *No.* "I hear congratulations are in order." Ugh, I sounded trite. CJ was marrying his high school sweetheart and gaining an instant family with her two daughters. At last getting the children we could never have, and CJ and his bride-to-be could have their own now too. It wasn't too late.

"Thank you," he said after a pause. "I hear you're still seeing Seth."

"Yes." This was really awkward. I supposed Pellner had told CJ. They were still in touch. CJ was the chief of police in Fort Walton Beach, Florida. His taking that job without consulting me was what had finally ended the chance we'd had to reunite. But it was why I was calling him now. He had access to databases that I didn't. "I need a favor."

I heard a sigh. That didn't bode well for me.

"What?" CJ asked, sounding wary.

"I need you to run a license plate for me. And not tell anyone."

"Sarah." He paused. I could picture him running his hand over his face the way he did when he was frustrated. "Why not ask Pellner?"

"I don't know who to trust. It's not that I don't trust Pellner." I added that bit hastily before CJ could say anything. "But I'm afraid there might be a bad guy in the department and that if I asked Pellner the bad guy would find out."

"What have you gotten yourself in the middle of this time?"

And there it was. Another reason our marriage had ended. CJ's lack of faith in my ability to handle things. His need for me to change back to the eighteen-year-old girl he'd married instead of accepting the woman I was. But maybe I was the one who was overreacting. It wasn't that unreasonable of him to ask this. It was more the way he asked and his tone of voice that got to me.

"I can't tell you." I paused to collect myself. I couldn't take my anger and frustration with the kidnapper out on CJ. "I wouldn't ask if it wasn't important."

"You know I can't use the system for personal business. I'm always on top of our young officers to make sure they aren't looking up the address of some hot girl or guy they saw on the road."

"Someone was following me. They scared me." I waited. And waited. "You know me, CJ."

It reminded me of something I had said to him almost two years ago. One of the other situations I had ended up being in the middle of. He'd done what I had asked then. I hoped he would now.

Another sigh. "Give me the plate number."

I read it to him and heard clicks on a keyboard. I almost shook with relief. I didn't say anything while I waited. Didn't want to jinx this or have CJ change his mind.

"It's owned by a Gregory Kiah."

"What's his address?"

CJ surprised me by rattling it off. "But that's not important because the car was reported stolen."

"Oh." It was a good thing I was sitting because I felt myself collapsing in. I hadn't realized how much I was counting on this being the bit of evidence that would lead me to Stella's kidnapper.

"No more favors, Sarah." There was another pause. Another sigh. "I'm not in love with you, but I'll always love you."

"Same, CJ. And I won't bother you again." I ended the call and tried to figure out what to do next.

Chapter Thirteen

After leaving the auction parking lot, I made sure no one was following me. What had that been about? Someone trying to scare me? Someone who wanted the stuff in the box? Again, I had no answers, just more and more questions.

I called Harriet and filled her in. She was heading over to pick up her niece to take her to the grocery store and said she'd check in later. Harriet also gave me a report on how far along she'd gotten pricing things. She'd done enough that I decided to focus on trying to find Stella. But first I drove through Dunkin's and got coffee and two glazed donuts. Not the best lunch ever, but it was all I had time for. I ate as I drove to the Masquerade Costume Shop in Chelmsford, which was about ten miles north of Ellington. It was the one I'd found online last night.

It was a long shot because it was easy to get costumes on the Internet. But the costume had looked handmade not mass-produced. The shop sat in a depressed-looking strip mall—cracked asphalt, dead plants in splintering planters, and a drooping awning. A sign on the door said Open, so I parked and headed inside.

"Hi, honey. How can I help you?" A short woman as stout as an antique teapot stood behind a short counter. Gray permed hair. Friendly, smiling face. The shop itself had costumes hanging like pictures on the wall alongside photos of people in costumes. A red velvet curtain covered an entrance to the back of the shop.

"Wow. Your costumes are beautiful," I said as I admired a blue satin dress with layers of underskirts that looked fit for Cinderella.

"Thank you, dear. I made most of them myself. I'm Poppy."

"I'm Sarah. I'm going to a party, and a friend recommended I come here."

"Naughty or nice?" she asked.

That was an odd question. "My friend's very nice."

Poppy chuckled. "Do you want to dress naughty or nice? Witch or princess? I have to say you look more like a princess than a witch. Although witch costumes are very popular. You wouldn't believe the number of people who come in wanting to be sexy witches or nurses. Not my cup of tea, but I have the costumes. The customer's always right." She finally took a breath. "If you want to be a sexy witch or any kind of witch for that matter I have something for you. Or I can design something special just for you."

I spoke up before she could go on. "I want to be Alice in Wonderland."

Poppy frowned, and my heart beat a hopeful beat or two. "I had a lovely Alice in Wonderland costume, but it isn't here."

"Where is it?" I asked.

"Someone rented it and didn't bring it back."

"Maybe they will before the date of my party."

Poppy shook her head. She glanced over her shoulder and leaned over the counter. "It's evidence."

I forced myself to widen my eyes so I looked surprised. "Really? Of what?" I would play along with her.

"A murder. Some poor woman was found dead, dressed in my beautiful costume. The state troopers showed up here. Tracked me down by the labels. It sounded like they were accusing me of murdering the poor dear."

It must have been Trooper Kilgard. I gasped like I was shocked by the news. "That's awful." And it really was. "Did you know the woman who was murdered? What was her name?" A name would be a wonderful lead.

"I have no idea. She's not the one who rented it."

I widened my eyes again. "She wasn't? Who rented it?"

"A terrible man. Gregory Kiah."

The man whose car had been stolen. I had a feeling Gregory hadn't been here at all. That whoever had stolen his car had been. "Did you wait on him?" Maybe I could find out what he looked like.

"No. My employee did. She gave a description to the police. Worked with a sketch artist." Poppy leaned in, lowered her voice. "She said it was like being in a movie. Kind of thrilling."

Not thrilling at all from where I stood or for poor Alice in Wonderland. "It must have been nice to help the police by providing a description of that Gregory Kiah person." I reminded myself to breathe as I waited for her reply. Hoping she'd share what her employee had told the police.

"It was the least she could do. I mean some maniac comes in here and rents a costume and kills someone. You bet she told them."

"What did he look like?" This might be the big break I was looking for.

Poppy leaned in again. "From what she said, he looked average. And not a tattoo or birthmark to help identify him. Brownish hair, average height, small diamond stud earrings. She was sorry she couldn't be much help to the police. She took a picture of the sketch when they weren't looking and gave it to me. I showed it to everyone in the shops around here, but no one recognized him. I want everyone to be safe."

"Could I see the picture? Just in case I run into him someplace." I gave a pretend shudder.

The woman grabbed her phone off the counter, opened her photo app, and held it out to me. "That's him."

I hold Poppy's phone and studied the face. The photo of the sketch was a bit blurry. But from what I could tell he had nice cheekbones, an elongated chin, and short hair. I didn't recognize him. How did he know so much about me and I didn't know him at all? Disappointed, I handed the phone back to Poppy.

"Would you mind texting it to me? I want to warn my friends. And would you let me know if you see him or find out more about him? I'll sleep better knowing he's been caught."

"I can do that."

I gave her my phone number, and my phone pinged with the photo. "How did he pay for the costume?"

"You seem awfully curious for someone who wandered in looking for a costume."

"I do. It's my biggest fault. 'Always with the questions,' my mom used to say. It drove her nuts." I wasn't giving up. "Do you make your clients show their IDs?"

"Normally." Poppy shook her head. "My employee is new. She didn't ask for his ID. That's how we ended up in this situation. Not having any information except for the name the man gave me on the phone."

"When did he call?" I knew I was pushing her, but any tidbit of information might lead me to Stella.

Poppy wrinkled her brow. "Thursday morning. He reserved the costume and said he'd pick it up Thursday evening. Which he did."

"How scary that you talked to someone who's a killer. Could you tell something was off? Did he have a creepy voice?"

"Not at all. He sounded normal. Friendly even."

"I bet his credit card information helped the police." I was taking a swag here, but I was running out of questions.

"He paid with cash."

All of this was extremely frustrating, because if Poppy had given any solid leads to the police, I would have gone straight to Pellner to tell him what I knew about Alice in Wonderland's death and Stella's kidnapping.

"I've been too trusting, expecting people to do the right thing. Well, not anymore."

And yet here she was telling me all kinds of things. "Thank you." As I turned to walk out of the store, I looked around the room. There were three security cameras. One pointing at the front door, one at the counter, and one at the curtained door to the back. "Could I watch the tape?" I asked, lifting my chin toward a camera.

"Why would you want to do that?" Poppy demanded.

"To see what the costume looked like." Whew. That sounded reasonable.

"I'd let you, but we had the cameras installed after we found out about the poor woman's death."

Rats. Every time I got my hopes up, they were smacked

down like pesky gnats. I would have to try another angle to find Stella.

"What about a costume, dear?"

"Let me think on it. I'm not sure I want to dress as Alice in Wonderland anymore."

"You'd make a lovely Sleeping Beauty. Or a sexy witch."

"I'll keep that in mind." On to plan B. I called Harriet as I walked to my car. "Want to go to Rhode Island with me?" I explained what I knew about Gregory Kiah.

"Sure, I'll go," Harriet said.

"Thanks. I'll pick you up around six."

As I was driving home from Chelmsford, a cop car came up behind me in Ellington and flashed its lights. What now? I pulled into the parking lot of a church, and the cop pulled alongside, driver's window to driver's window. It was Pellner. *Don't talk to the police.* Rule number one. But what could I do? Pellner would be suspicious and would follow me home if I hadn't stopped. Better Pellner than Awesome at least.

Pellner was a few inches taller than my five six. Muscular. He had dimples, but they didn't soften his face. In fact at times they made him look downright scary. "I need you to come down to the station. We got an ID on Alice in Wonderland."

My heart revved like it did when I found a great bargain. "Who is she?" Maybe this was the break I needed to find Stella, because nothing else was panning out.

"Follow me to the station, and we'll talk."

"Can't you just tell me here?"

"No."

"Why do you need me at the station?"

Pellner rolled up his window instead of answering.

That was odd. I nodded and watched Pellner head off. What was I going to do? I couldn't let the kidnapper think I was telling the police about Stella if he found out I was at the station. I had to do something to mitigate that risk. I pulled out my phone and sent a text in response to the last one the kidnapper had sent this morning about going to the auction. I got pulled over by a cop and have to go to the station. I'm not going to say anything about Stella. Or you. I hoped the kidnapper would believe me.

I sat for a minute waiting for a reply, but didn't hear back. I put my car in gear to head to the station. Pellner had stopped at the entrance to the church parking lot and was waiting for me. There was no escaping this, but I did want to find out who Alice in Wonderland was. I stuck my phone in my purse and followed him.

Ten minutes later I was walking down a corridor behind Pellner. He stopped in front of a room, opened the door, and stepped back to let me go in first. Such a gentleman. I walked in, spotted Trooper Kilgard sitting behind a desk, and stopped. I glanced over my shoulder at Pellner. *Traitor.*

"Have a seat," Trooper Kilgard said. Her hair was pulled back in a bun again, and her eyes still had no warmth.

I did as I was told because what choice did I have? Pellner sat in the chair next to mine. The desk was gunmetal gray, the chairs hard, and the walls beige. I was surprised I wasn't in an interview room.

"Pellner, Officer Pellner told me you'd identified Alice in Wonderland." I wondered why I was here. Why Pellner hadn't just given me the name.

"Yes. Her name is Crystal Olson. Do you know her?"

I thought it over before I shook my head. "I don't remember anyone by that name." Did that make me sound guilty of something? "I don't know anyone by that name."

"Maybe a photo will prod your memory."

They wanted me to look at the photos? Why? As far as they knew I had just had the bad luck of finding her.

Trooper Kilgard opened a manila folder in front of her and slid a color photo of Crystal over to me. It looked like Crystal was on the autopsy table. The makeup had been washed off her face, but her eyes were closed.

I shook my head again. "I don't know her as far as I can tell from that photo."

Trooper Kilgard opened the manila folder again and handed me another picture. Crystal was alive in this shot. Her chin was tilted up. She had a sexy smile and her makeup was flawless— pink lips, a light blush, and a smoky eye. Deep blue eyes. And thick, dark hair tumbling down her back like a forties movie star.

I wondered where they had found this photo of her. "She looks kind of familiar, but I can't place her." I'd thought she'd looked familiar the night I'd found her, but still couldn't come up with why.

Pellner leaned in. Tapped the photo. "She looks like you."

I flinched. "No. She doesn't. Crystal has brown hair." We didn't look alike. I looked back at the photo. "Okay, her eyes look almost the same color, but that's it." I shook my head.

Trooper Kilgard handed me another photo. This one a straight-on shot where it seemed like Crystal was staring directly at me.

"Her face is the same shape," Pellner said. "And the tilt of her nose."

I took in a sharp breath. Let it out slowly. "Okay, there is some resemblance." Too much resemblance. My stomach cramped. "What do you know about her?"

"She was a high-end prostitute working out of Lowell," Trooper Kilgard said. "The photo is from her website."

Lowell. That's where Seth and I had met at a bar just over two years ago. It was about twenty minutes north of here if there wasn't much traffic. "Lowell?" I knew it had its share of crime. It was an old mill town with a university. It seemed like an odd place for a high-end prostitute to be working, but what did I know about hookers?

"She lived in the same apartment building Seth used to live in," Pellner said.

That was weird. Seth had lived in Lowell until he'd bought a house in Bedford last year. "Are you saying there's some connection?" Seth wouldn't be involved with a prostitute unless he was prosecuting one. He was a victim here too. Kilgard and Pellner must know about the attempted kidnapping.

"None that we've found," Pellner said.

"Yet," Trooper Kilgard said.

"Did they live in the same building at the same time?" I asked.

"They overlapped by about six months," Trooper Kilgard said. "Did you ever run into her there?"

I guessed that meant Trooper Kilgard knew Seth and I were in a relationship. Somehow that made me uncomfortable. "Not that I remember. But it's a big apartment complex, and I wasn't there very often." I sounded way more defensive than I wanted to.

"You aren't remembering much here, are you?" Trooper Kilgard said.

I was hoping Pellner would jump to my defense, but he stayed quiet. "How did she die?" Time to change the topic.

"We suspect an overdose. She has a history with drugs," Trooper Kilgard said. "But toxicology will take weeks to get back. You're sure you don't know her?"

"I'm positive. I don't think I know any prostitutes." There I went again with the ambiguous statements. How did Crystal fit in with the kidnapper? It didn't seem like any of this was very helpful. But maybe this bit of news would make Seth look up old cases with prostitutes. Maybe that would be the link to the kidnapper. What would Seth think when he found out she had lived in the same building as he had? "Did she have a record? A pimp?"

"One arrest several years ago for drug use. It helped us identify her quickly."

"Do you have her phone or computer so you can find out who her clients were?" I asked. Maybe one of her clients had some connection to me.

"We haven't found either yet," Pellner said.

That was disappointing. We all sat there staring at one another for a few moments. "I need to go," I said. There was nothing I could help them with. At least not right now.

Trooper Kilgard nodded her head. I was out of there and in my car calling Seth before Pellner had time to stop me. I didn't reach Seth and didn't bother leaving a voice-mail because after I thought about it, I realized Seth would already know this.

Chapter Fourteen

Harriet and I left at six p.m. Pawtucket, Rhode Island was about an hour south on the 95 on a good day. My local friends always teased me for putting "the" in front of the number of a road. But that's what I'd grown up saying in California. And I still called them freeways instead of highways like they did here.

Traffic was thick, and heading south was slow even on a Sunday. They did this weird thing in Massachusetts that allowed people to drive on the right shoulder on some portions of the freeway during rush hour. It freaked me out so even though this wasn't rush hour, I stayed in the middle lane. I told Harriet about Crystal Olson as I drove.

"That must be scary to find out there's some resemblance to you."

"It's creepy. Unsettling." I repressed a shiver. My whole life was unsettled right now.

"I could do some digging and see if I can find out anything else about her."

I thought it over, weighed the risk of the kidnapper finding out. "Okay."

"Maybe there's a link to the kidnapper among her customers."

"Or maybe there's a link between one of her customers and me."

Harriet nodded. "Good point."

"The police have to be taking a deep dive into who they were too." I hoped they'd find her phone or computer or even whatever phone carrier she used for her service soon. Harriet and I were quiet most of the rest of the way there. Harriet tapping away on her phone. An hour and fifteen minutes later we were pulling up in front of Gregory's house. Harriet hadn't found anything out about Crystal Olson that I didn't already know.

"Why don't you park a couple houses down from Kiah's house," Harriet said. "Then let's just take a stroll around the block."

I did as instructed, and soon we were walking down the street. There was a chill in the air. Harriet and I were dressed almost alike in sweaters, leggings, and light jackets. I had on flats, and she had on boots. The neighborhood was a mix of ranch houses and duplexes or two families as they called them here. Modest homes on modest lots. At Gregory's house—a one-story ranch or rambler—lights were on, curtains were open. We slowed in front of his house, both of us craning our necks, looking for glimpses of Stella. No one was in the front room. There was a car in the drive with a rental sticker on it.

"Gregory's identity could have been stolen along with his car," I said. I'd described what the man who'd rented the costume looked like on the drive down and showed her the blurry picture Poppy had sent me.

Harriet nodded. "In all likelihood that's the case, but it never hurts to check out a lead."

I wondered if Harriet had a gun. All I had was my hairspray and bottle of wine. But the heft of my purse felt good. We turned at the corner and discovered an alley ran behind the houses.

"Let's take a walk down the alley," Harriet said. We passed garbage cans, single car detached garages, swing sets, and dogs in fenced yards. They barked. A lot. But Harriet kept moving, so I did too.

We stopped behind Gregory's house. No fence. No signs of a dog. Patchy grass. Lights were on in the basement, and again there weren't any window coverings. "It doesn't look like he's a man with anything to hide," I said.

"Let's take a look anyway," Harriet said.

"Why don't you stay here and watch for anyone who might happen by. I'll go peek in." I didn't want to get Harriet in trouble if I got caught. Harriet nodded, and I crept forward. I dropped to my knees and peered in the basement window, stood, and repeated the process at the window on the right side of the house. Then I creeped up the steps leading to a back door. Peeked in. A kitchen with a small table and chairs off to one side. Stella wasn't tied to a chair.

"Well?" Harriet asked when I got back. We continued down the alley.

"If he's guilty of anything, it's of being a neat freak. Lots of tools and a workshop in the basement. A partially built bookcase. No chains hooked into the walls or duct tape lying around. Kitchen had a small table with four matching chairs. Nothing out of the ordinary. No sign of Stella or Gregory."

"Let's go knock on his door then."

"And say what?"

"That you live in the area and heard his car had been stolen. That someone stole your car too."

"Oh, you're good at this," I said.

Harriet laughed.

"If whoever answers looks like the guy from the costume shop, I'm not going in."

"Agreed."

"You don't have to go in with me." Although as a hostage negotiator Harriet was probably better equipped to handle this than me.

"There's safety in numbers. Maybe while you talk, I can get away and take a look around."

A few minutes later we sat on a couch across from Gregory Kiah, who slumped in an overstuffed chair. He'd bought my story about my car being stolen too. Gregory looked nothing like the man who'd rented the Alice in Wonderland costume, but that didn't necessarily mean he wasn't involved. His head was shaved bald. A well-trimmed mustache and goatee combo covered his upper lip and chin. He'd already told us he was originally from Liberia and had fled with his family during Charles Taylor's reign of terror.

"When was your car stolen?" Gregory asked as he shook his head, disgusted.

The answer would be a lie, and my face tended to contradict my words, although I'd been working on that. "A couple of days ago." Being vague seemed best. "Do you have any idea who took yours?" Gregory seemed honest enough, but maybe he'd loaned the car to a friend or even used it himself and reported it stolen.

"No."

"It couldn't have been a friend or a family member who needed to borrow it?" Harriet asked.

"They would have asked, not just taken it. My spare keys are still here." He nodded toward the front door where a decorative piece read "Home" and had hooks for hanging keys. Several sets were there. I should tell him not to do that. That someone could break the window on his door and get the keys all too easily.

"Where was your car parked when it was taken?" I asked. "Mine was on the street."

"Mine too. I told the police all this." He opened his mouth to say something else.

Harriet stood. "May I use your restroom?"

I knew that she was going to search as much of the house as possible looking for Stella while I distracted Gregory.

"Of course. Down the hall, second door on the right."

"I thought maybe there's a ring of people who might connect us to each other. And that we could figure out who did this if we compared notes."

"Shouldn't we leave that to the police?" he asked.

"I don't think a couple of stolen cars are high on their priority list. At the very least it's not as important to them as it is to me."

Gregory nodded. "You're right. In Liberia the police were corrupt for the most part. But I believe it's different here."

"It is different here. But they are busy and spread too thin. Crimes against people take a priority over stolen property." Gregory nodded again. "Where do you work?"

I asked. Minutes later I knew he worked for an IT company, went to a Methodist church on Sundays, played pickup basketball on Tuesday nights, and loved American reality TV shows. I shared as little as possible and made up everything I said.

Harriet walked back into the room with a slight shake of her head. No signs of Stella. I wasn't sure whether to be relieved or not.

"Do you have any security cameras?" Harriet asked.

"No."

"How about neighbors? Do any of them have security cameras?" I asked.

He puckered his lips together as he thought. "The people across the street have a doorbell with a camera."

I stood. "Thank you. I hope they find your car and get it back to you."

"Yours too."

There were lights on at the house across the street. Harriet and I crossed over and rang the doorbell. Like Gregory had said, it was the kind with a camera on it and an intercom. I looked around to see if there were other cameras, but didn't see any. Although I knew from past experience that cameras could be very small and easily hidden. But weren't most security cameras big to scare people off?

A voice came out of an intercom. "What do you want?"

"We were talking to Gregory Kiah about his stolen car and wondered if your security system picked anything up," I said.

"It did. I gave a copy of the recording to the police."

"Any chance I could take a look? My car was stolen

too. A couple blocks over. My doorbell picked up a figure but not much more."

Harriet gave me a small nod of approval.

A moment later the door opened. A dark-haired woman in jeans and a green *Providence, Rhode Island* T-shirt stood there. She had a laptop in her arms that she opened. She turned the computer toward Harriet and me. "I hope we aren't going to have a rash of crimes around here. It's a good neighborhood."

"Yeah, me too," I said.

The woman clicked open a file, and we watched for a couple of seconds. Gregory's car was clear in the photo. A slender person in a black hoodie walked up and slid a jimmy between the window and the door, bold as could be. He got in and seconds later drove off. His face never showed.

"That's all I've got," the woman said.

"Thanks for showing us," I said. Harriet turned quickly and started down the walkway. I looked after her in surprise and followed suit. I guess she didn't want to answer questions if the woman started asking them.

"What did you say your name was?" the woman called out as we hurried down the sidewalk.

"Poppy Smith," I called over my shoulder. I didn't want to alarm the woman after she'd helped us.

"What street do you live on?" she yelled.

I kept going like I hadn't heard her. Harriet walked up the block past my Suburban with me hustling along, trying to keep up with her longer stride. At the corner she turned and looked back. "Coast is clear. We can head back to your car now."

Chapter Fifteen

"That was a bust," I said as I drove north on the 95. It was eight fifteen.

"Not completely."

"How so?" I asked.

"We know Stella isn't at Gregory's house and that he probably didn't have anything to do with her kidnapping."

"Probably?" I switched lanes. Thankfully, the traffic was much lighter. My app showed that we'd be back in Bedford in 57 minutes. I hoped to beat that and sped up.

"None of his behaviors suggested he was lying," Harriet said. "He maintained eye contact. Didn't twitch his mouth or nose. It's not always a foolproof method, but my gut said he was telling the truth."

"One suspect down and how many people live on Earth? Seven billion left to go?"

"It's better than no suspects down." Harriet leaned her head back against the headrest and closed her eyes. "What's your next move?"

"A late dinner at DiNapoli's while I go over everything I know." More likely all I didn't know. "Want to join me?"

"I can't. I'm sorry. I need to spend some time with my niece."

"How's she doing?" I asked.

"We haven't killed each other yet, thanks to your getting me out of the house."

"Not bad then."

Harriet yawned.

"Sleep if you need to. Being a caregiver is exhausting."

"Thanks, Sarah." Harriet closed her eyes and slept the rest of the way home. I wished sleep would come that easily for me.

After I dropped Harriet off, I drove home, sat in my car, shot off a text to Awewome, and called Seth.

"Any word on who tried to kidnap you?" I asked, trying to keep my voice concerned but not shrill. Because every nerve was standing like a tin soldier. I had too many thoughts like bowling-sized balls twirling above my head— Stella, Crystal, Seth, the kidnapper. If I could catch just one of those balls, maybe the rest would fall into place before they all crashed down.

"They're working on it."

"Who are they?"

"Several different agencies."

"But they haven't figured it out yet?"

"I don't think they have a clue."

That meant I had to find one for them. I filled him in on my visit with Trooper Kilgard and Pellner. I left out my trip to Pawtucket. "Did you know Crystal Olson?" I asked.

"No."

I should have been that decisive with Trooper Kilgard. "Did you ever see her around the apartment complex?"

"I'm sure I didn't. I would have noticed someone who looked like you."

"It's disturbing," I said.

"It's almost like someone left Crystal there for you to find."

Oh, no. Trust Seth to take two and two and come up with the right answer. "It is." There. I managed to find a response so I hadn't lied to Seth and I hadn't compromised Stella's safety.

"But how would anyone ever think you'd be at that house to find her?"

This was a much harder question to answer without lying. "Exactly." That wasn't really a lie. I was just agreeing with the question. I hated all this evasiveness. Skirting the truth didn't suit me.

"Come over?"

It was tempting, but I couldn't work on tracking the killer if I was with Seth. "Are your guards still there?" I hoped they were for his safety and also because it gave me an excuse to not go over.

"They are. Is that a no then?"

Leaving would be much harder than not going over at all. "It is. What's your day like tomorrow?"

"Court in the morning."

"Is it safe for you to go?"

"As safe or safer than any place."

Metal detectors. Armed guards. I hoped safe.

"I have to ask you about something, Sarah. I'd rather have asked you in person, but since you aren't coming over, I need to get it off my chest."

His tone was so serious that I braced myself. I'm not sure I wanted to hear what was coming next.

"I heard from Awesome that you're thinking of buying

a house. Why didn't you ever talk to me about that? I have a house. I was hoping, maybe unrealistically, that someday we'd be sharing it."

My heart fluttered with joy for a moment, a glimpse of a shiny future out ahead of me. But then reality hit. If hearts could drop, mine just had. And now I'd have to flat-out lie to Seth. Sins of omission didn't seem as bad somehow. "Thinking of buying something is way different from actually buying something." It sounded lame. I would feel terrible if Seth made a big life decision without talking to me at this point in our relationship. "I wouldn't have bought a house without talking to you, and I don't have the money now anyway. I've always liked looking at real estate. You know that."

"I didn't."

I'd hurt him. The tone of his voice screamed it. I almost couldn't stand myself, and I just hoped, when the truth came out, after I found Stella—*please let me find her*—that Seth would understand.

"I need to go," Seth said.

"Okay then. Love you, Seth."

"Love you, Sarah." Seth disconnected.

The words gave me hope, but they were said flatly. At the end of *How the Grinch Stole Christmas,* the Grinch's heart grew three sizes when he realized that Christmas is about more than just presents. Mine was swollen with the pain of a thousand lies.

I arrived at DiNapoli's door just as Rosalie was turning the sign to Closed. I hadn't realized it was already past nine thirty. I wasn't that hungry, but I needed to be around people who loved me if only for a few minutes. Rosalie spotted me and motioned for me to come in. The place was empty except for Angelo and Emil. *Oh, boy.* Why was that my reaction every time I saw the man? He was heading to the back of the restaurant.

"We were just sitting down to eat. Join us," Rosalie said.

I wanted to make an excuse and leave now that I knew Emil was here too. But my stomach rumbled just loudly enough for Rosalie to hear.

"Come in and eat with us," she insisted. "There's pizza in the oven. It will be ready soon."

"As long as you let me help clean up until then."

Rosalie nodded. Emil walked out from the back just then with a broom in his hand. I hung up my jacket and started putting chairs up on the long line of tables as Angelo and Rosalie worked in the kitchen. I'd found some of the tables along with various chairs at garage sales I had attended. Nothing matched, but it was charming somehow. Twenty minutes later a timer went off, and Angelo pronounced the pizza ready.

He gestured to the table on the right side of the room where I'd left the chairs down. Emil opened a bottle of Chianti. Rosalie grabbed a big salad on the counter in front of us, and Angelo carried a pizza toward the table.

"Bianco. Your favorite, Sarah. It's like I knew you were going to turn up tonight."

Bianco was white pizza with cheese and garlic. If heaven had a food, it was surely Angelo's bianco pizza.

"Can I get anything?" I asked.

"Grab some silverware and napkins please," Rosalie said.

I did as instructed, carried the utensils and napkins to

the table, and set it. When I finished Emil lifted a strand of my hair and examined it.

"Dough free," he said with a deep chuckle.

"I've heard it's the latest craze for conditioning one's hair. People are paying hundreds, and you did it for free," I said. It felt good to be silly for a minute.

Emil chuckled again. "Well, it's working for you. Your hair couldn't be any silkier." He held out the chair next to him as Rosalie beamed at us and Angelo winked at me. They were about as subtle as grizzlies in a tea shop. They sat opposite us. Emil poured us all wine, and we toasted to good friends and good food. Angelo passed out pieces of pizza, cheese oozed over the sides. I took some salad when it was passed to me, arugula with walnuts, goat cheese, and pomegranate seeds, with Angelo's light vinaigrette to dress it.

Just as I took my first bite of pizza, Emil asked if we'd heard there'd been a murder in town. I suddenly found it difficult to chew and swallow. Angelo and Rosalie turned to look at me.

"I'm sorry, Sarah. That was a terrible time to bring it up." Rosalie frowned at Emil.

"She found the body," Angelo said.

Emil raised his eyebrows. "I'm sorry. Did you know her, Sarah?"

Maybe that would put an end to any romantic interest if there even was any. I finally managed to swallow. "I didn't know her."

"Have they identified who it was?" Emil asked.

"I was at mass this morning, and there was a lot of talk, but no one had heard who she was," Rosalie said.

Apparently church, like almost every place else in

Ellington, was a hotbed of gossip. "Did they say anything else?" I asked.

"No. Everyone was gossiping about it and the lack of information," Rosalie said.

I guess the police wanted to hold back that Crystal had been dressed like Alice in Wonderland because that might be something only the killer would know. With the Ellington information pipeline, it was amazing that detail hadn't gotten out. But it was disappointing that Rosalie didn't know anything new. How would I ever find Stella?

Emil set down his fork. "Do you find dead bodies often?"

More than anyone should.

"No," Rosalie said. "Of course not."

"I have on occasion," I said. And even if I hadn't found the body, I'd ended up tangled in more than one investigation to help someone out. Even the police last January.

"You're an interesting woman," Emil said.

"That's one way to look at it. Someone else might say unlucky." Stella would definitely say that. I changed the topic to my upcoming garage sale and the rest of the dinner passed without controversy.

Rosalie looked at Angelo. "Will you help me with the dessert?"

"It's just cookies, right?" Angelo said.

Rosalie poked him with her elbow as she smiled at him. "You can help me clear the table."

Angelo looked at her with a puzzled expression and then glanced over at Emil and me. "Sure I'll help. Anything for the woman I love."

"I can help," I said.

"No, no," Rosalie said. "You're our guest. Sit. Emil pour some more wine for Sarah."

Most nights when I ate here alone with Rosalie and Angelo, they let me clear the plates, and sometimes they even let me do the dishes. I could only hope that Emil didn't pick up on the blatant messages.

"That was awkward," Emil said as soon as Rosalie and Angelo headed to the kitchen.

"I'm embarrassed. I'm seeing someone, and for all I know you are too."

"Nope. I'm free, but I think I left my heart in Italy."

"Ah, sorry." I knew a lot about hearts and breaking.

"It's okay. I'm a survivor. Came home to be surrounded by my loving family."

"They are an amazing family to be surrounded by. Living in Italy must have been wonderful," I said.

"It was. My girlfriend—now ex-girlfriend—runs an art gallery in Rome. It was a fascinating world. Very different from the one I grew up in. Poor in Cambridge."

People always thought of Harvard when someone mentioned Cambridge, but there was another side to the place too. One where people struggled to survive from day to day. Interesting that Emil didn't talk about what he had done for work in Italy. An international man of mystery.

When my phone rang I was surprised to see it was already eleven fifteen. The night had flown by. The number was blocked, but of course I answered anyway. It was him—the kidnapper. "Hold on," I told him as I stood.

"Are you okay?" Emil asked. "You just got very pale."

"Um, yes. I just have to go. Please apologize to Rosalie and Angelo for me." I brushed past him and hustled out the door before I said more.

"What?" I snapped when I was out on the sidewalk.

"Is that any way to greet me?"

It's the only way.

"Did you get what I asked you to this morning?"

Did he really not know or was this part of his game? "I got it. Lot five."

"Perfect. You need to take the pocket watch and the rest of the lot to the Queen of Harts at midnight."

"Where's the queen of hearts?" Was he talking about a deck of cards?

"You think you're smart. Figure it out."

I stared at my phone. He'd disconnected before I had a chance to ask anything else.

I ran home to my car, climbed in, started it, and turned on the seat warmer. The box of stuff was still on the backseat where I'd put it when I picked up Harriet. I reached around, grabbed it, and hauled it to the front seat. I stared down at the items willing them to give me some kind of answer. They didn't.

Queen of Hearts? There were no stores or restaurants by that name that I knew of. I searched on my phone for Queen of Hearts and Ellington, Massachusetts. Nothing came up. I broadened my search, but didn't find anything in the surrounding towns. I tapped my fingers on the steering wheel. Who could I call who might have some idea of what the kidnapper was alluding too? It had to be someone who would still be up this time of night.

I dialed a number. Miss Belle answered a few moments later. "I'm sorry to bother you this late." I had helped sell Miss Belle's collection of mysteries to raise money for the local library last summer. She'd lived in Ellington for many years and knew almost everyone across all walks of life.

"You know I'm something of a night owl. What can I do for you, dear?"

"Have you ever heard of a store or restaurant or business around here called the Queen of Hearts?"

"Not a business but a woman."

"There's a woman here called the Queen of Hearts?"

"Was. Belinda Hart. H-a-r-t. She had a big brood of kids, but she called herself the Queen of Harts. Everyone always got a kick out of that. She's buried in the cemetery off Great Road. Her tombstone is a six-foot obelisk topped with a tiara."

"Thank you. That's a big help."

"You're welcome, dear. Anytime."

I loved that Miss Belle didn't ask me why I needed to know this. I had plenty of time to get to the cemetery, but I was reluctant to go. It wasn't the dead I was afraid of but the living.

Chapter Sixteen

I was alone. There was no one to call on such short notice. No one who wouldn't require a lot of explanation anyway. No one who I wanted to wake at this time of night or put into danger if there was going to be any. I drove around the perimeter of the cemetery. I didn't see any cars parked or people lurking. Not that that was much comfort. I parked on a side street, as the cemetery was officially closed. Fortunately or maybe unfortunately I could still walk in.

I slung the strap of my purse over my shoulder and picked up the box. It was just big enough that I needed to carry it with both hands. It left me feeling a bit defenseless in case something happened even though I was still relying on the wine bottle and hairspray as weapons. Tonight, if I wanted to use them, I'd have to drop the box and grab my purse off my shoulder before I could use it. Not good. Not good at all.

The cemetery was planted with tall oaks, pines, and shorter maples. During the day in full bloom it looked lovely, but tonight the leafless trees looked like skeleton hands stretching toward the dark sky. The half-moon played peekaboo behind clouds that scurried across the sky. The wind lifted my hair, blew it in my face, and then tossed it aside. Not helpful. My eyes adjusted to the dark.

The half-moon provided a little light, as did the lights out on the street. But it was darker than I liked. Much darker. Especially since I didn't know why I was here. I creeped along the paved path toward the interior of the cemetery where the older, taller grave markers were. I'd figured that out as I'd driven around the perimeter.

I stopped every once in a while to listen for other footsteps. I had a terrible feeling that I hadn't been sent here for any good reason. But so far I hadn't heard a thing. When I reached what seemed to be the middle of the cemetery, I stopped again and looked around. The moon peeked out. I spotted the tiara monument about thirty yards to my left and headed toward it.

That was when I heard voices. Hushed voices—both male. But not hushed enough that I couldn't tell some kind of drug deal was going down. *Great!* How to ruin a night in ten easy lessons. There was a lot of back-and-forth about "show me the money" and "not until you show me the drugs."

"Where's Alexer?" one of the men said.

"Not until you show me the money," the other answered. A raspy voice.

Elixer? Was that what he meant? I wasn't up on street drugs, but maybe that was the name of one. The men sounded like they were between the tiara and me. I stepped off the paved road onto the soft grass and circled around, hoping to wend my way to the tiara without being seen.

I scurried from one monument to another. Crouching when necessary. Trying to keep the voices away from me. I checked my phone. Almost midnight. I had to get this box there now. I peeked out from behind a grave marker. The coast seemed clear, the voices farther away or at least softer. I made my move and dashed over to Belinda's grave. Just as I set the box down, the alarm on the clock went off.

It sounded like Big Ben in the quiet night, and I froze.

"Who'd you bring?" a male voice demanded. "You double-crosser."

"It wasn't me. It must be you."

"Let's go find out who's the liar."

There was no time to fumble with the alarm and turn it off. I turned and ran as footsteps pounded toward me. I tripped on a root and fell, barely catching myself before my face hit the soft dirt. A gunshot banged, and I threw my arms over my head, as if that could save me.

"Let's get out of here," one of the men yelled.

The footsteps pounded away. If they hadn't shot each other, who had fired the shot? I still wasn't alone here or safe. I crawled to the nearest grave marker. Was that rustling a person or a bit of breeze scraping branches together? I couldn't stay here all night listening. I kept my head down and snuck from marker to marker, but they kept getting smaller as I headed toward the entrance. Now or never. I leaped up, dodged around a tree, and smacked right into someone.

"Come on."

It was Emil. He grabbed my hand. Gave it a yank. We ran to the front entrance, out onto the street, around the corner to where my Suburban was parked. I was gasping by the time we got there.

"What are you doing here?" I was bent over, hands on knees. I looked over sideways and up. I saw the lump of a gun under his jacket. "You shot someone?"

"I shot into the dirt. To scare them off. I have a concealed carry permit."

It was hard enough to get a gun permit in Massachusetts. Let alone a concealed carry permit. Rosalie said he was in "international business." Now I wondered what the heck kind of business it was. I straightened up. Leaned against the Suburban. "How did you just *happen* to be out here?"

"You looked scared when your phone rang." He shrugged. "So I followed you." He tilted his head toward the Suburban. "It's not like it's hard when you're driving that. What were you doing out here?"

My Suburban had been a problem in the past because it was big and white. "My problems are mine, not yours. As are my reasons for being out here." The last thing I needed was for a man with a knight-in-shining-armor complex to stumble into the kidnapper's way and accidentally put himself and Stella in an even worse situation. I dug my keys out of my pocket and unlocked the car. I sighed and turned toward Emil. "But thank you."

I drove home watching my rearview for headlights to see if I was being followed. Emil had gotten in his own car, but had peeled off a couple of blocks ago. There wasn't much traffic in Ellington this time of night. Why had the kidnapper sent me to the cemetery? Had he just wanted to scare me? Or was it something worse, like he had hoped the drug dealers would kill me? If Emil hadn't been there. If the drug dealers had found me. *Just stop.* They didn't.

I had just turned onto my block when headlights flashed behind me. I squinted at my rearview mirror. Great. A police car. Just what I didn't need. Instead of stopping at my house, I drove on by, turned right, wound around past the town hall, and then to the parking lot behind the library. The car pulled next to me. Pellner for the second time today. This time he climbed out of his car.

I wanted to bang my head against my steering wheel. I rolled down my window as I tried to figure out what to say about why I had driven here instead of just stopping at my house. I couldn't risk Stella's captor seeing me talking to the police. Who knew if he had put up another camera? A smaller one that I hadn't spotted.

"Why are we here?" Pellner asked.

"You flashed your lights at me, so you should know."

He blew out a breath. "Why did you stop here instead of in front of your house?"

I guess my weak attempt at a joke didn't sit well with him. Pellner's dimples were deep, and that was never a good sign. "I think the neighbors get nervous when the police are around all the time. They're starting to think I'm a jinx." I had no idea if that was true or not, but it sounded good.

Pellner stared at me for a moment, but didn't press the issue.

"What's up?" I asked.

"I talked to Chuck this evening."

Rats. Pellner called CJ "Chuck." I'd always hated that. CJ had promised he wouldn't say anything about my call. "Oh." I wasn't going to say more until I knew what was up.

"He found out you'd found another body, and he was worried. Called to see if I'd check on you."

Okay, I guess CJ hadn't told Pellner the real reason I'd called. "Pellner, you don't need to check on me." Not at all. Not this week when being seen with him could hurt Stella. "I'm fine." My voice quavered a little. Oh, that was convincing. "You have five kids and a wife to worry about. Plus, keeping the town safe."

"What are you doing out so late anyway?"

This just kept getting worse. I didn't want to answer him. I didn't have to answer him, but he'd think something was off if I didn't. "While I was heading home, I drove by the cemetery. Just a few minutes ago. I thought I heard a gunshot, and I saw two guys running out."

Pellner's eyes went wide. He clicked on the mic on his shoulder and repeated what I'd just told him. "I've got to go," he said. Pellner slid into his car and took off, lights flashing. Whew. No more questions at least for tonight anyway.

I dragged myself up the stairs toward my apartment. I hoped whoever was sitting outside Mike's door was someone I knew who wouldn't hassle me as had happened in the past. Usually it was Francesco, Diego, and one or two other guys taking rotating shifts. When my foot hit the top step, I glanced to my right. Mike himself was sitting there. Oh, no. He'd never been the one sitting outside the door. The whole reason he was here was to keep him safe.

"Where have you been?" Mike asked.

What? Was he my father? This was the third man tonight who was worried about me, and I was over it.

"Not really your business," I told him.

He stood up. His body tense. Mike could be helpful or menacing. Tonight he didn't look helpful. I thought about lying and saying I'd been with Seth. But he knew Seth. He'd helped Seth. Their history went way back to a private high school they had attended. And Mike could easily find out if I had been with Seth or not. The easiest thing to do would be to give partial truths. I had a lot of that going on these past couple of days, and I didn't like it.

I gave an exaggerated sigh. "If you must know I drove a friend to Rhode Island and back. She doesn't see well at night." I hoped he hadn't seen my car in the parking lot on the side of the house while I was at DiNapoli's or me coming and going.

Mike reached out toward me with his hand. I pulled back so he dropped it. "You have dirt on your face." He looked down. "And on your knees."

He was right. My jeans had two big brown marks from when I'd fallen over the root. "The friend I drove to Rhode Island was helping a relative plant a tree. It's dirty work." I made a couple of swipes at my knees while I said it so I didn't have to look Mike in the eye. I straightened. "Any word on the threat against you?" I hoped this would distract him.

"We think it was a false alarm."

"Does that mean you're going back to Boston?" *Please, please, please, say yes.* I would have crossed my fingers like my five-year-old self if I could have done it without him seeing it.

"Not yet."

That was a disappointment. I hoped my face didn't show it. I went for neutral with a side tilt of my head. "Why not?"

"I've just got this itchy feeling. Something's up."

Rats. I'd worried about this exact situation when Mike and his brothers had first showed up. "Dry skin? I've got some lotion that might help." Mike's eyes got icier. Apparently he didn't appreciate my humor. There was a lot of that going around lately.

He lifted his chin and looked down at me. "You okay? There's a chair wedged under the door to the basement."

"I'm tired," I said as I turned toward my apartment.

"You know what they say," Mike said.

I walked to my door and unlocked it. I was too tired for mind games with Mike. "No. I don't."

"You have an itch, you've got to scratch it."

That's the last thing I needed. I looked back at him. "Scratching makes everything worse, Mike."

Chapter Seventeen

I wanted to fall into bed and pull the covers over my head. But when I looked at Stella's phone there were a bunch of messages and missed calls from Awesome. I shot off a few texts. Still at practice. The director's a perfectionist. But he's good and I'm excited to be here. Miss you. Love you.

My face was flushed when I finished and reviewed what I'd written. My hands shook a little. I couldn't bear to type "talk soon" to Awesome. Moments later a kissy face emoji popped up. Awesome might never forgive me for keeping Stella's kidnapping from him, but it was a price I'd have to pay if I could bring Stella back to him. I couldn't risk her life   not before I was certain I couldn't find her myself. The kidnapper knew too much about me. I only had one more day on my self-imposed schedule to find her before I talked to the police.

I took a quick shower and climbed in bed. Went over the day in my head. Was I any closer to finding Stella? I didn't think so. Why had I been sent to the cemetery? It didn't make that much sense. The kidnapper knew the clock would go off at midnight. The stuff must have been his. Was he hoping the drug dealers would find me? *Kill me for him*, I thought again. Or did he want the police to know there were drug deals going down at the cemetery, but didn't want to tell them himself?

What did that say about him? Was he using me as some kind of vigilante because he didn't want to be one? Had he killed Crystal or did he know who did? But why kidnap Stella to clean up problems in the town? Too many questions, and I was way too tired to figure them out.

Monday morning came too early, after another restless night that involved dreams of a lot of men trying to tell me what to do. I showered, drank some coffee, and searched Stella's phone. Today I was going to try to track Stella's ride share, find out who the driver was, and talk to him or her. During the night I'd realized I hadn't done a thorough search of Stella's phone—other than looking through her texts with Awesome and shutting off her location tracker. I was going to see what else was on her phone—go through all of her text messages and emails. I should have thought of doing this before, but between almost sleepless nights and the stress of the whole situation, I'd forgotten. It made me worry what other things I hadn't thought of. I knew I wasn't even close to the top of whatever game I was playing.

I also wondered why I hadn't heard from the kidnapper last night or yet this morning. Did he know what had happened at the cemetery? And if so how? Was he one of the drug dealers? Since I again didn't have any answers, I focused on Stella's phone. I read for the next half hour, but didn't find anything out of the ordinary.

I opened her ride share app. It was for a local company instead of one of the bigger national ones. She'd ordered a car at seven a.m., requesting an arrival time of eight ten. I gripped the phone tighter. Whoever picked her up could be her kidnapper. According to the app the car was a black SUV with license plate XORSOX. How could I find someone to run this plate? I looked at the photo of the driver. Seriously? Why did it have to be him?

It was Elmer Norman, the town curmudgeon. The one I had just outbid for lot five. It didn't seem possible that he was the kidnapper. Why would he have me outbid him at the auction or send me to the cemetery? I needed to know what had happened after Elmer picked Stella up, but he'd be about as likely to want to help me as CJ would, which was never.

Who would have ever thought that Elmer would be a ride share driver? And yet his ratings were fairly high. That didn't go along with his reputation. Maybe the stories about him were exaggerated, or maybe he'd changed his ways. As much as I didn't want to talk to him, I had to. At least he'd be easy to find.

I drove to Dunkin's and bought two cups of coffee and a half dozen assorted donuts. Back at my apartment I used my phone to order the ride share. I requested Elmer. It said he would arrive in twelve minutes. I put my hair up in a ponytail and put on a Red Sox cap. I pulled it low over my face and added a big set of sunglasses even though it was cloudy out. Maybe if he didn't recognize me as the person who outbid him, things would go more smoothly. Maybe he hadn't even seen my face at the auction. I hoped he hadn't.

A black SUV with the license plate XORSOX pulled up. I'd have to talk fast. How had Stella ended up getting in the wrong car? If that's what had happened. I didn't know for sure. I'd requested a ride to the shopping mall in

Burlington, which was about twenty minutes away, hoping that would give me time to ask all the questions I needed to. I climbed in the back seat. Elmer looked a lot like the picture on the ride share app with a broad forehead and jawline. Stubble stuck out every which way, as if he only saw the need to shave every third day or so. His nose was smashed flat at the bridge, like someone had decked him one too many times. Given his reputation, that wasn't surprising.

I stuck out the donuts. "These are for you."

Elmer glanced in the rearview, and I looked down so he'd see the brim of my hat. He grabbed the box and tossed it on the seat next to him.

"I'm diabetic, have high cholesterol, and my doctor said gluten is causing inflammation."

Great. I should have brought him hard-boiled eggs. Although maybe he was following a vegan diet too.

He opened the box, snatched a donut, took a big bite, chewed, and swallowed. "I told my doctor to go to hell. I know vets with better sense."

"I brought coffee too. Black." I held out the cup, again keeping my head down. "I brought some sugars and creamer if you need it."

"Naw. Black's the only way to go. I'm not supposed to have caffeine either, so thanks."

I couldn't decide if he was happy or mad. Elmer pulled away from the curb, chomping on his second donut.

"My landlady Stella recommended you."

"I've known her since she was in diapers. Taught her sixth-grade science class."

The town curmudgeon had taught young kids? "She's a gem," I said.

"Strangest thing. I was supposed to pick her up a couple of days ago, and she didn't come out of the house. She usually comes right out after I pull up. I was about ten minutes late. I went up and knocked on her front door."

"That doesn't sound like her. What did she say?"

"Nothing. She didn't answer her door. I eventually left. But it bothered me. Sure I was late, but I could have gotten her to the airport on time. Unlike her not to let me know she didn't need me or to cancel the ride."

"Were there any other cars around when you pulled up?"

"A gray one pulled away from the curb and flew down the street as I rounded the corner. Typical Masshole driver. You shouldn't drive like that on a side street."

"What kind of car?"

"Looked like every other gray car on the planet. What happened to car designers? No one takes a risk anymore. No classic Thunderbirds or Mustangs. No fins." He shook his head. "They all look the same. Bland."

"Did you notice the plate?" Although that car might have been stolen too. In that case the license plate number wouldn't be important, but I had to turn over every stone until I found Stella. The person who'd tried to kidnap Seth had been in a black van. But maybe, after he'd ditched it in the Cambridge Reservoir, the kidnapper had to use his own car. I needed a break.

"Massachusetts plates 294—hey, why are you asking all these questions?" He looked in the rearview again. I didn't duck my head in time. He tightened his grip on the steering wheel and swerved to the curb. "I know who you are. Sarah Winston." He spit my name out like something tasted bad in his mouth. "Get out."

"You've got to be kidding."

"I'm not."

"Just tell me if you got the rest of the plate number. Please."

He glared at me, face red. "That's all I saw. Get out."

I climbed out, and he sped away from the curb. Fortunately, it wasn't that far of a walk home, and at least I had a tiny bit of information. Gray car, Massachusetts plates, starting with 294.

Harriet had to take her niece to physical therapy this morning, so I worked at John's house alone. Working here when I should be out looking for Stella was beyond frustrating. Even if I couldn't price everything in time for John's sale, even if he fired me or wrote a bad review and Zoey got all future business, it was less important than finding Stella. It was day three since she'd been kidnapped. My personal deadline. But the kidnapper had said to go about my routine, and here I was following his orders again.

I would work for a little while. Maybe something would come to me. I picked up one of the many tramp art picture frames John wanted to get rid of. He and his husband had decided to go more modern when they moved to Boston. I was keeping an eye out for fifties and sixties furniture for them when I went to garage sales and thrift shops.

My phone rang. It was Alice Krandle.

"Sarah, you did such a wonderful job with my garage sale."

"Thank you." It was nice to hear something positive with all that was going on.

"I decided to sell more of my things. Can you swing by tomorrow so we can talk about another sale?"

The difficulty of working with Alice and my need for

income did a brief war with each other. Income won. "Of course. What time works for you?"

"Around nine-thirty?" she asked.

"Sure. I'll see you then."

I roamed the house pricing things and worrying, for a couple of hours until my phone chimed. It jerked me back to reality, which was somewhere I didn't want to be right now. I glanced down with trepidation, but it was Damaris Christos, a therapist in town. What could this be about?

Chapter Eighteen

A half hour later I sat across from Damaris at the Dunkin's in Bedford. Damaris was as beautiful as her Greek name, with thick, dark hair, huge brown eyes, enviable long eyelashes, and she didn't even wear makeup. She looked like she was around my age. I couldn't imagine what she wanted. Damaris had moved to town in January and had sent me her business card after I was in the press for a murder I'd been embroiled in. I guess she had thought I might need therapy, but I hadn't taken her up on it. I hoped that wasn't why we were here today.

I knew how hard it was to start a new business, but if she was so desperate that she was calling people to drum up clients, things must not be going well for her. Damaris flicked her hair back across her shoulder, and she seemed nervous. I thought therapists were supposed to be good at hiding their emotions. It made me feel even more unsettled.

"What do you need?" I asked. One of us had to start with conversation. Drinking coffee and awkwardly glancing at each other was getting us nowhere.

She leaned forward, perched on the very edge of the hard, plastic seat. Easy to clean, not comfortable to sit on very long which I supposed was the whole point. I watched as she changed the expression on her face. Set it to neutral.

"I run a therapy group for family members who have loved ones who are incarcerated."

I nodded. "I've heard about it. At the Congregational church on the town common, right?" What did this have to do with me? Perhaps she wanted me to run a garage sale to raise money for her group. I felt a little warm glow. I'd be happy to do that. Charity garage sales gave me a lot of joy, and I could help my adopted community—after I got Stella back. I would get Stella back or die trying. I repressed a shiver at that unwelcome thought.

Damaris flicked her hair again. "Yes." She put her hands around her coffee cup like she wanted to warm them. "I have to be careful what I tell you because of the confidentiality between a therapist and her patients."

I nodded encouragingly. "I'd be happy to help in any way I can." Just spit it out. I had things to do.

"Something disturbing has come to my attention, and it concerns you."

I had my cup lifted halfway to my mouth, but I froze. After a moment I managed to set my cup back down. "Just tell me."

"One of the group members came to me and told me a splinter group has formed off my group." She took a drink of her coffee. "They have a grudge against you. A sort of 'we hate Sarah' group. Since you helped the police send their loved ones to prison."

I knew my mouth was hanging open, but it took me a few moments to close it. "Who are they?"

"I'm sorry, but I can't give you that information."

"But what if they want to hurt me?"

"From what my client told me, there's been no mention

of violence. It's more just venting." She shifted in her seat. "And now that I know about the situation, we will be concentrating on not blaming others for the actions of their loved ones."

That was all well and good, but Damaris didn't know about Stella being kidnapped. Maybe it was someone in the splinter group who was doing all of this. "This is very unsettling. Scary. I think I have a right to know who they are."

Damaris stood. "I shouldn't have told you as much as I did."

"Then why mention it at all?"

Damaris bit her lip. "Don't worry. It's under control."

"That's not an answer."

"If you want to discuss your fears concerning this, here's my card."

My fears? She had a group she couldn't control. Instead of helping them, she'd somehow fired up at least some of them. When I didn't take the card from her, she put it on the table next to me and strode off. A slow burn of anger built in me as I stared down at her card. I picked it up and ripped it into tiny pieces. Not that it made me feel any better. How was I going to find out who was in the splinter group?

When I got home I checked the Congregational church's calendar. The incarcerated loved ones group met today at four. It wasn't like I could show up for the meeting, and I couldn't think of anyone I knew to ask if they could go. And even if I did know someone, asking them to spy for me wouldn't be fair to them. I paced back and forth across my living room a few times before I made a phone call.

"Frida, I need your help," I said. Frida Chida had her own cleaning business and also cleaned the church. We'd started out very suspicious of each other when her former employer had been killed, but she had helped Miss Belle out for me last summer. I hoped Frida would help me now. Plus, Frida had lived in Ellington for a long time and knew a lot of people.

"What kind of help? Honestly, your apartment isn't that big. I'd think you could clean it yourself."

That was Frida for you. Blunt and to the point. "I don't need you to clean for me." I filled her in on my conversation with Damaris. "I really need to know who is in the splinter group."

"And you want me to be cleaning outside of where they meet to see who goes in there?"

"Yes. You've lived here all of your life and would probably recognize the people in the group." Maybe this wasn't such a great idea, but I was feeling very desperate right now.

"I don't like the idea of spying on people who already have their share of problems."

"I understand that." I didn't feel great about asking her to do it.

"But I also don't like the idea of people sitting around bad-mouthing you with all the good you do for others."

I gripped my phone a little tighter, trying not to get my hopes up.

"I'll do the best I can to find out who's in the group."

"Thank you, Frida. And please don't do anything that makes you uncomfortable."

"I won't. You know me."

I guess I did.

I made a Fluffernutter sandwich, which consisted of white bread, peanut butter, and marshmallow fluff. It was my go-to comfort food, but today it tasted terrible. I forced myself to eat it because I couldn't help Stella if I couldn't function. I was running on almost empty the way it was.

As I ate, I went over people who might be mad at me because their loved one was incarcerated. The list was longer than I liked, and, worse, most of those people probably had extended family and friends who I knew nothing about. Even if Frida got me some names, I might just be chasing rainbows. I'd go nuts just sitting here, so I decided to price more things for my anniversary sale.

At three thirty I looked out my window at the Congregational church. It stood tall in the bright spring sunlight. There were several entrances. I had a great view of the main one that went into a vestibule that led to the sanctuary. A side door that I could also see led down to the classrooms where Sunday school and other events were held. There was also an entrance around back, out of view, that led to the kitchen. It seemed like people who attended the group session would most likely use the side entrance. If I had a pair of binoculars I could watch who went in around four.

But that wouldn't help. According to the church website, there were other activities at four like choir practice and after-school programs. I'd be better off continuing to distract myself by doing more pricing for my sale. Frida would call or come over soon enough. Hopefully then I'd have another lead and I'd find Stella.

I'd stacked some things to price in the corner of the living room to the left of the window. My apartment had a sloping ceiling on that side and a short five-foot-high wall. I grabbed some boxes and carried them over to the trunk in front of my couch. Last year, I'd collected vintage Christmas ornaments to make my mom a wreath like one my aunt had that my mom loved. The wreath was really cute, but I'd ended up with more ornaments than I needed. It was a problem when I started collecting something new. It was easy to buy more (although not always cost-effective) on sites like Etsy and eBay.

The ornaments were called Shiny Brites. Before World War II, almost all of the glass ornaments on American Christmas trees had been imported from Germany. To ensure Americans could still buy them during the war, Max Eckardt had teamed up with the Corning Glass company to produce machine-blown glass balls. Max had convinced Woolworths to sell them, and they had been an instant hit.

People still loved them today because they remembered their grandmother or mother having them. The ornaments were clear at first, but they soon added color to them. Which was why I was sitting here pricing red, silver, blue, and green ornaments. I soon realized I didn't want to part with any of them. Maybe I should make a wreath for myself. As I priced I rehashed everything that had happened in the last three days. Nothing new, no inspiration came to me. There wasn't much I could do until I heard from Frida or Stella's kidnapper.

At five fifteen I heard loud voices out in the hall arguing and went running out to see what was going on. Frida and Mike's brother Francesco were toe-to-toe at the top of the stairs, yelling at each other.

"Let me by," Frida shouted. Frida was a thick, sturdy woman from all her years as a cleaning lady. Last summer I'd helped find her a job working for Miss Belle that put less stress on her body and more joy in her work life.

"No one gets by me without ID and purpose of visit," Francesco said.

"She's here to see me, and this has got to stop," I said. "I'll take this up with Mike later. Come on, Frida."

Francesco stepped back, and Frida charged by him, jabbing an elbow into his stomach. He didn't react, but Frida rubbed her elbow. Francesco shrugged. I interpreted the shrug as "take up whatever you want with Mike; nothing's going to change."

I fixed Frida a cup of English breakfast tea, and she settled on my grandmother's rocking chair. I sat on the sofa with my own cup of tea. Frida had burgundy streaks in her gray hair and wore black knit pants with a worn Patriots' sweatshirt.

"So?" I asked.

Frida frowned at her tea and then over at me. "It's not good, Sarah. I swept, mopped, and then dusted. I think Damaris caught on because she eventually closed the door. But first I heard her talking about not blaming the police or others who locked their family members or friends up."

"Could you see their reactions?" I held my tea, warming my hands.

"Yeah. Fortunately the door has a big window. Some people leaned in nodding, but another group sat back and crossed their arms over their chests."

"How many leaned back?"

"I counted five."

That was consistent with what Damaris had said. "Did you know them?"

"Only one. Louisa Crane. Do you know her?"

I thought for a minute and then shook my head. "I don't." I hadn't helped with a case with someone whose last name was Crane. "What do you know about her?"

"Not much. I cleaned for her once about six months ago when she was moving from one apartment to another. It's not like we run in the same social circles."

I briefly wondered what kind of social circles Frida ran in. "Does she have money?" Maybe that would be some sort of indicator.

"Not if the apartment I cleaned was any indication. The whole building seemed to sag. Old linoleum peeling up in the kitchen. Yellowed roller shades at the windows."

"But she had enough to pay you."

Frida nodded. "With a generous tip."

Hmmmm. Someone who'd come into some money? "Do you know where she moved to?"

"I don't. If you have paper and pen, I can write down descriptions of the others." I went into my bedroom and found a notebook in my nightstand. I had pens on the top of the trunk from pricing ornaments. I gave both to Frida and watched as she wrote, brow creased in concentration. Ten minutes later she handed the notebook to me and stood.

"I've got to get going."

After I thanked Frida and she left I read over all the descriptions. They could have fit half of America. Black, Latinx, Caucasian, tall, short, jeans, slacks, leggings. A few tattooed arms, too far away to see the detail of what they were. Red Sox hoodie, plaid flannel shirt, white button-down, sleeves rolled up, pink dress, blue tee. Three women and two men.

I set the notebook aside and looked up Louisa Crane on my phone. She had a Facebook account, but her privacy settings were high, so I couldn't see anything she'd posted. Her profile picture was an avatar of a crane—the bird, not the piece of construction equipment. I tapped my finger on my thigh while I thought about it. The last name seemed familiar. I tried again, typing "Crane" and "crime."

Louisa Crane's nephew had attempted to kidnap a baby at the mall. All I had done was stick my foot out to trip him. Then I had caught the baby as the nephew fell. That had happened about eighteen months ago. The nephew should still be in jail. Was that really reason enough to resent me? To do this to me? I had no choice but to try to figure that out. If Louisa was the one doing this, either she had help or she could change her voice.

Another thought occurred to me, and I searched for how to change your voice. There were plenty of articles that went from the ridiculous, with a suggestion to purse your lips when you talk, to the frightening, like apps that you can download to disguise your voice.

In that case it would be easy for a woman to be behind Stella's kidnapping. My phone rang. It was a blocked number. I tensed as I answered.

"I hope you are having a pleasant day, Sarah."

"As you can imagine, with Stella kidnapped, I'm not."

"'Kidnapped' is such a harsh word. Borrowed? Held?"

"And you almost got me killed last night at the cemetery."

"Tsk, tsk. That would be a devastating blow to the town."

"Wow. A comedian and a criminal." I don't know what had gotten into me to speak to him this way. It probably wasn't doing Stella any good.

He laughed, but it was a maniacal sound that wasn't at

all comforting. His grip on sanity sounded very thin. "I have another small task for you."

I wasn't in a position to say no. "What?" A train sounded its horn, and I heard the bells that indicated crossing gates were going down. A clue? I tightened my grip on my phone. Maybe not. He could be driving some place. But there was only one place in Ellington with a train track with crossing gates. It was on the far west side of the town. But I had to act calm. Normal. As if nothing had changed. I'd had plenty of practice doing that of late.

"There's a barn out on the west side of town beyond the hockey rink. I left a package for you. Take it to Alice Krandle. Oh, and do it right now. Have it to her by 8:08." He disconnected before I could say anything.

There was more than one barn on that side of town. It was already almost six. How was I going to find the package and get it to Alice by 8:08?

Chapter Nineteen

I didn't like that he was involving my client in this mess or that he knew Alice was a client. Did her earlier call to me have anything to do with it or her garage sale? I drove past the third barn on this side of town. The sun was going down because I'd wasted so much time driving around. The first two barns I had spotted were behind houses with lights on in the house and people in their yards. They didn't seem like great spots for leaving a package.

I continued to drive around. The next barn I pulled up to was close to the crossing point for the train tracks. It was set back from the road on a piece of land. No houses were close to it. No animals grazed in the field that surrounded it.

I assessed the situation. The land was surrounded by one of the low stone walls so iconic to New England. I'd have to climb over it and tromp through a field to get to the barn. The light was fading rapidly. The field was overgrown with knee-high dried grass, and who knew what could be lurking under it—snakes, spiders, rodents? But it had to be done. I found a place to pull off the road as close to the barn as I could get. But it was still a good fifty yards in front of me.

The wind whistled around me as I swept the darkness with a Maglite flashlight CJ had given me a couple of years ago. Not only did it have a great light, it had a heft to it that gave me some sense of security. Getting hit with this thing would hurt, and it was easier to carry around than the wine bottle that was still in my purse, which I'd left in my car.

I looked down into the ditch I had to cross before I got to the stone wall. Ditches were always deeper than they looked from above and the banks always steeper. I started down, stumbled, and righted myself. Fortunately, the bottom was dry, and climbing the other side was easy. I used the flashlight to sweep for critters but didn't see any, so I scrambled over the stone wall without dislodging any stones.

I walked through the field toward the barn. The air smelled of dirt and weeds. I heard some skittering noises. Hopefully, it was just the wind on the dry grass. Seconds later my flashlight swept across something metallic. I scanned again and crept closer. It was an old bear trap. Opened, ready to spring with rusted teeth. Had the kidnapper left it for me or was it just a bonus for him? Stepping in one would do a lot of damage. I found a sturdy rock and tossed it on the spring, snapping the trap closed. The noise made me jump. Maybe vermin of the animal variety were the least of my worries; a human who set booby traps was a much bigger concern.

My pace slowed to almost a crawl. Scan, step, scan, step. It seemed like I'd been out here for hours. Thankfully, I didn't spot any other traps. The owners, whoever they were, should be contacted to make sure nothing else like that was in their field.

Now I faced the sliding barn doors. Were they booby-trapped? Staring at them wouldn't do any good. But maybe I could mitigate the risk. Instead of grabbing the handle and sliding the door open from the middle, I stepped to the far end of the door, grasped it as best I could, and tugged it far enough open that I would be able to slip into the barn. No gunshots sounded. No one had rigged a shot-gun to shoot when the door was open. I took that as a good sign. What if I'd gone through all of this, I was in the wrong barn, and the package wasn't here?

I peeked around the door and flashed my light into the barn. The floor was covered with a thin layer of straw or hay—I could never remember which was which. The musty smell made my nose itch. A shoebox tied with string sat in the middle of the old barn. As far as I could tell there were no contraptions set up around it to harm me. I also flashed the light up over the door. No pots of hot oil or honey and feathers were there either.

The walls were lined with old leather harnesses, rusted shovels, rakes, and pitchforks. It was basically a scene out of every scary movie set in a barn. I hustled over to the package and reached for it. Then I stopped. What if it was on something that would cause a chain reaction when I picked it up? Or what if it was a bomb that would blow as soon as it was moved? I scraped some hay away from the package with my foot. It looked like regular old wood floor under it. I knelt next to the box, getting my ear as close as I could without touching it. No sound. But did bombs even tick anymore with everything going digital?

I stood up and reached down, hoping that I wasn't going to have some kind of Indiana Jones experience complete with rolling boulders, poison darts shooting at me, and the barn collapsing. *Don't be ridiculous.* I grabbed the shoebox. It weighed almost nothing. I sprinted out of the barn clutching the box to my chest. I retraced my path as best I could and got back to my car unharmed. I had ten minutes to get to Alice's house.

I'd driven like the proverbial maniac, racing down side streets, careening around corners, and made it with two minutes to spare. But now I sat frozen. How could I take something unknown into my client's house? What if it were a bomb or poison or a body part? Yes, my imagination had gone wild while I drove over here. The dilemma weighed on me. Take this package unopened to Alice or open it and possibly hurt Stella?

I flipped on the inside lights of my Suburban, untied the string, and lifted the lid of the shoebox. The kidnapper had never said I couldn't open it, and I still had a couple of minutes before I was supposed to deliver it. The box was filled with crumpled newspaper. I pulled piece after piece out of the box, tossing them aside. But there wasn't anything else in the box. Why would the kidnapper want me to take this to Alice? Did the pieces of newspaper have some significance? I picked them back up, one by one.

Each piece contained a front-page article about me from the local newspaper. The time I'd saved kittens from a drain along with the unfortunate picture of me in action, my T-shirt wet; it was obvious I was cold. An article about my saving the child from being kidnapped, one about me being accused of murder, and one about me finding a beloved piece of art. All my escapades of the past two years here in crumpled black-and-white.

Why? I opened the last piece of paper, and a ring fell into my lap. I picked it up and realized that it was Stella's engagement ring. Something brownish-red was dried on it. *Please, don't let that be Stella's blood.* But I could picture her fighting to keep the ring. My eyes blurred with tears. Tears of anger. I swiped at my eyes so I could read the last article. It was about my brother, who'd been accused of murder and then had gone missing. Until now, that had been the most stressful time of my life.

I smoothed out each piece of paper. These had to be some kind of clue, right? Some test. I read each article again, embarrassed all over again that the town's residents thought I was a hero. Last spring the town leaders had wanted me to ride in a parade after saving the cats, baby, and artwork. Fortunately by the time the actual parade had rolled around, they'd found someone else to fawn over. Me on the back of a convertible waving like a homecoming queen? No thank you. I took the empty shoebox, got out of the car, and set it on Alice's porch without bothering to ring the bell. As far as I was concerned that fulfilled the instructions the kidnapper had given me. I headed back to the car thinking about all the articles, all the things that had happened.

I climbed in and sat there unsure what to do next. Seconds later I bolted up, grabbed my phone, and made a call. "Harriet? I think I know where Stella is."

Chapter Twenty

Thirty minutes later I had a team of friends assembled at the Bedford Farms Ice Cream shop. I had an empty cup of Almond Joy ice cream at my elbow. My dinner. And yes, I was amazed I had any kind of appetite, but maybe hope gave it to me. Around the table with Harriet and me were Frida, Frida's son who'd served in the military, and two of his friends who were also prior military. They'd all helped protect Miss Belle last summer. Charlie Davenport was with us too—she'd served in Vietnam and was as smart and tough as they came. Charlie had not only helped me when my brother disappeared, but I'd also purchased my pink ruby ring with her assistance. We were waiting for one more person who was driving in from Dorchester.

Everyone eyed one another while we waited for Gennie Elder, Stella's aunt. She was a retired mixed martial arts fighter or a cage fighter as I called her. I just hoped she didn't kick me from here to Jupiter when she found out her niece had been missing for three days and I hadn't told anyone but Harriet. Gennie strode in five minutes later and pulled up a chair.

All I had told anyone on the phone was that I was in

trouble and needed his or her help. That each person said yes without question humbled me. In my two years of living in Ellington, I'd found people I loved and ones who loved me. Who could ask for more?

After a deep breath, I explained the situation. Gennie turned whiter than my ice cream and then flushed an angry red as I talked. I couldn't tell if she was mad at me or furious with the situation. Frida had taken Gennie's hand and gripped it. Harriet talked about the situation too. How she had some resources looking into things. She glanced at me while she said it. I'd asked her not to contact anyone and she'd promised, but who was I to judge? Harriet's comments seemed to calm Gennie down.

"I think Stella is being held in an old barn west of town," I said.

Gennie leaped up. "Let's go get her."

"Please sit for just a minute. Let's talk this through and see if my logic makes sense."

Gennie nodded and sat back down—on the edge of her chair. I told them about the phone call and hearing the train in the background as I'd talked to the kidnapper earlier this evening. How he had sent me to the barn to pick up the package, about the newspaper articles with my past, scary connections to two different barns.

"Hearing the train was Stella's kidnapper making a mistake. But the articles were to taunt me. He didn't think I'd figure it out." And I'd come close to missing the significance of the two articles about the barns and my experiences in them, to not putting it all together. I told them about the trap I'd seen in the field, explained again why we couldn't call the police.

We formulated a plan. I was going to drive home, park,

and go to my apartment. I'd turn on lights to make it look like I was home. Then I'd sneak out one of Stella's windows and walk to the alley where Harriett, Gennie, and Charlie would be waiting in a car. Frida, her son, and his friends would meet us on a side street near the barn. Everyone stood. Hopefully, in less than an hour Stella would be safe. I hadn't mentioned Stella's ring and the possibility that there was dried blood on it.

I pulled Gennie aside. "I know you must be upset with me, but I did what I thought was the right thing to do."

Gennie gave a brief nod.

"If she's not there, I'm going to the police," I said. Three days. It was the bargain I had made with myself.

"Let's take it a step at a time before you make any decisions." She hugged me. "I'm sorry you're going through this, but let's get going."

Forty-five minutes later we stood outside the barn. Fortunately, it hadn't been Mike or one of his brothers outside the door when I'd gone back to my apartment, changed into all black clothes, and left again. The man had just nodded at me and gone back to reading his book.

Everyone had worn dark, comfortable clothing like I'd suggested. Charlie was out in the field somewhere watching with a pair of night-vision binoculars. She would call my phone if she saw anything worrisome. Gennie, Frida, Frida's son, and his two friends were stationed around the barn. Harriet had brought some kind of scope with forward-looking infrared capabilities that included detecting people through walls. She held it up, but didn't detect anyone inside the barn. But I still believed Stella was in there. Harriet insisted on going in with me. She had a gun, so I agreed.

The barn door was still open from when I'd been in there before. We slipped in and stood for a moment listening.

"You're sure she's here?" Harriet asked.

"Can I borrow your scope?" I asked.

Harriet handed it over, and I scanned the floor. I knew from an experience last May that some barns, even very old houses, had spaces below them where livestock were kept in the winter. I spotted a blurry image of one person and my heart almost stopped from relief. "Look about halfway across the barn." I gave Harriet the scope.

Harriet used it, nodded, but continued to scan. She looked up toward the loft. "Looks like there's just one person in here."

"Now to find how to get down there."

The barn floor was covered with hay. Done deliberately to cover the entrance? I turned on my Maglite and scanned the floor.

"There's a disturbed spot in the middle," Harriet said.

"It's where I found the package," I said. An old rake and a broom hung on one wall along with other farm implements. Harriet and I grabbed them and went to work. Moments later we uncovered a trapdoor. Harriet yanked it up. I jumped down with my flashlight. The space was only about five feet deep. There was Stella, tied to a folding chair, mouth duct-taped, dark green eyes squinted against the sudden light.

I cried out with relief as I ran to Stella. "Harriet! She's here."

Harriet jumped down too. I ripped the duct tape off Stella's mouth while Harriet slashed the ropes with a knife she'd pulled out of a pocket.

"How are you? Any injuries?" I asked. As soon as Harriet freed Stella's hands I grabbed her ring finger and looked at it. No damage. I took her engagement ring out of my pocket. "I thought it was dried blood."

"No. He didn't touch me." Stella's voice was husky as if her throat was raw. "Just ketchup from the fast food he brought me." She put her ring back on with shaky fingers.

Once all the ropes were cut, Harriet and I got on either side of Stella and helped her up.

"I'm sorry." Tears were flowing like Victoria Falls down my face.

"It's his fault, not yours," Stella said.

I set the chair Stella had been tied to under the trapdoor, got on it, and pulled myself back up into the barn. All that lifting and moving things at garage sales gave me good upper-body strength. I kneeled on the floor as Harriet helped Stella up onto the chair. Stella shook as I grabbed her arms and pulled while Harriet boosted her up. Once Stella was out, I helped Harriet. Stella's olive skin was dirty, her hair tangled, but there weren't any visible bruises.

"Did you see his face?" Harriet asked.

"I didn't," Stella answered as we left the barn. "I'm not even sure it was a man."

I had my arm around Stella's waist, and she leaned in to me. We were shoulder to shoulder.

I wanted to ask her what had happened. How she'd been taken. But my questions could wait. Gennie ran to Stella and wrapped her in blankets I'd brought. Someone handed her a bottle of water.

"I'll call 911." And I'd follow up that call with one to Awesome. The call I dreaded making.

Chapter Twenty-One

Ten minutes later police cars and emergency vehicles swarmed the barn. There was an old drive on the backside of the barn that Frida's son and his friend had found. They'd opened the gate so everyone could drive in. The call to Awesome had been one of the worst calls of my life. In seconds he'd gone through disbelief, shock, anger, and then calm. The controlled calm scared me the most. I didn't want to be alone with him anytime soon.

Awesome careened up to the barn in his SUV. Jumped out and gathered Stella to him like she was the world's most precious gem. He hadn't even glanced at me. He didn't speak to me even though I'd been standing with my arm around Stella. I missed her warm presence next to me when Awesome swept her up into his arms, carried her to his car, and drove her off. I assumed to a hospital to be checked out.

I realized it was going to be a long night and I would have to answer a lot of unpleasant questions. "Harriet, I can leave you out of all of this."

"Don't lie for me. I agreed to go along with this and I'll

take full responsibility for my role. After all, what can they do to me? I'm retired."

Maybe she couldn't get in trouble with the FBI, but there could be legal consequences.

Crime scene techs showed up, and soon police tape was stretched around the barn and the field. People from Seth's office showed up, but not Seth.

An hour later Harriet and I were at the police station. Separated. I didn't know where she was, but I sat in a vacant office by myself. No one knew yet about the connection between Stella's kidnapping and poor dead Crystal Olson. I had my arms wrapped around my stomach. It cramped just thinking about it. I worried about the kind of legal trouble I might be in for withholding information about Crystal and Stella. I only hoped that, with my finding and rescuing Stella, all else would be forgiven.

Since they hadn't taken my phone, I called Vincenzo DiNapoli, one of Angelo's many cousins. Vincenzo was a shark of a lawyer with rumored mob connections. He'd gotten Mike Titone off charges before. I reached an answering service, not surprising at this time of night, and left a message saying I was at the Ellington police station and possibly in serious trouble. I knew the drill while I waited to hear back from Vincenzo. Keep my answers short and don't volunteer anything. How sad was it that I knew that? And how could I not volunteer anything about Crystal Olson's death?

The minute I said anything about Crystal, the two state troopers would be brought in. The thought of facing Trooper Kilgard again was worse than thinking about Awesome, who probably wanted to kill me at this point. He could probably do it a thousand different ways and hide my body where no one would find it. Then there was Seth.

I'd tried to call him once but it went to voicemail. I didn't leave a message. His attempted kidnapping was probably connected to this too. What would he think when he found out I'd withheld information not only about Crystal's death but about his own kidnapper? Oh, lord, and Mike Titone. He might be the scariest of all when he found out he'd been sent out here by the kidnapper to make my life more difficult. After going through the list of people who were going to be mad at me, maybe facing Trooper Kilgard wasn't all that frightening.

All the justifications I had made in my head the last few days—not to say anything to the police about Stella and Crystal—suddenly didn't make much sense. I tried to reach Seth again. This time by sending a text. Are you okay?

I waited, watching the dots move across the phone until a heart appeared. I'm sorry I can't be there. The office door slammed open behind me, hitting the wall and making me jump. Pellner stood there. His deep dimples indicated that this wasn't going to go well. I wanted to cry or better yet run. I did neither. Instead I sat quietly, waiting to hear what he had to say.

He tossed a notepad onto the desk and sat in the desk chair on the other side. "I don't even know what to say to you."

That's how it started. He went on with the "how could you" and "what were you thinking" and "do you realize what could have happened to Stella" comments.

"Do you think I didn't agonize over what could have happened to Stella?" I wanted to jump up, slam my hands down on the desk, and get in his face. None of that would help. I folded my hands in my lap and squeezed until my knuckles turned white. Pellner noticed.

"He gave me a set of rules I had to follow or he said I'd never see Stella again. He could have killed Stella."

"Or you." Pellner leaned forward. "Tell me about these rules." He sounded skeptical.

I listed them for Pellner. Even the one about Mike Titone. Let the chips fall, as they say.

"Why Mike Titone?" he asked.

I lifted and dropped a shoulder. Oh, to hell with it. "He's given me some help with things in the past." I'd recently gotten out from under all the things I owed Mike for. Some of his help I didn't want Pellner or anyone else to ever find out about. I'm sure Mike felt the same way.

"How did you know the kidnapper would have followed through?"

And there was the can of worms, Pandora's box, the genie out of the bottle. The question that led right to what had happened with Crystal Olson. "I couldn't take the risk. Not with Stella kidnapped and in danger."

Pellner tapped a finger on the desk. "Does this have anything to do with the body you found?"

I wished he hadn't figured that out. But Pellner was no dummy, so I wasn't surprised. "I'll talk after my lawyer arrives."

Pellner rocked back in the desk chair like I'd punched him. "Your lawyer?" His voice dropped. Threatened.

"Yes."

He put his forearms on the chair and leaned in. "Sarah, it's me. You can tell me."

I shook my head. I couldn't. "Vincenzo should be on the way."

Pellner shook his head too. Disappointed. How did his

five kids ever get away with anything? That look was almost enough to make me spill everything I knew. Almost.

Pellner and I sat there staring at each other—well, I felt Pellner's stare. I'd broken mine off after the first few seconds and looked at the scratched surface of the metal desk. I finally cracked. "Do you know who owns the barn?"

Pellner frowned at me. I didn't think he was going to answer, but he relaxed his shoulders. "Yousef and June Ghannam."

"The same people who own the house Crystal was found in?"

Pellner nodded. "Yousef was my dentist. At one point they thought they'd try their hand at farming. They quickly realized they didn't have time with their dental practice."

"Do you think they had anything to do with Stella's kidnapping or Crystal's murder?"

"It seems unlikely."

"Do they have kids?" Maybe they had children that I'd run into at some point.

"A daughter who is going to college in Scotland."

"Have any of them ever been in trouble before?"

Pellner shook his head. "Do you have any connection to them?"

"Not one that I know of. I go to a different dentist."

"I shared information with you, Sarah. Now, why don't you tell me what you know about Crystal."

"I appreciate that you did. But I'll wait to say anything further until Vincenzo arrives."

Pellner leaned back again, and we sat in tortuous silence—for me at least—until we heard a knock on the door fifteen minutes later. I looked up. Pellner had a puzzled expression on his face as he looked over my shoulder.

I turned to see why. Instead of Vincenzo, Emil Kowalski, Rosalie DiNapoli's nephew, stood there.

"What are you doing here?" I asked.

"Vincenzo is out of town and asked me to fill in for him." Emil wore tan cashmere slacks and a burgundy V-neck cashmere sweater with a white, button-down shirt peeking out above the V.

"You know this guy?" Pellner's dimples deepened even more.

I nodded. "No offense, Emil, but I need a lawyer not a businessman."

"I am a lawyer. Mostly international criminal law, but I maintained all my bar credentials here in Massachusetts too." He stepped up to the desk and shook Pellner's hand. "If you don't mind giving us the room, I need to have a word with my client."

After Pellner walked out, unhappily I might add, Emil took his vacated chair. He pushed up his sweater sleeves and rolled up the sleeves of his cuffed white shirt. After that he extracted an expensive-looking silver pen and a leather-covered notebook from his pocket. Finally, he directed his gaze at me. I hadn't gotten over the shock of having him here and not Vincenzo. Vincenzo I trusted. Emil I wasn't sure about.

I shifted in my seat. "Don't I have to give you a retainer to be your client?"

He smiled, open, warm. "It's covered under your agreement with Vincenzo."

What was my agreement with Vincenzo? I had some vague recollection of giving him ten bucks one time. "I didn't realize I had an ongoing agreement with Vincenzo."

"According to Vincenzo you do. I trust him. Don't you?" Emil cocked his head briefly to one side as he said it.

"Yes. Of course. He's helped me out before." Me and a few of my friends. Vincenzo had helped me and not charged me much. I wondered why. Maybe since I knew Angelo I got the friends-and-family discount.

"Why don't you just start at the beginning and finish with how you ended up here." Emil waved a hand around.

"It's complicated."

"It always is." He leaned forward. "I'm here to help you." His voice was soothing. What did I have to lose?

Chapter Twenty-Two

"My friend, Stella Wild, was kidnapped."

"Are you talking about the opera singer Stella Wild?"

"Yes. You've heard of her?"

"Not only heard of her, but I heard her sing in Italy. Multiple times. She was mesmerizing. And then, poof—she just disappeared from the opera scene."

I didn't want to tell him about Stella's past woes with drugs. "She's singing again, and she's still amazing. Last fall she was in a production of *The Phantom of the Opera* and she was supposed to leave last Friday to appear in another staging in LA."

"Then I hope I get to hear her sing again sometime. But let's get back to what happened with the kidnapper."

Emil jotted down notes as I talked. His handwriting was sloppy, and he seemed to use some kind of shorthand. If anyone ever stole his notes, good luck to them at being able to decipher his handwriting. Maybe he did that on purpose. He'd occasionally stop me and ask me a question, but he mostly just listened and wrote. If I paused, he looked up at me encouragingly, but waited patiently for me to continue.

It was almost midnight when I finished talking. I yawned.

"Do you want to go home and finish this tomorrow?" Emil asked.

"No. I have information the police are going to need. Stella might be safe, but her kidnapper is out there." Seth's almost kidnapper and Crystal's probable murderer. "I have to do this now."

Emil gave me a brief nod. "Okay, then my next move is to get hold of the DA and get you immunity for explaining what you know. I'll make some phone calls."

"Um, I'm seeing the DA."

Emil smiled. "I'm aware. Aunt Rosalie filled me in. That will probably work to our advantage."

I hoped so. But part of me worried how this could impact Seth's career. His mother would have even more reason to dislike me after this. "Wait. Harriet Ballou could be in trouble too. She helped me out. She needs immunity too."

Emil stood. "I'll be right back."

"Be right back" turned into another hour. But by then I had immunity for any crimes I might have committed in the last few days, as did Harriet. I almost couldn't believe it. A few minutes later Emil and I walked down to a bigger conference room. Pellner, the two state troopers, two assistant DAs, and Awesome were already in there. I was relieved I didn't have to face Seth yet. Awesome leaned against the back wall, arms crossed, jaw clenched. He wouldn't meet my eyes. Harriet sat there with a woman. Her own lawyer perhaps. I'd have to pay for Harriet's legal expenses since I had dragged her into this mess.

By now they all had to know, from information Stella must have given them, that I'd known about her kidnapping for several days. And if Stella hadn't already told them, I'm sure Frida, her son, his friends, and Gennie had all been interviewed too.

"Before Sarah starts, I just want to remind you that, because of her actions tonight, Stella is safe. Sarah put herself at risk to save Stella. The kidnapper is the monster here." Emil looked from person to person as he spoke. "Not Sarah."

No one nodded in agreement. Awesome's jaw didn't unclench.

"And Sarah did what she thought best. What any of you would have done to protect a loved one."

I started speaking. I gave just the facts—talking almost robotically. Taking out the emotional turmoil I'd gone through during the past few days. I didn't try to justify my decisions. Although my voice betrayed me a couple of times by shaking. When I got to the part about being sent to find Alice in Wonderland, knowing that she was connected in some way to my kidnapper, all hell broke loose.

Awesome shook his head in disgust. Pellner looked so disappointed it almost broke my heart. Only Harriet and her lawyer remained stoic. But Harriet knew most of this story already.

"She obstructed our investigation. Lied to us," Kilgard said. "She's got immunity?" She looked at me with her psychopath eyes like she wanted to leap across the table and do me in. I couldn't really blame her.

Emil put a hand on my quivering arm. "Let's let Sarah continue," he said.

I cleared my throat, looked at a spot above Kilgard's head, and started talking again. I told the story about what had happened in the cemetery.

"Why didn't you tell me what was going on when I saw you that night?" Pellner asked.

"Or me. At any point. *Any point,*" Awesome said. His voice like a grizzly's growl.

Emil started to say something, but this time I put a hand on his arm. "I couldn't risk it. The kidnapper may have some link to the police. He knew as soon as I called about Alice in Wonderland. Like I said earlier, he docked me twelve hours after I made that call. Twelve fewer hours before he killed Stella." I paused. Swallowed. "I told you. I gave myself three days to find her with the least amount of risk. And I found Stella." Thank heavens. I'd found her. But I knew the trust I had with these men was broken. Maybe forever. While that thought hurt, I'd gotten Stella back.

Who knows what she was thinking about me though. Stella might hate me as much as Awesome seemed to. Then there was Seth, who wasn't even here. Sure, he'd sent me a heart emoji in his last text and said he couldn't be here. But couldn't he have checked in on me for a minute, even if it were only on the phone?

"Sarah, go on," Emil said.

I explained about having Elmer Norman pick me up and the partial license plate number he'd given me. Awesome looked hopeful, but the car was probably stolen, a dead end. I left out the part about calling CJ and about visiting Gregory Kiah. There was no reason to drag either of them into this mess.

Awesome shook his head while I talked about assembling my team of friends to help me rescue Stella. He muttered something that included the words "stupid" and "reckless." At this point I didn't care anymore. Stella was safe. That was all that really mattered. A half an hour later

I finished the story. No one seemed too concerned that a group of people had formed an anti-Sarah group, that one of them—maybe all of them—could be behind all this. Maybe they were all going to go over and join the group.

Harriet spoke briefly, confirming what I'd said.

"Just one more thing," I said. It struck me while I was talking. "The realtor who is the agent for the house where Crystal was found also had the listing for the store where I was sent to find the Alice in Wonderland doll. Anyone in her office would have access to both buildings."

"We'll check it out," Rodriquez said. "You stay out of it."

I bobbed my head, knowing that this was probably just one more lie to add to the long list of them. Staying out of it would be difficult for me.

"We'll need your phone and Stella's phone," Kilgard said. "Maybe it won't be too late to find a way to track the perpetrator. Of course, that's a lot less likely than it would have been three days ago."

She turned those empty eyes back on me. I just stared back into those blank lagoons of brown, too tired to be intimidated. Then I grabbed my purse from where it hung on the back of my chair and dug out the phones. I handed them to Emil who slid them across the conference table to Kilgard.

Emil stood. "That's it then. If you have any questions for Sarah, contact me." He passed out business cards. Emil looked at me. "Let's go." His voice was gentle, nonjudgmental.

As I stood I took one last look around the room. Pellner and Awesome didn't look at me. Kilgard continued her hard stare. Harriet smiled and mouthed, "Don't worry."

Her lawyer, if she was one, looked relieved. At the door Emil stepped back so I could leave first.

Awesome caught up with us in the hall. "I need a word with Sarah." His look at Emil seemed to say "don't try to stop me."

Emil opened his mouth, but I put a hand on his arm. "It's okay. Give us a minute." Emil frowned, but walked further on down the hall. I'd take whatever Awesome had to dish out like a woman. I didn't mean by crying or sniveling. But by being strong and empathetic. I gathered myself as if I were going to get punched.

Awesome glanced up and down the hall. It was empty except for the two of us and Emil. He leaned in close, bent his head down toward me. "Please tell me that you didn't send me those texts? The ones that were supposedly from Stella."

My back was trapped against the wall. Awesome's breath was hot on my nose. I could almost feel the waves of tension radiating off him like a force field. If this had been a dark alley, I would have been terrified. But I knew, angry as he was, Awesome was a good man and would never hurt me.

I looked straight at him. "I did." His muscles tensed. "And I would do it again if it meant saving Stella." I hadn't meant to add that last bit, but every word was true. Sometimes you had to do things you didn't want to. This had been one of those times. I slipped by Awesome to Emil. I felt like a wooden toy soldier walking away.

"Are you okay? He looked angry," Emil said.

"I can't blame him." I made it all the way to the parking lot before my shoulders sagged.

* * *

Emil parked in front of my house. Seth sat on the top step of the porch. It was almost two thirty in the morning. I sighed, uncertain if I was happy to see him or not. I almost laughed at myself. Not long ago I had been offended he'd only sent me a heart emoji and a note saying he was sorry he couldn't be there for me.

"Do you want me to walk you up there?" Emil asked.

"No. Thank you." I looked at Seth and then back at Emil. "Thank you for everything tonight."

"It's my job."

"Driving me home. Offering to walk me to the door isn't part of your job."

He grinned. "I'm a full-service lawyer."

I even managed a brief smile back. "You're a good man."

He tilted his head toward where Seth sat. "Go get it over with."

"Okay." I opened the door, but turned back. "Thank you."

"You said that. Go. We'll talk tomorrow."

Seth trotted down the stairs and pulled me into his arms as Emil drove away. We just stood there with my head resting on his shoulder. The fabric of his jacket was cold. Maybe it was time to give him a key. I breathed in the spring night air and Seth. The first moment of peace I'd had since the first phone call from Stella's kidnapper.

"I'm sorry," I murmured into his shoulder.

"Don't. Don't. I'll walk you up to your apartment." He looked at a car parked on the street and pointed toward the apartment.

His guards must be there with him. Of course, they would be. It didn't sound like he planned to stay, which disappointed me. On the other hand, I was exhausted and discombobulated. Being alone was probably best. I clutched his hand as he went in and up the steps to my apartment. Mike's brother Diego sat outside Mike's door doing another Sudoku puzzle. A bag of chips and a Coke were by the chair. He gave us a brief nod. Mike. I'd have to talk to him tomorrow. Explain that the threat that had brought him out here to Ellington might be tied to the kidnapper.

Seth and I settled on my couch after I got us two glasses of water. They sat in front of us on the trunk. Seth's arm was slung around me, protecting me. I'd been very worried about his reaction to all this. Feared he'd be gone. But here he was. For now anyway. It seemed like we were both waiting for the other to say something. I drank half my glass of water.

"I didn't know what the right thing to do was. Do you hate me?"

Seth shook his head. His chin brushing back and forth across the top of my hair. "No. Of course not. You were in an untenable situation."

"But you must have at least second-guessed what I did."

"I've had a lot to think about since Emil called." Seth pulled away from me. Rested his arms on his legs and dropped his head in his hands. He sat that way for several seconds before sitting back up and turning to look at me. "I don't understand why you didn't trust me. I would have taken precautions. You didn't have to do this alone."

"I did what I thought was best. I wasn't completely alone."

"You trusted Harriet, a woman you barely know, before trusting me."

"It's not that I didn't trust you. It was about keeping you safe after I found out about the kidnapping attempt. And you were listed in his rules—no contacting Seth. If there'd been a leak, Stella—" I couldn't say it again. That Stella would have been killed. I hoped Seth would come to understand that, if not now then at some point. I didn't want to lose him. "Thank you for the immunity."

"I had to recuse myself. You know I'd do anything for you, but I couldn't put the office at risk of criticism."

"It could happen anyway. They might say your staff would do whatever to please you."

Seth nodded. "That could happen. But we followed procedure."

Another thing to worry and feel guilty about. "I don't want to hurt your career."

He folded me into his arms. "Screw the career. How many times do I have to tell you that? I care about you. I love you. I'd rather quit and work with you on your garage sale business than lose you."

My heart burst. "I love you too." While Seth could say "screw the career" all he wanted, and he had said it before, I didn't want to be the one to put him in a position where he'd have to choose. He was smart and helped a lot of people. I wasn't the only one who should matter to him. I could picture his mother if he ever decided to chuck his career for garage sales. I couldn't decide if I should laugh or cry.

"You weren't really planning to buy a house?"

"No. It was a spur of the moment lie when I was trying to save Stella."

Seth nodded, opened his mouth to say something, but shook his head instead.

"Are we okay?" I asked as he stood. "Can't you stay?" I realized how much I didn't want to be alone.

He hugged me to him, but didn't say anything for a

minute. "I have an early start in the morning, and I imagine you need to catch up on your sleep."

He had often spent the night under those circumstances.

"And I still have the guards. At least for tonight. If I stay here, one will be in the hall and one on the couch."

"Wait, you won't have guards after tomorrow? The kidnapper is still on the loose."

"I'm not sure how much longer they'll be with me. They can't guard me forever."

I wasn't going to press him further. A few minutes later, as I watched him leave, my unease returned. Despite his lovely words about his career, it felt like the canyon between us might still be there. I'd hurt him by trusting Harriet over him. Even though he said he loved me, I wasn't sure how much he liked me right now. I hoped I could build a bridge back to his side.

Chapter Twenty-Three

I woke up at seven thirty Tuesday morning. Earlier than I wanted to, but I needed to talk to Mike and to buy a new phone before I went over to Alice's house to work. Thank heavens my phone number would roll over from one phone to another.

After I showered, I made some coffee, procrastinating because I didn't want to face Mike. I thought over my conversation with Seth last night. We'd left some things unsaid. Like it could have been Seth I'd been trying to rescue instead of Stella, and we both knew it. Seth might not have the guards for long, and the kidnapper was still on the loose. That was worrisome.

I didn't think Stella had come home last night. And I didn't hear any noises from her apartment now. She was probably with Awesome or her family. Somewhere that she felt safe, if one could ever feel safe again after what she'd been through. I also thought over the grim looks on Awesome's and Pellner's faces. Would they ever be able to forgive me? Would Stella? Perhaps the only way to earn their forgiveness would be by finding the kidnapper.

Before I could start searching for the kidnapper I had

a few other things to take care of. I drained the rest of my coffee, set my shoulders, and headed over to see Mike. Francesco slouched on the chair, arms folded, head tipped back. He stood when he saw me.

"I need to talk to Mike," I said.

"Lemme check with him." Francesco went into the apartment, closing the door behind him.

Nice. I waited a couple of minutes. Mike opened the door and came out, his hair wet from a shower.

"You wanted to talk to me?" He didn't look surprised. Maybe he'd somehow heard the whole story by now. He had lots of resources.

I nodded. "Let's go to my place." I didn't want to have all three Titones sitting there judging me.

"This about that itchy feeling I had?" Mike followed me down the short hall and into my apartment.

"Maybe. Coffee?" I asked.

"Sure." Mike plopped down on a chair at the small kitchen table I had. It was covered in a vintage tablecloth with bright red salad bowls, jars of green olives, and salad tongs on a white background. One side of the table was pushed up against the wall. Three mismatched oak chairs were around the open sides.

I poured the coffee into vintage Fire King jadeite mugs. I loved their soft green color and sturdy rounded handles. "Is black okay? I don't think I have any cream or sugar."

"Then I guess it's okay."

I pulled out a chair across from him. Blew across the top of my coffee like that would cool it off. Mike waited, watching me. I straightened my shoulders. I'd been doing that a lot. Sitting up, shoulders squared, somehow it gave me a bit of courage. I launched into the story once again. However, in this retelling I left out the parts about Crystal since it was an ongoing murder investigation. Mike's face remained impassive, but those blue eyes seemed to get icier as I went along.

"I think that maybe the kidnapper planted the threat to scare you out here to complicate my life." I lifted my chin slightly.

Mike leaned back. "You coulda told me."

I shook my head. "What if someone close to you is behind this?"

"To what end?"

"You've helped me out lots of times. Maybe someone doesn't like it."

"Nah. Everyone close to me knows the slate is clean between us. I made that clear."

"It doesn't mean someone doesn't resent me." It seemed unlikely, but no stone unturned. "Who told you there was a threat in the first place? Who got you to come out here?"

Mike stood, walked to my apartment door. He paused, hand on the knob. "My brothers. I won't tell you who gave them the information."

Mike left without saying anything else, even though I called out to him. We weren't done with this conversation. Finding out who had told his brothers there was a threat wouldn't be easy and maybe downright impossible. I checked the time. I had just enough time to get a phone and get to Alice's house to work.

After I bought a new phone, as I drove to Alice's house, I pondered Mike and his brothers. Why wouldn't Mike tell me who gave the information to his brothers? Who was he protecting?

Who did I know that had connections to Mike? The list was short: Vincenzo, possibly Emil through Vincenzo, and Seth. Seth couldn't be involved in any of this. He was a victim himself. Vincenzo had no reason to do this. He was a successful attorney—at least he appeared to be. Emil was the wild card, but he'd seemed surprised when I'd mentioned Stella. Authentically surprised, not faking it. But I'd been exhausted by the time I talked to him. Would I have really noticed if there had been subtext? Did I know him well enough to pick up on it? I shook my head. I didn't have the bandwidth to figure this out now.

But there was something else I could check. I pulled up and parked in front of Alice's house at 9:15. Instead of going in I grabbed my phone and looked up the realtor's office I'd mentioned to the police last night. Five realtors smiled out at me. I recognized one because she was one of Ellington's selectmen—selectmen were the chief executive body for the town. We'd clashed a bit once, a year ago, when someone had complained about a sign I'd put up, which was why I was so careful with placement now.

And of course I recognized the woman who I'd met the night of Crystal's murder. She also had the listing for the empty store the kidnapper had sent me too, and the property the barn was on. None of that could be a coincidence. I'd have to do more digging, but it was nine-thirty. Time to meet with Alice.

When Alice didn't answer my knock, I let myself in with the key she'd given me. Alice was in the living room. On the floor. Not moving. With a broken Lladró figurine smashed on the wood floor beside her. I stared down for a moment. Frozen. But then I noticed the lift and fall of her chest. Not dead. *Not dead!*

I called 911 with my new cell phone.

"Are you safe?" the dispatcher asked after I described

Alice's condition. She looked very pale, but her breathing seemed okay.

"I-I think so." Alice's house was silent except for the normal creaks and groans of old houses. I jumped when the furnace clicked on.

"Stay on the line."

I grabbed a fuzzy blue afghan off the couch and covered her with it. The broken Lladró was worrisome. I sat down on the floor beside her and took her hand. Poison, stroke, heart attack?

"The door's unlocked," I told the dispatcher. And then I questioned myself. What if the dispatcher was the kidnapper? What if help wasn't coming? But then I heard sirens. Most times I didn't want to hear a siren. Today I was happy to.

Alice came around shortly after the paramedics arrived along with a police officer. For once it was someone I barely knew, but she curled her lip at me in derision. I guess the whole force knew what was going on. Probably half the town did by now too.

Alice insisted she was fine. "It was my blood sugar. I didn't check it this morning, and I ate something I shouldn't have. I passed out. That was all. I just need a glucagon injection." She told the EMT where to find the medication.

The police officer did a walkthrough of the house after Alice gave her permission. The officer didn't find anything amiss. She left, casting one last stink-eyed look at me as she did. The paramedics packed up shortly after and suggested Alice make a doctor's appointment forthwith.

"That police officer didn't seem to like you," Alice said once we were alone.

I was sweeping up bits of the Lladró even though Alice

hadn't wanted me to. "Just sit and rest. Can I make you scrambled eggs?" I might not be a great cook, but I could handle fixing eggs. "The protein would be good for you."

"It would be nice," Alice admitted. She stared at the floor as she said it. "Make some for yourself too."

Alice wasn't one to sit or let people do things for her. She must not feel well. As I whipped up the eggs I wondered if the kidnapper had a hand in this. But why target Alice? Although he'd wanted me to take the shoebox to her yesterday evening. A few minutes later I took two plates of eggs with some cheddar cheese mixed in out to the living room and handed one to Alice. "I'd be happy to drive you to your doctor."

Alice nodded. "Okay. But I'll pay you for your time."

I didn't answer. I wouldn't accept money for helping someone out, and I had a nagging worry that even though everyone agreed that Alice had passed out because of low blood sugar, maybe there was another reason.

An hour later Alice was sitting on her couch again. On the drive back to her house she had said the doctor had scolded her for not taking better care of herself. While Alice had been in with her doctor, I'd stewed about Stella's kidnapper. I hoped the police had found something in the barn or on my phone that would help find him. Stella sent me a text asking if I was okay. After all she'd been through, Stella was worried about me.

I told her I was fine. She said she was staying with Awesome. That he was so freaked out that he'd actually taken leave to be with her. I couldn't blame Awesome, and it made me happy for Stella that someone cared about her that much.

I spent an hour pricing while Alice napped on the couch. I was going to sell this batch of things through my online garage sale that I'd been running for over a year. A few minutes after Alice woke up and assured me she was fine, I drove home. It was after one as I pulled into the four-car parking lot on the side of the house. My phone rang. Caller unknown. I hoped it was a new client.

"How are you today, Sarah?"

Rats. The kidnapper. "Better than I was yesterday."

"Why's that?"

"I think you know, but I'm happy to spell it out for you."

"Oh, please do."

"Stella's safe, and the police are going to find you." *If I don't first.*

"Did you think you'd won? I let you find Stella." He laughed.

He'd let me win? "No, you didn't." I didn't like the uncertainty in my voice. "You just want me to think that because you lost."

"Oh, Sarah, the only way I could have made it any easier for you is if I would have sent you a map with an *X* that marked the spot where she was."

Was that true? I'd thought I was so clever last night, figuring things out.

"Honestly, if you hadn't put together where Stella was with the train horn and the articles, I would have been very disappointed in you."

"Well, I'm glad I didn't let you down. But why don't you just turn yourself in? The police are probably outside your house right now with the evidence they found at the barn."

"Ooohh, I'm so scared. Let me check out my front window. Nope. No one's there."

"Just leave me alone," I said.

"Did you think it was over because you got Stella back? Do you really believe Alice just had low blood sugar? The game's just begun, Sarah. No one you care about is safe. Let's have some fun."

Chapter Twenty-Four

I hung up. He was toying with me. He was scared, not me. Before I thought much about what I was doing, I ran down the block to DiNapoli's. I hoped Emil was there. I needed to go to the police, but I didn't want to go alone. The kidnapper didn't know it yet, but there were new rules this time, and he was going to have to play by mine. He no longer had a hold over me.

By the time I got through the door at DiNapoli's, I had convinced myself that the kidnapper was lying to scare me. He'd slipped up, and we both knew it. At least I hoped that was true. His comment about Alice had me worried. Although, he'd probably heard about the call to Alice's house through a police scanner app and just tried to use it to his advantage. To make me think he was still in control.

Angelo was teaching a class to the left side of the restaurant as the last of the lunch crowd finished their meals. A group of people stood around a table watching Emil carry a large tray of meatballs toward them. He frowned in concentration and hadn't noticed me.

"Emil," I called. He jerked up, the tray tilted, and meatballs rolled all over the place. All I could do was watch as meatballs plopped to the floor in small splats. Some of the group ran over and managed to catch them as they rolled off. A woman helped steady the tray.

I clapped my hands to my mouth. Angelo's mouth formed a wide *O*, and Rosalie started laughing. Fortunately, everyone else joined in.

"Sorry about that," Emil said to the group as he set the tray on the table. He looked at me. "Give me a minute to wash my hands."

"I didn't think you'd be having a class this early," I said to Angelo.

"We moved the time up because of Emil's schedule today. He has something going on later this afternoon."

I watched as Emil walked over to the sink, soaped his hands into a foamy lather, and then rinsed. He grabbed a hand towel as he walked toward me. I pulled him over to a corner of the restaurant as everyone got back to the meatballs.

"I need your help. The kidnapper called me. He said— he said that this was just the beginning. That the game was still on. He even said he let me find Stella."

Emil flung the towel over his shoulder and studied my face. "How are you?"

"I'm furious. He said that no one I cared about is safe." I took a deep breath. "I have to go to the police. I'm playing by my rules this time, not his."

"Okay."

"I don't want to face the police alone. Will you go with me?"

"Of course." Emil paused, looked up at the ceiling. "Do you want to go in the front door of the station or arrange a meeting elsewhere?"

I thought it over. "Elsewhere since we still don't know

if the kidnapper really has inside information with the police. He knew about what happened to my client Alice Krandle."

Emil frowned. "What happened to Alice?"

I quickly explained.

"My car's parked out back. Let me put this towel away and grab my jacket."

As soon as Emil left my side, Rosalie rushed over. "Is everything okay?"

"No, but it will be." My voice shook a little.

"You come back for our family supper tonight." The meal they had after the restaurant closed at nine thirty.

"If I can, I will. Thank you."

Rosalie patted my arm and went over to the counter to help a customer. It gave me a minute to call Seth.

He answered almost immediately.

"I heard from Stella's kidnapper again." There was a long pause. I took the phone away from my ear and looked at it. We were still connected. "Seth?"

"Sorry. I closed my office door. You have to come stay with me. The guards are still with me around the clock. You'll be safe."

That was tempting. Nothing sounded better than hunkering down and hiding some place. Especially if it involved Seth. "I can't."

"You have to."

"I need him to think I'm doing what he wants. I think it's the only way to catch him. For the police to catch him." That sounded better. "Emil is setting up a meeting with the police right now." Seth made a snorting sound. "I take it you don't like him."

"The jury is out on him. But he has nothing to do with you staying with me."

I wasn't going to argue about Emil with Seth. I needed Emil right now. "Mike is next door. There's always someone outside his door. I'm fine."

Another pause. "If Mike leaves, you can't stay in the building by yourself."

I didn't want to stay there by myself. "Hopefully Stella will be back soon. And that means Awesome will be too." Even though Awesome was mad at me, he wouldn't let anything happen to me. At least I didn't think he would. Emil returned to my side.

"Let's go," he said.

"I have to go," I told Seth.

"Will talk later. Love you."

"Love you, too." I blushed a little as Emil watched me hang up.

Emil and I were riding in his silver classic Ford Mustang. I was no expert on cars, but even I knew this was a classic car. The engine rumbled as we took off.

"Nice car," I said.

"My passion project."

"You restore cars?"

"A friend does most of the work."

"Nice. Where are we headed?"

"The library. Pellner set it up so we can use their meeting room."

Emil had accomplished a lot while I was on the phone with Seth. "Isn't that a little close to the police station if the kidnapper has connections there?" The library was across the street to the right of the police station.

"It will be okay. Close enough that everyone can get there, but far enough to be out of sight."

Minutes later we were sitting around a table at the back of the meeting room in the library. That way people who passed by couldn't glance in and see us. The door was locked, so no one else could get in. Beige carpet, chairs, table, and walls gave this room a dystopian feel. Seated around the table were the two state troopers, Pellner, Harriet—who'd I'd called and asked to join us on the way over—Emil, and me. Awesome stood in a corner even though he was officially on leave. No one smiled. Expressions went from grim to grimmest. Awesome won by a long shot—not that I could blame him. I wanted to run out of here. A vacation was starting to sound like a really great idea, but I had too many sales coming up to take any time off.

Emil started. "Sarah got another call from the kidnapper. I'll let her explain the call."

I focused on Harriet. She wore a black business suit with a red silk blouse under it. Probably clothes left from when she worked for the FBI. While she looked serious, she didn't appear to want to throttle me like everyone else did. I once again managed to say everything without adding a lot of emotion.

"He said no one I cared about was safe." I glanced at Awesome, who looked directly at me. I thought I saw a flicker of sympathy, but it might have been wishful thinking. I wrapped it up quickly. "I hung up on him." I paused. "I'm not sure he's telling the truth about leading me to

Stella. I think there's a good chance his ego won't allow him to believe anything else."

"Now you're a psychologist along with being an amateur sleuth," Awesome said.

"It's likely Sarah is right," Harriet said, swiveling in her seat to look at Awesome.

Under any other circumstances, I would have wanted to say "ha take that," but this was too serious.

"We all need to pool our resources to catch him without petty infighting or holding grudges," Harriet said.

"And what resources do you have?" Awesome asked Harriet. His voice lacked his usual calm demeanor.

"I worked on the FBI's Crisis Negotiation team for twenty-four years." Harriet's voice was calm. "I still have contacts, and frankly I'm damn good at what I do."

"Oh, are you?" Awesome said.

"I can hear the frustration in your voice. And I understand it, but we need to work together," Harriet said. "We all want the same outcome. To catch whoever is doing this."

"You were in law enforcement, and yet you kept Sarah's secret," Awesome shot back.

"I gave Sarah my word before I knew the exact situation. And"—Harriet glanced at me—"and as Sarah knows, I didn't keep my word entirely. I reached out to a few people who were helping behind the scene. They looked into Sarah's background and people she's close to."

That was news to me.

Awesome's shoulders slumped a little. "You're right. I apologize."

I wished that apology would extend to me, but I doubted it did.

"Sarah, we'll need your phone," Kilgard said.

I pulled it out of my purse and passed it over to her. Maybe I needed to just buy something cheap to replace this one until the kidnapper was caught. I couldn't keep buying expensive phones only to hand them over to the police even though I knew I'd get them back eventually.

"How am I going to keep 'everyone I care about' safe?" I asked. I thought about friends here—Carol and Brad Carson, the DiNapolis—friends on base, my brother, my family in California. How long was this guy's reach? "Warning all of them is going to scare a lot of people. But if something happened to someone because I didn't warn them . . . "

"It's not up to you to keep them safe," Rodriquez said.

We developed a plan that included warning my friends and family to take precautions and the police increasing patrols and alerting the security force on base. I agreed to let the police know when I heard from the kidnapper. Pellner gave me the number for a burner cell phone to use to contact him that wouldn't go through dispatch.

What I wouldn't agree to was the idea that Kilgard should move in with me. No thanks to that. Kilgard looked relieved when I balked at that idea. I think it was suggested because no one trusted me to do the right thing when the kidnapper called, and I couldn't say I blamed them.

"I saw that you're having a garage sale event on Saturday on the town common," Kilgard said. "I think you should cancel it."

What? "I'll think about it. I've done a lot of advertising, not just here but all over New England. It may be hard to cancel at this late date." Face it. I didn't want to cancel. All the more reason to track down the kidnapper.

"Just a minute ago you were concerned for the safety of those around you," Kilgard said.

"But this is different. Out in the open. The public will be there," I said.

"Exactly my point," Kilgard said. "More people who could be put in harm's way."

"I don't think there's much of a risk, based on the kidnapper's past actions," Emil added.

"Is it worth taking the chance?" Rodriquez asked.

My heart would be broken if I couldn't celebrate my two-year anniversary. "I'll consider it. I don't want anyone hurt because of me."

"Anyone else," Awesome said.

The weight of my guilt pounded down on me, but at least I knew what I needed to do next.

Chapter Twenty-Five

At two o'clock I sat in a small anteroom on one of four chairs with nubby gray fabric. The walls were painted grayish blue. The lighting was soft. No buzzing fluorescents in here. Framed degrees from a college in Philadelphia and Harvard. The magazines were all shiny new issues on topics ranging from home décor to gardening—nothing political or controversial unless one was anti-gardening. However, the low-volume music, instrumentals, made me want to plug my ears. I suspect the music was supposed to be calming, but it was having the opposite effect on me.

I didn't have an appointment with Damaris Christos, but I hoped she'd make the time to see me. When Awesome had asked if I was playing psychologist, it had made me think about Damaris again. A few minutes later I heard the muffled sound of a door closing, and Damaris came out of her office. She didn't look happy to see me. However, at this point I was getting used to that from people.

"I only have a few minutes, but you can come in." I followed her into an office that looked very much like the waiting room. Fortunately, no music played in here. I selected another nubby fabric-covered chair. Damaris sat next to me, not behind the desk. I guessed this was to show that we were on the same team.

"The police are probably going to show up here to talk to you about the anti-Sarah group," I said. I didn't really know if that was true, but I hoped it was. "I wanted to let you know."

"How could you, Sarah?" Damaris got up and sat behind her desk, putting space between us.

Wow. For a psychologist she didn't seem to understand her action spoke volumes. Damaris picked up a pen and started clicking it open and closed until I wanted to snatch it out of her hand.

"I have built up a rapport with my clients and am on the edge of a breakthrough with them. If the police barge in, it could ruin everything." She set the pen down. "These people already feel victimized by what they've been through. This is a disaster."

I tamped down my ire as I realized Damaris still hadn't seen the news and had no idea that Stella had been kidnapped. Now that I thought of it, not much had been in the news. If the kidnapper wanted notoriety, he wasn't getting it. That might unhinge him even more.

"Someone is threatening me and people who are close to me. It could be someone from your group."

"No offense, but the way you run around town questioning people, there's probably a long list of people who might threaten you."

Well, offense taken. I didn't run around questioning people like some vigilante in a bad movie. Most of the time anyway. "Please tell me who is in the 'I hate Sarah' group."

"Again, I can't. You have to trust that I'm making progress with them. The group is on the verge of disbanding." She tossed her thick hair over her shoulder with a flick of her head.

Her hair flicking was dismissive. It made me want to reach over and yank it, but that wouldn't help anything. I couldn't pressure her more without talking about Stella. I wasn't willing to do that, but the police might be. I'd leave the scare tactics to them. This time I was the one who pulled out a card. When she didn't take it, I put it on her desk. "Call me if you change your mind. Someone wants to hurt me and the people I care about. You don't want that on your conscience."

When I got home I heard Stella singing in her apartment. The sound almost made me weep with gratitude that she was back, safe. I knocked on her door, anxious to see her. I hoped she didn't hate me. When the door flung open, it was Awesome standing there, not Stella. He glared down at me and blocked the door.

"Who is it, Nathan?" Stella asked.

He started to close the door. "It's just a—"

"It's me, Stella."

"Sarah," she shrieked.

She pushed past Awesome, and we hugged. More like clung to each other. When we pulled apart we both looked each other over as if trying to make sure the other was okay. Stella took my hand and pulled me into the apartment. We sat on her couch, turned toward each other.

"If you can't be civil to Sarah, go run an errand," Stella said to Awesome.

"I don't want to cause any trouble." I looked back and forth between them.

"Any further trouble," Awesome muttered, but he closed

the door and leaned against it. He'd been doing a lot of leaning lately when we were in the same room together.

"I'm sorry," I said to Stella. "I feel terrible."

"As you should," Awesome said.

"Nathan, I mean it. Just stop." Stella looked over at him, but her expression was soft and loving not angry.

His face softened in return. The intimacy of the moment made my heart patter harder.

Stella looked back at me. "Don't feel terrible. You didn't do anything wrong. You found me. Saved me."

"It's just that if it weren't for me—"

Stella took my hand again. "You stop it too. You are as much a victim as I am."

Awesome made a choking noise that made Stella give him another look.

"Can you tell me what happened? And if it's too soon, I understand." I knew that she'd been kidnapped sometime between the time she had scheduled the ride to the airport and the time Elmer Norman had come to pick her up.

"After I scheduled a ride to the airport, there was a light knock on my door. I answered it, and a masked man shoved his way in. I guess I was tased or something, because the next thing I remember, I was in a room in a house somewhere."

I gripped her hand tighter. "You weren't in the barn the whole time." That was a relief.

"No. Not even for a whole day. At least I don't think it was a day. Time passed differently down there. Then you saved me." Stella squeezed my hand one more time and let go.

"Are you back here for good?" I asked. It was lonely in the building without her. I missed hearing her sing and seeing Tux. I wanted to ask how she was doing, but I knew it would take her time to get over being kidnapped. If one ever got over such a thing.

"I'm not."

"Staying with Awesome?"

"No. I'm heading out to Los Angeles to explain things to the director in person. It's too late to do the play, but it will be good to get out of town for a bit." She glanced at Awesome, and he nodded.

I assumed leaving town was to get her far away while the kidnapper was still on the loose. It was a good idea even though I would miss her. Stella would be safer there than here, which seemed a little ironic. "Is Awesome driving you to the airport?" I glanced at him. "Because if he can't take you, I can."

"He's doing more than that. He's flying out with me and staying for a few days." Stella smiled over at Awesome.

Wow. I was surprised Awesome would leave in the middle of the search for Stella's kidnapper. Either he really trusted his team or his desire to make sure Stella was safe was more important. "That's good. When are you leaving?" I stood as I asked.

"This evening." Stella stood and hugged me. "Be careful. He's—he's still out there."

"I will." I planned to be careful, but I also planned to find the guy.

When I got back to my apartment, I looked in my refrigerator to find something to eat. I hadn't eaten since I'd had the eggs at Alice's house. I pulled out the leftover pasta I'd brought home from DiNapoli's the other night and heated it up in the microwave. Once it was ready, I took it over to my kitchen table and started eating. Seth had texted me earlier letting me know he was attending a bar association meeting in Boston tonight. He knew it was going to run late, so he planned to spend the night at his parents' brownstone in the city. My thoughts kept wandering to Damaris. I didn't know much about her. I also didn't know anyone who knew her, so there was no one to ask for information.

Camping outside her office to see who came and went seemed invasive. Not to mention impractical with all I had to do. But an Internet search wouldn't hurt. I finished my pasta, rinsed my plate, and left it in the sink to wash later. I grabbed my laptop off the trunk and sat on the couch. I checked to see if there were other people in Ellington with the last name of Christos. There weren't.

After that, the first thing that popped up when I typed in Damaris's name was a link on a site to find a therapist. It listed her specialties, which included PTSD, relationships, and trauma.

That was followed by a paragraph about her philosophy, which included "wanting to get to know you" and to help you find your "superpowers" so that "you can live a meaningful life." Superpowers? Really? Did superpowers include forming groups that targeted other people? Whatever. That kind of thinking wouldn't get me anywhere.

According to the website, Damaris had earned her undergraduate degree at a university in Philadelphia and her graduate degree from Harvard. *Harvard*. I remembered seeing the degrees hanging on the wall in her office, but it hadn't hit me in the moment. Seth had graduated from Harvard law school. Did they know each other? Had they dated? Now I was just being ridiculous, making leaps from two people attending a school with over twenty thousand students to dating.

I had wondered how she had ended up in Ellington of all places, but maybe it was because of Seth. Ugh. There I went again. The website also listed her hourly fees and what insurance companies she was in network with. I added Philadelphia to her name in the search bar. A surprising number of articles came up.

Her father had been the supposed head of the Greek mob in Philadelphia in the eighties. When Damaris was thirteen he had been incarcerated for racketeering, money laundering, and prostitution rings. Two years later he was killed in prison while serving his sentence. Wow. That was a lot for a teenage girl to have to deal with. My sympathy meter turned up a notch for her. It was no wonder she had studied psychology. She was probably trying to fix herself. I hoped she had found her superpower.

By eight o'clock I'd only found out a bit more about Damaris. She'd organized a nonprofit in Philadelphia for crime victims, and she was still on the board. Damaris had certainly thrown herself into community service by starting the group at the church. Given her background I could see why she had. The mob connection and prostitution ring her father had run seemed worrisome. Was Damaris behind getting Mike out here? I yawned. Damaris was a puzzle that I'd have to try to solve later. I'd have to ask Seth if he knew her. Figure out if I could ask Mike. I flipped on the TV. *The Phantom of the Opera* was on. I watched until I couldn't stay awake any longer.

Wednesday morning at nine I sat at a table in the community center on Fitch with a group of women whose children were all enrolled in the Air Force Exceptional Family Member Program or EFMP. It was a program for people who had a family member with a special need. Needs ranged from kids with autism, cerebral palsy, or cancer to spouses with asthma.

My friend Rebecca Nichols, whose daughter had a rare disease, had asked me to come to the quarterly moms' morning out meeting. It was a potluck breakfast. I had brought bagels and cream cheese. My plate was heaped with food—an egg and bacon casserole, ham and cheese croissant sliders, loaded breakfast potatoes, and French toast. This was the first time since Stella had been kidnapped that food looked really good and I wanted to eat.

However, as I looked at the food I realized I hadn't heard from the kidnapper since yesterday when he had said the game wasn't over. It worried me. But Rebecca was starting to talk and I needed to pay attention.

"We were thinking of throwing a garage sale to raise funds for some of the families who have things they need that aren't covered by the military," Rebecca said. Rebecca had light red hair, a sprinkle of freckles, and a get-it-done attitude.

I knew that the military paid for medical expenses and would fly a dependent child and parent somewhere else to see a specialist if needed. They even got a per diem for food and hotel. "What kinds of things do you need?" I asked.

"My son has cerebral palsy," another woman said. "It's severe, and he can't do anything for himself. He turned fourteen recently, and he's the size of a full-grown man. We need a van that can accommodate him, and that's one thing that isn't covered." The woman had dark circles under her eyes. Her thin shoulders were rounded under her sweater. "Trust me, I know we have it better than a lot of civilians, and I'm grateful for that. I just don't see how we can afford the van we need. And without it, getting him to medical appointments and therapies is becoming impossible." She took a big shuddery breath.

The woman next to her put an arm around her. "My husband is deployed. My daughter has autism, and she's a wanderer, which is usually caused by sensory overload. If we could put a swing set in the backyard, she could play outside on her own. But we need a privacy fence for our backyard to keep her safe. It's okay with the housing people if we put one in, but now that the housing is privatized, we have to pay for the fence."

The government used to own and run housing on bases. Over the past twenty years most of the housing had transitioned to being owned by private companies, and there were a lot of problems. This was just one of them.

"My husband is enlisted," the woman continued. "We just hit the threshold where we aren't eligible for food stamps anymore. There's no way we can afford the fence."

My heart hurt for these women.

The rest of the women around the table shared their stories, talking about what had been going on in their lives since their last meeting. Not everyone needed something money could buy, but they all needed someone to talk to.

"Another need is for respite caregivers," a woman said. "The government will pay for some, but there just aren't enough caregivers to go around. We help each other when we can. But we're all exhausted." Most of the women nodded. "I forgot to renew my ID card, and my expired one was confiscated at the commissary. My husband is TDY somewhere, and I have no way to get hold of him."

TDY stood for Temporary Duty. It was more or less like a business trip, but they could last up to 179 days. That left the other spouse home handling everything on his or her own, as military spouses often did. Almost every military spouse understood what it was like to have a husband gone and unreachable at times.

"Do you have a power of attorney?" I asked. If she did she'd be able to get a new ID on her own.

"I can't find a current one. I'm supposed to leave for a trip with girlfriends to San Francisco. We're booked at the Marines' Memorial Club in San Francisco, but without my ID, we won't be able to check in. I know it's my fault, but this is supposed to be my respite."

"I'm so sorry," I said. "I hope you can work it out."

Another woman spoke up. "My four-year-old son needs an adaptive tricycle. They can cost from five hundred to two thousand dollars. Like the others, we just can't afford it. His physical therapist said it would be good for his co-ordination and socialization. Not to mention he'd get more exercise."

"How can I help?" I asked. As I'd listened, I'd begun to formulate a plan, but I wanted to see what they had to say first.

"We thought you might have some advice about the best time to have a sale and how to set it up," Rebecca said. "Where to have it too."

"I have an idea, if you are interested," I said. Everyone, well almost everyone nodded. One woman was frowning at me for some reason. "I'm having a garage sale on the town common on Saturday to celebrate the two-year anniversary of my business. Why don't I turn it into a fund-raiser for all of you?"

"That would be wonderful," Rebecca said. "We knew you did the one for Eric and Tracy Hunt to bring Eric's dog over. But we didn't expect you to do something for us. We just wanted some advice."

"I'm full of advice, but it would be an honor to help you all out," I said. "I know it's short notice, but if you all are willing we can make it work. I can ask some friends to donate things for a silent auction. That really helped last time."

Everyone chatted excitedly as we tossed around ideas. Everyone except the woman who had frowned at me. She finally spoke up.

"Zoey Whittlesbee could do the sale for us," she said. "She has a garage sale business too. It's new, and she could use the publicity."

"That's fine if you want to work with her," I said. I hoped my voice and face were neutral. I wasn't doing this for publicity. Although realistically doing a good deed usually yielded something back. There had been an old *Friends* episode in which Phoebe had challenged Joey to do something that wouldn't benefit him. It was almost impossible.

"Zoey thinks the garage sale should be on base," the woman said.

"That's an option, but more people will be able to come if it's on the town common. You need to do what's best for your group. Another option is to have Zoey do one sale on base and me do one in town." I wished I wouldn't have said that. All I needed was to have Zoey view this as some big competition between us. "Why don't I step out for a minute and let you discuss it."

"You don't have to do that," Rebecca said.

"No, it's fine. Really."

Chapter Twenty-Six

I walked out and sat in the little gazebo. The air smelled of damp dirt with a hint of things that were starting to grow. A few minutes later Zoey's friend charged out of the community center and took off toward the housing area. She didn't even notice me sitting in the gazebo. Or if she did, she didn't want to acknowledge me. Rebecca came to the door and motioned for me to come in.

"I didn't mean to cause a problem. Everyone seems to have enough of them," I said as we walked back to the meeting.

"You didn't. And, like you said, Zoey can always do a sale too. We just liked your enthusiasm. And, between us, Zoey can be difficult."

I would have liked to ask Rebecca more, but needed to work out the details for the garage sale while we finished our food. Most of the ladies would be contributing things, while others agreed to help out the day of the sale.

When we were finished, Rebecca walked me to my car. "Thanks for this. You didn't have to turn your garage sale into a fund-raiser for us."

"I'm happy to do it." I'd planned to use the money to

rent a cabin at Lake Winnipesaukee in New Hampshire and surprise Seth with a getaway, but this was more important. "I don't mean to pry." I totally did. "But you mentioned Zoey is difficult. How so? And if you don't want to talk about it, that's fine."

"She's one of those people who volunteers to do things, but then just wants to have a bunch of underlings to boss around. No one wanted to say it out loud, but if she ran the garage sale, we'd be doing all the work. Zoey would show up long enough to grab some glory."

Zoey sounded annoying, but that didn't make her some kind of homicidal kidnapper. Somehow that disappointed me. "Do you know if she's independently wealthy?" I was still curious about how she had the money to offer to buy all of Alice Krandle's stuff.

"Not that I know of. If she was, I don't think she'd be living on base. The houses aren't that great."

"Has she done any garage sales for people on base?"

"A few. I went to one of them. It was like Martha Stewart herself had designed it. Very fancy."

I'd done one high-end garage sale where everything was arranged to look like a fancy store. It was a waste of time and money as far as I was concerned, but the customer is always right.

"She also did a sale for a neighbor of mine."

"Do you know if your neighbor made any money?"

"Not much. Zoey made her buy expensive tags, signs, and an open-sided tent for the sale. It took hours of organization. She would have been content just to throw stuff on tables and hope for the best."

That wasn't the best way to do a garage sale either. I took a middle-of-the-road approach for my sales. "Okay.

Thanks. I'll be in touch soon with final details about the sale." We hugged our good-byes. As I drove away I remembered Trooper Kilgard wanted me to cancel the sale. I couldn't let those women down.

I decided since I was on base I'd stop by the thrift shop and say hi to my friend Eleanor. Maybe she'd know something about Zoey. At the sale for Alice Krandle, Eleanor had said Zoey wanted to be the only garage sale organizer in town. How far was Zoey willing to go to accomplish that?

At eleven I went into the thrift shop through the back door. I hadn't been here for a couple of weeks because I'd had one of those terrible spring colds that I hadn't wanted to expose anyone to. Since I'd recovered, I'd been busy with my clients' sales. The storeroom was shockingly clean and well organized.

I'd been here at times when donations were stacked everywhere and you could barely walk through the room. Now clothes were hung neatly on racks, toys were on low shelves, and stray boxes were up high on shelves above the clothes. I walked into the shop, which was equally neat, but there seemed to be less merchandise than usual. Eleanor was at the front of the store behind the cash register, looking at her phone.

"Eleanor, the storeroom and store look amazing." I didn't add "if rather empty."

"It's all Zoey Whittlesbee."

"She must have spent hours in here." I'd taught her well apparently when she'd worked for me in January.

"Oh, no. That's not it. She's convincing everyone to hire her to do garage sales, and our donations are way down. Three quarters of our recent donations are leftover items

from the sales, and most of it isn't worth trying to sell."
Eleanor shook her head. "I'm not begrudging anyone the
chance to make money off their stuff. It's just, from what
I've heard, they aren't."

"What do you mean?"

"Zoey has people signing contracts, but almost everything is an add-on."

"Like?"

"Tags are extras. Signs are extra. She even charges for
her time posting the sale online. I think she's the only one
making any money."

"It doesn't seem like she'll stay in business very long
at that rate."

"Maybe not on base, but she has a rich aunt in Concord
who knows everyone and has done a couple of huge sales
there. I guess Zoey raked it in."

That must be where Zoey had gotten the money to offer
Alice Krandle a lump sum. It still seemed like a risky way
to do business.

"Do you know what Zoey's husband does?" I knew he
was in the Air Force, but I couldn't remember his exact job.

"He's with the security force."

The security force worked closely with the Ellington
Police Department. He'd have access to all kinds of information. Did I really think Zoey could be behind Stella's
kidnapping? Was she that desperate?

"How long have they lived here?"

"About two years."

Long enough to know that Green Monster was a flavor
of ice cream at Bedford Farms. I'd moved off base about
two and a half years ago which is why I didn't know the
Whittlesbees except from the brief time Zoey worked for
me. During that time I'd never met her husband or kids.

I just couldn't imagine that I knew someone who would do this to me or Stella. The kidnapper said I knew him. I shook my head.

"Why do you ask? Is everything okay?"

"Yeah. Sure. Everything's fine." I'm not so sure Eleanor believed me, but she let it drop. Eleanor and I chatted for a few more minutes before saying our good-byes.

Next on my list was tracking down Louisa Crane. She was the last person I knew by name who had some connection to all that was going on. Damaris wouldn't be happy if she found out, but that was the least of my worries. Figuring out who the kidnapper was had to be a priority. No one—especially Seth and Stella—would sleep well until that was accomplished. After a quick online search, I found an address for Louisa in an apartment complex on the north side of Ellington.

It didn't take long to drive over there. A closed outdoor swimming pool was surrounded on three sides by four story buildings. It looked like each unit had its own balcony. Louisa lived on the third floor. I hesitated at the door before knocking. But what was the worst that could happen? I didn't think she was going to let me in and kidnap or kill me. It was more checking off a box. And I still had the wine bottle in my purse and hairspray in my pocket. I knocked, then slipped my hand in the pocket of my sweater to grasp the hairspray bottle.

Louisa answered the door and looked me up and down. "Sarah Winston." Louisa was a lumpy woman who looked to be in her sixties. She wore jeans, a tunic top, and had thick black socks on her feet. "I can't decide if you are brave or stupid coming here."

I couldn't agree more. "Probably some combination of both," I said.

"Come in since you're here." Louisa turned, and I followed her down a hall. A bedroom was off to the right, a bath to the left. The main living space included a small kitchen open to the tiny living room-dining room combo. Another bedroom was off the living room to the left. It didn't seem like anyone else was here, but I didn't relax my grip on my hairspray bottle just in case.

Louisa had a huge leather couch and matching recliner that took up most of the living room. A flat-screen TV was hung on the wall opposite the couch. All of it looked new, and I remembered Frida had said she'd thought Louisa had come into some money. Louisa's balcony overlooked the parking lot at the back of the building. Family photos hung above the couch. Louisa sat in the recliner, and I took a spot on the couch.

"Your apartment is lovely." I'd try to soften her up first.

"What? You think I robbed a bank?" Louisa asked.

Whoa. That didn't go as planned.

"If you must know, I won fifteen thousand dollars on a scratch-off lottery ticket."

"That's amazing. Congratulations. I've never won more than two dollars." Not that I played often. "You must be very lucky."

"Yeah, well, most of my life my luck has been of the bad kind." She peered at me with a "why are you here" look.

"I know about the anti-Sarah group that meets at the church." Soft-pedaling didn't seem to be a good idea.

"I knew Frida Chida was up to no good when I saw her outside the room that day."

I wasn't going to throw Damaris under the bus and tell Louisa that was how I'd first heard about the group.

"Did you know Crystal Olson?" I thought I'd go back to the very beginning of what had happened with the kidnapper.

"The hooker that got herself killed."

I'm not sure how she "got herself killed," but I'd let that slide. "Yes."

"My nephew went to high school with her in Lowell."

Chapter Twenty-Seven

What? I'd known that Crystal had lived in Lowell, but this was another connection, and I'd take any tenuous link I could find right now. However, Louisa's nephew couldn't have murdered Crystal because he was in prison for attempted kidnapping. *Kidnapping!* He couldn't have kidnapped Stella either, but maybe he had something to do with it.

"They mostly called her by her middle name, Alexer, in high school. She thought Crystal sounded trashy, which in my opinion suited her just fine even back then."

Translated without the Boston accent it was Alexa if you took off the *r* and changed it back to an *a*. "Alexer" sounded familiar. I sat straighter. The night in the cemetery. I'd thought I'd heard them ask about Elixer, but maybe they'd said Alexer. I'd thought it was a street drug not a person. Crystal/Alexa had been dead by the time I was in the cemetery, but not many people would have known about it by then. Why had I been sent to the cemetery that night? Was Alexa a clue I'd somehow missed? But a clue to what?

"Do you know if she sold drugs?"

"Don't know. But if you're willing to sell your body, why not drugs too?"

Louisa had a point. But I couldn't see how any of this connected to Stella's kidnapping or me. Unless, like I'd originally thought, the kidnapper had known that a drug deal was going down and just wanted to put me in harm's way that night. I'd put that thought aside for now and focus on who else I'd run into during the past few days.

"Do you know Elmer Norman?"

Louisa snorted. "Everyone knows Elmer. Used to be such a regular guy. Great teacher."

"What happened?"

"His wife died unexpectedly about five years ago. Maybe six. Heart attack. After that he hated everyone. Developed a temper as hot as a stove burner on high. Had to give up teaching, which he'd loved." Louisa shook her head. "He wouldn't let anyone help him out."

That was heartbreaking. "What about Alice Krandle? Do you know her?"

Louisa shook her head. "Can't say that I do."

I had saved my most difficult question for last. "Do you know why your nephew tried to kidnap that child?"

Maybe there would be some motive that would connect him to Crystal's death and Stella's kidnapping.

Louisa was shaking her head. "It was a mess. His wife had lost another baby. Fifth time. He just lost his mind when he saw the cute little thing at the mall." Louisa shook her head some more. "He wasn't ever the brightest kid, but he'd never been in trouble before that."

That story didn't add up to someone who was out to seek revenge on me unless he'd completely snapped. I knew what it was like not to be able to have children. How hard it was. "How's he doing now?"

"Remorseful as all get-out. He knows what he did was wrong, and he doesn't blame you." She crossed her heart. "I swear that's true."

I hoped it was. I stood up. "Thank you for chatting with me."

Louisa stood up too. "I suppose I owe you an apology for being part of the group that was against you."

"Who else was in the group?"

Louisa started down the hall toward the front door. I followed. "Doesn't matter. It's disbanded. Damaris made all of us realize we were wrong to blame you. Almost everyone."

Louisa wasn't bound by any patient-psychologist relationship as Damaris claimed she was. "Please tell me who." My voice held a desperate note. "Someone has been threatening me and people I love. I don't want anyone else to get hurt."

"Someone you know has been hurt?"

"Yes. And I'm afraid it won't end with them."

Louisa pursed her lips and gave me the once-over like she was weighing whether or not she should say anything. She nodded once as I waited. "It's Zoey Whittleshee."

Zoey. "Thank you."

"I don't wish you any harm, and Zoey don't neither. But she isn't happy with you."

I said my good-byes. Why was Zoey in the group? As I started my car I remembered that she was good friends with someone I'd helped get arrested last January. Someone who was awaiting their trial.

I went home for a quick Fluffernutter sandwich and a cup of coffee. One of Mike's men had been sitting outside his door when I'd gotten home. He was still there when I left to go price things at John's house. I was surprised Mike hadn't gone back to Boston by now. But maybe Seth had asked him to stay to keep me safe.

On the drive over I assessed my feelings. In some ways I felt lighter knowing Stella was far away from here, but in other ways I was waiting for something bad to happen. The kidnapper's silence was creating a lot of anxiety for me. I parked in front of John's house and Harriet pulled in beside me. After we went in we got right to work. Harriet was more talkative than usual. I think she was trying to distract me from my dark thoughts.

"I'm sorry I broke my word to you," Harriet said.

"I shouldn't have put you in that position in the first place. Did whoever you talked to find anything out?"

"Not yet."

"Do you think they'll ever find the kidnapper?" I asked Harriet. I was holding a tramp art box that was five by three by three. The intricately carved lid slid off the box. When it was closed it looked like it was all one piece. It had taken me awhile of playing with it to figure out how to open it.

"Yes. There are lots of people looking for him now. He can't stay hidden forever. What are you going to price that at?"

"Sixty. I've been doing a lot of research and found something similar online." I filled out a tag for the box. "What if he just disappears? That would be the smart thing for him to do."

"Most criminals just aren't that smart."

"It's hard for me to relax. I keep waiting for my phone to ring."

"You could not answer it."

I managed a partial smile. "You know that's not going to happen. But he has to realize without Stella it's not like he can make me do anything." Harriet nodded, and we got back to work. Harriet looked things up when I couldn't figure out a price. I set a few things aside to ask my friend who was an antique dealer to help me find prices.

Forty-five minutes later my phone rang. I put it on speaker, expecting to hear the kidnapper. Instead, the song "White Rabbit" by Jefferson Airplane was playing. My parents loved Jefferson Airplane, and one of their early dates had been to see them in concert. A line in the song was "Go ask Alice." Harriet and I stared at each other over the phone. I shivered.

"You can't make me do anything anymore," I said.

"Go ask Alice if that's true or not." The call disconnected.

"I have to go to Alice," I said as I leaped up. I grabbed my purse, still heavy with the wine bottle.

"I'm going too. I'll drive," Harriet said.

We stepped out, I quickly locked the door, and we ran to Harriet's car.

I called Pellner at the number for the burner phone he'd given me and told him about the song. My worries about Alice's safety. We slid into the Porsche, and Harriet was speeding off before I'd closed my door completely.

Chapter Twenty-Eight

Harriet drove with controlled confidence. Tight turns, darting around traffic on Great Road. She ignored the honks that followed us. I kept trying to call Alice, but she didn't pick up. I pictured her passed out on the floor again. Maybe with low blood sugar or maybe something far worse had happened. Harriet slowed when we got to Alice's street.

"It could be a trap," she said as we drove toward Alice's house.

"I hadn't even thought of that." I rolled down my window as if I'd hear the kidnapper.

"What's that smell?" Harriet asked.

We looked at each other. "Gas."

Harriet slammed the car in reverse, backed down the street. I called Alice again. Still no answer. I hung up and called Pellner with an update. But as soon as Harriet stopped, I sprang out of the car and sprinted toward Alice's house. I'd only made it ten feet when I was yanked to a stop. Harriet had me by the back of my shirt.

"Let me go," I shouted.

"It's not safe."

We heard a whoosh, and then the house exploded. A fireball went straight up. We were close enough to feel the heat. Bits and pieces of wood and glass were flung into the air. We ran back toward Harriet's car as debris started landing around us.

"Maybe she wasn't home when you called her," Harriet said.

I punched the recent calls on my phone and tried calling Alice again. It rang and rang until it went to her voicemail. "There's no answer." We both looked toward Alice's former home. I crumbled to my knees.

An hour later we were in the library meeting room with Pellner, the state troopers, and Seth. Harriet and I had a slight smoky smell wafting around us. Our clothes were smudged, and even Harriet's calm demeanor seemed to have vanished. There was a water bottle in front of each of us. I opened mine and drank some. My throat was dry and scratchy. Guilt, sorrow, anger swirled like a tornado of emotions through me.

Trooper Kilgard led the meeting. "Who hates you, Sarah?"

"Hey," Seth said, "Stop right there."

"It's okay, Seth." I didn't want him to defend me. I could handle Kilgard myself. In my dreams anyway. Her eyes didn't seem quite as creepy today, but maybe I was just getting used to her. "Trust me. I've thought this over. A lot."

"And?" Kilgard said.

This was going to be really awkward with Seth sitting right across from me. If he was next to me, at least I wouldn't have to see his face. "I can't imagine any of the people I'm going to mention would actually take any action. However, Seth's mom isn't a big fan. She thinks I'm hindering Seth's career. She wants him to be with someone else." I glanced at Seth. His lips were pressed together.

Pellner and Rodriquez took out their phones and started frantically flipping through them like they didn't want to be any part of this bit of information.

"There was a woman who wanted very much to marry Seth. She's engaged now, but drops by his house a lot. Then there's the plethora of women he's dated." I paused. "Any of the women I mentioned would have to have an accomplice. Like I said, I can't imagine any of them actually doing this. Dislike is a long way from kidnapping, arson, and murder."

Trooper Kilgard took notes while I talked. Seth had leaned back and crossed his arms over his chest.

"Anyone else?" Trooper Kilgard asked.

I nodded. "There's a woman, Zoey Whittlesbee, who worked for me briefly last winter. I trained her, and then she opened her own competing business organizing garage sales. She's said some nasty things about me to try to damage my reputation." I took a drink of water. "She wanted to do Alice's sale. Zoey offered to buy everything for one lump sum, but Alice turned her down and hired me. When Alice told me how much money Zoey had offered to buy her things, I was shocked."

"Why?" Trooper Kilgard asked.

"Zoey's just starting out for one thing. I've since heard she did a couple of big sales in Concord, but I still wonder how she had enough money to offer a lump sum. Especially since she would have no guarantee she could make it back."

"That's unusual?"

"Highly unusual. Also someone took down all the signs I put up giving directions to Alice's house for her sale. I don't have any proof it was Zoey, but it must have been."

"Why do you think that?" Trooper Kilgard asked.

"When I left Alice's house that afternoon, Zoey was parked across the street from my car. She was just sitting there. When she saw me, she started her car, flipped me off, and left."

Seth gave me a "why didn't you tell me that" look. But he'd been dealing with his own problems, and, with all that had been going on, I really hadn't thought about it when I was with him. "But again, it doesn't seem like she'd dislike me enough to do all of this." She *would* hate me once Trooper Kilgard showed up on her doorstep. "Zoey is an Air Force spouse. She lives on base."

"Anyone else?" Trooper Kilgard asked.

"There's all the people in the group that I told you about before who meet with Damaris Christos the therapist. Zoey is part of it." I paused for a moment. "Damaris went to Harvard around the same time as Seth did." I glanced at Seth. His face flushed slightly. "But it's a big school."

Rodriquez looked at Seth. "Do you know her?"

Seth nodded. "I do. We went out a couple of times. Nothing serious."

Rodriquez flipped a pen around in his hand. "Have you seen her since?"

"At some alumni events and we had lunch after she moved here." He looked over at me.

I wasn't mad that he'd had lunch with her and hadn't mentioned it. We didn't have the kind of relationship where we had to report every little thing we did to each other. I'd had lunch with my friend James a couple of weeks ago, and I hadn't told Seth. Okay, so maybe I was a little irked. Damaris was a beautiful woman.

"This is kind of out there," I said. Trooper Kilgard whirled her finger in a "get on with it" motion. "I told you earlier about the anti-Sarah group. What if Damaris is really egging them on instead of calming them down like she told me?" Louisa Crane had vouched for Damaris, but what if she'd been lying? Damaris had known Seth for a long time and maybe she'd twisted her relationship with him and resented me.

"Who would know you worked with Alice?" Rodriquez asked me.

I guess we were moving on. "Like I said before, Zoey would. Also anyone who attended the sale or saw the ads for it. I placed a lot of ads. It wouldn't be hard for someone to figure out."

"Is that it?" Rodriquez asked. Everyone nodded.

"Is there any word on Alice?" I asked.

Trooper Kilgard was shaking her head before I finished. "It's too soon to go through her house." She stood up. "Okay. Let's get on this."

For once I'd rather have stayed in the room with her. It would be easier than talking to Seth after throwing his mom's name out there. We all stood up except for Seth.

"Sarah, can I speak to you for a minute?" Seth asked.

I looked longingly at the door. Watched everyone hustle out. Harriet lingered by the door. "Harriet drove me over here. I don't want to make her wait."

"I'm fine," Harriet said. "I can wait."

Traitor.

"I'll give you a ride home," Seth said.

"I have to go back to my client's house," I said.

"Then I'll give you a ride there," Seth said. He sounded irritated, and it was a tone I wasn't familiar with.

"Okay." I might as well get this over with. I waved to Harriet, who shut the door behind her. Seth stood and started pacing back and forth on the other side of the table. But he didn't say anything. I didn't either.

I couldn't take it though. "Seth   "

"Sarah—"

We both stopped and waited for the other one to continue.

"I'm sorry I had to say those things about your mother and your past relationships." I stood and walked around the table to him. I took his hand and pushed him gently into a chair. I pulled out a chair and turned it toward his.

"I can't believe my mother makes you feel so horrible. I'll talk to her."

"No. Please don't. That will just make things worse. Not that having the state police show up will help our relationship." I felt queasy just thinking about that.

"I trust that Kilgard will make some discreet inquiries instead of rushing off bullheaded to question my mother. That's the advantage of having a wealthy, well-known family. It's not right, but that's the way life is." He shook his head. "I don't want anyone to ever make you feel less than the strong, smart, accomplished woman you are."

He reached over to kiss me, but the door was flung open, and a group of excited children rushed in for story time.

"Sarah, I can tell something is on your mind. What's going on?" Harriet asked as she drove me back to John's to get my car. She'd waited for me instead of leaving, just in case I needed someone to talk to, and I did.

"You're going to think I'm crazy."

"One thing I know about you is that you're not even close to being crazy. And trust me I've seen crazy."

Harriet and I had never really talked much about her career in the FBI. At first because I didn't know her well enough. Then the kidnapper took up all my time. But, from what I did know, she truly had seen crazy.

"Okay, then. What if this isn't about me, but it's about Stella." I watched Harriet to see her reaction.

Harriet wrinkled her nose for a moment. "Stella? What makes you think that?"

"Something Emil said to me. It didn't sink in right away. I flipped on the TV last night, and the movie *The Phantom of the Opera* was on."

Harriet nodded. "I've seen it."

"You know it's about a man who is fixated on an opera singer and kidnaps her."

"Yes. But what does that have to do with Stella?"

"She's an opera singer, and she was in *The Phantom of the Opera* last fall."

Harriet made an *O* with her mouth. "What did Emil say that made you think about that?"

"He heard her sing a long time ago in Italy. He said she was mesmerizing."

"Okay, but what does any of that have to do with you? The person seems bent on tormenting you, not Stella."

"But what if by going after me, by creating rifts in Stella's life with the people she's closest to, he's trying to keep people away from her so he can have her to himself?" There, I'd said it. The thought was there when I woke up this morning. But with the meeting on base, the terrible explosion that I could hardly bare to think about, and the meeting with the police, I hadn't been able to do anything with the thought. "He could be trying to get to her through me. Someone hurting people you love is much harder than being hurt yourself."

"That's true." Harriet paused for a moment. "Doesn't the Phantom kidnap Christine, let her go, and then he kidnaps her again?"

"Yes." I gasped. "Do you think he'll go after her again?" I picked up my phone. "I'd better warn her."

"Wait. Before you do. You said Awesome is with her. He must be aware that, until the person is caught, it's a possibility. Why didn't you bring this up at the meeting we just had?"

"Because it's farfetched. Maybe I'm just desperate to not have this be about me."

Harriet traced her finger over the steering wheel while she thought. I watched as her finger went up, over, and around again and again. She had a fabulous manicure with dark pink nail polish and a row of rhinestones across the nail on her index finger. I glanced at my hands as I waited for her to comment. No manicure. The garage sale business was hard on nails.

"The problem with all of this," Harriet finally said, "is that I get how someone would know about your connection to the police and Seth. That's been fairly public. But your connection to Mike Titone? From what you've said that isn't as well-known."

"Mike has stayed here multiple times by now, and, while much of the time he's stuck up in the apartment, the last few trips he's been out and about more." I'd seen him walking back from DiNapoli's with a pizza box in his hand on his last trip. "It might not be the closely held secret he thinks it is."

"Yes, but he could be connected to Stella, not you. Which

brings us back to your theory that it could be someone who is really after Stella. Any thoughts on who?"

"None. I know she had a troubled relationship in California and problems with drugs. But how would anyone there know anything about me?"

"It wouldn't be that hard to figure out if they came here."

"Who is new in town that knows Stella?" It was a rhetorical question. One for me to think over not Harriet. "Someone with a connection to Stella."

Harriet pulled up in front of John's house. She looked at me with a crease between her eyes. "What about Emil?"

Chapter Twenty-Nine

I twisted toward her. "My lawyer, Emil?" *Duh, Sarah.* There weren't a lot of people named Emil roaming around Ellington.

"How well do you know him?"

"Not well at all, but he's Rosalie's nephew, and he works with Vincenzo."

"What?"

I thought about Vincenzo and gossip I'd heard about him. "There have always been rumors that Vincenzo had mob connections. Vincenzo has helped Mike before." Mike said his brothers had been tipped off. Could that tip have originated with Vincenzo? "And Emil's working with him."

"He also said that Stella was mesmerizing."

I shook my head. "Anyone who has heard her sing would think that."

"What did Emil do before he showed up here?"

"He said he was in criminal law in . . . Italy." Home to the Mafia. "I'm looking him up."

Harriet and I both grabbed our phones and started

typing away. We both read in silence. "This doesn't look good," I said.

"Which part? Emil's getting all those reported Mafia bosses off the hook for their crimes or all the photos of him attending various versions of *The Phantom of the Opera*?"

"Lots of people have a favorite show they see over and over again."

"What about the picture of him at a ball dressed as the Phantom?" Harriet turned her phone to me. There he was— a handsome devil with a beautiful Christine on his arm.

This was getting worse and worse. And Emil liked costumes—at least he was willing to dress up as the Phantom. "His girlfriend makes a lovely Christine. She's probably the one who decided how they'd dress. Women usually do in those instances." I looked at the picture again. "There's not a hint of scandal in any of the articles about him as a lawyer." Or anything about him being fascinated with Alice in Wonderland.

"There are lots of scandals in Italy. Some of it is just done more quietly with payoffs and such."

"It just can't be. He's helping me." Rosalie would be heartbroken if Emil was involved in a crime or multiple crimes at this point. I pushed away a vision of Alice's house blowing up. Then I looked at John's house. Was it safe? Was he? I had to get to the bottom of this.

"Or making sure that he knows what you are up to."

I shook my head. "No. It's not him." He *had* shown up at the cemetery. "I was with him when I got one of the calls. That proves it isn't him."

"Calls can be taped in advance."

"I take back this whole theory. It's not directed at Stella but at me. Like you said—that makes more sense."

Harriet nodded. Didn't say more. But I had a feeling she'd be digging into this, and I had no way to stop her.

I dragged myself up the stairs to my apartment at four thirty still dirty from the explosion at Alice's house. Diego leaped up when he saw me. "Are you okay? Let me get Mike."

I started to say no, but Diego was already in the apartment before I managed to say anything. I wondered how bad I looked to make him react that way. I swiped a hand across my face and some mascara came off on it. There were probably tear tracks too. A minute later I was sitting on their couch flanked by Mike and Francesco. Diego stood in the doorway, back against the doorjamb. That way he could keep an eye on the steps and listen to me.

"Do you want something to drink?" Mike asked.

"Water?" Francesco suggested.

"Wine?" Mike said.

"Whiskey?" Diego asked.

I almost laughed at the three w's they'd suggested. "Water would be great."

Mike got me a glass. "What's going on?"

I sketched out what had happened. "And then her house exploded, and she's dead." I could barely get the words out. I saw it happen all over again. I'd felt helpless. "Because of me."

"Not because of you," Diego said. Mike and Francesco chimed in with similar reassurances.

"Why are you guys still here if the threat to you is over?" They all exchanged looks. "Did Seth ask you to stay so I wouldn't be here alone?"

Mike finally nodded. "He did. And we're happy to do it."

"Thank you. It's nice not to be here alone."

I got up and walked over and stood by Diego. I had to ask one more thing, but I wanted to watch their reactions. "Do you know Emil Kawolski?"

"Name sounds familiar," Mike said.

I didn't watch him. I watched Francesco's much more expressive face. His eyebrows popped up, and he whipped his head toward Mike. "He's been in Italy. Just returned recently," I said.

"Interesting," Mike said.

Francesco continued to watch Mike.

"He's working with Vincenzo," I added.

Mike stood. "That must be why the name is familiar. I've got a call I need to make. Let us know if there is anything else we can do."

After a round of hugs, I went back to my apartment. I showered and spent the rest of the evening on my laptop trying to find connections between Emil and Mike. Of course I didn't find anything, but, then again, Mike was very good at secrets.

Thursday morning I went to Dunkin's drive-thru for coffee. Right after I picked it up along with two coconut donuts, my phone rang. The ID said it was the Masquerade Costume Shop. At least it wasn't the kidnapper.

"Sarah? This is Poppy from the Masquerade Costume Shop."

"Hi, Poppy. What can I do for you?"

"I think I can do something for you," Poppy said. She sounded a little breathless.

"That would be great." I really needed a break.

"Of course, I called the police first, but I wanted to let you know. There's been a bit of a mix-up."

That wasn't too surprising given the interaction I'd had with her at the shop. "What kind of mix-up?"

"Gregory Kiah ordered the costume, but he wasn't the one who picked it up."

I already knew that, but it was nice of her to call me. "Thank you for letting me know."

"Remember that picture I showed you?"

"The one done by the sketch artist?"

"Yes. Exactly. I printed it out, framed it, and put it up on my counter with a sign saying, 'Do you know this man?'"

I gripped my phone. "Did someone?"

"Well, a man came in and said it looked like one of the grocery baggers at that little Italian grocery store in Ellington."

"Danucci's?" I asked.

"Yes. That's the one."

I'd met Mac Danucci last June when I did an athletic equipment swap for the school board. The superintendent of schools had been murdered in a closet off the gym during the event. I shuddered at the memory of finding her.

"Well, you seemed very concerned when you were in here. But hopefully the police will make an arrest soon. Did you decide which way you wanted to go with your costume?"

Costume? Oh, I'd forgotten that I had told her that was why I was in there. Ugh. Keeping track of lies had more layers than Poppy's Cinderella costume. "The event was canceled. If they reschedule, I'll be back in." I needed to visit Danucci's and talk to Mac.

Chapter Thirty

Danucci's hadn't changed much since the last time I was in there a few months ago. Still dark and dingy. I think the only reason Mac was still in business was because he stayed open until three in the morning when all the other grocery stores in town closed earlier. I'd suspected Mac of nefarious deeds last June, but hadn't ever dug any real dirt up on him.

I recognized the cashier—a teenage girl who had quizzed me mercilessly one time when I'd come in and asked if Mac was here. Only after I had convinced her that I wasn't a bill collector, bounty hunter, or law enforcement had she told me where to find him. I still wasn't sure if she'd been joking or not.

"Mac?" I asked her.

"In his office," she said over her shoulder as she scanned things for a customer. Did she remember me or was she too busy to feel protective today? Mac's office was at the back of the store. I threaded my way through the dim aisles. The lighting in here, unlike that of most grocery stores, was abysmal. A teenage boy who'd worked here for some time was shelving boxes of generic granola. I always spoke to him, but he never responded.

Since the first time I'd seen him, I'd thought his eyes looked older than his years. I said hello as usual, but he continued to shelve at the pace of a sloth. But he must be a good worker because he had been here for a long time. Mac's office door had a big Leave Me Alone sign on it. I knocked once and went in after I heard a muffled "come in."

Mac sat at his desk, a bulletin board with OSHA warnings and signs to wash your hands tacked all over it hung on the wall behind him. Like last time, the air was scented with the tang of cigars even though there was a No Smoking sign posted on the wall. A large exhaust fan rattled and wheezed like it had inhaled too much smoke over the years. Mac didn't sound much better.

He wore denim overalls instead of his usual blood-stained butcher's apron. The overalls strained at the middle over a yellow, long-sleeved T-shirt.

"Well, there's trouble."

"Nice to see you too, Mac."

He looked longingly at his expensive-looking humidor, the only nice thing in the office. "Cigar?" he asked with hope in his voice.

"I don't smoke, but I don't care if you do." I did, but I wanted information. Having him relaxed would work better for me. I sat on a wobbly plastic chair across from him. "Will you take a look at a picture for me? It's someone who might work here."

Mac cast another glance at the humidor, but didn't grab a cigar. "Sure. Why are you looking for him?"

Interesting. I hadn't said if the person was a male or a female. But if the police had already been here, Mac might know who I was asking about. "A friend wants to find him." I lifted a shoulder and dropped it like it wasn't that important. "I think she's interested, if you know what I mean." That was nice and ambiguous. Hopefully, my face wouldn't give away the half-truth or how much this mattered to me. I handed over my phone while Mac nodded.

He patted a pocket. "Dang. I lost another pair of readers." He held my phone at arm's length and studied the photo. "Kind of hard to tell since it's a sketch not a photo."

"It's not the best. I've been having phone problems." And yes, the police taking my phones was a problem.

"Yeah, I don't recognize him." Mac handed me back my phone and stood up. He pulled an apron off a hook. "I gotta get back at it."

I stood too. "Thanks for taking a look." Mac ushered me out of his office, but didn't follow me out. Once his door closed, I heard the distinct click of a lock falling into place.

Maybe he just wanted that cigar, or maybe he wanted to make a call and didn't want me to hear him. Locking the door seemed suspicious, but there wasn't much I could do about it. Standing out here being frustrated wasn't going to accomplish anything. I went to the produce department and grabbed a couple of oranges that looked about a minute away from being tossed in the garbage.

I waited in line to be rung up, if you could call it that anymore. Once it was my turn, I whipped out my phone and showed the cashier the photo. Fortunately, no one was waiting behind me. "Any chance you recognize him? Does he work here?"

"The sketch is lousy," she said, squinting at it.

Yeah, yeah, I knew the sketch was crap.

"It kind of looks like the guy who plays Archie on that CW show *Riverdale*." She looked up at me.

"Does he work here?" I smiled at her.

She laughed. "I wish." She handed me my phone back, scanned my oranges, and bagged them.

"Thanks," I said as she handed me the oranges.

"It also kind of looks like Mac's daughter Victoria."

What? Did Mac realize that and lie or could he really not tell because of the poor image and lack of glasses?

"She has really short hair, big features, and broad shoulders. She's a swimmer, and she has a deep voice. I can see how someone might mistake her for a man."

A deep voice? I was reshuffling everything I'd been thinking. Why would she have something against me? "Does she work here?"

"Only when forced to."

"What about last week?"

"She covered for me Thursday, Friday, and Saturday."

"Have the police been by with this picture?" I asked.

"I've been here since nine and haven't seen anyone."

I thought that over. Why wouldn't they have already followed up on this? Although if Poppy had called the police, it was probably the Chelmsford police. It might take a bit for the news to go from one department to the other. "Okay, thanks."

I headed toward my Suburban in the parking lot as an Ellington police SUV pulled in. Whoever was driving spotted me and parked by my car. Just as I arrived at it, Pellner came around the side of the SUV.

"What are you doing here?" he asked.

He didn't sound happy to see me. I held up the bag with the two oranges. "Shopping." I hopped into the Suburban, started it up, and headed home as Pellner walked toward the store without a glance back at me. He'd find out soon enough that I'd been in there asking questions. He could just add it to his list of reasons to be mad at me.

I'd driven about two blocks when my conscience got the better of me. I made a U-turn and drove back to Danucci's. When Pellner came out, I was there waiting for him.

"I'm not sharing any information with you, Sarah. It's too dangerous," Pellner said as he walked by me.

At least he was talking to me. "I already know the picture looks like Mac's daughter."

He stopped and wheeled around. *"What?"*

"Didn't you talk to the girl at the register?"

"I did. She said the picture looked like some actor."

"She told me that too. Then she said it also looked like Mac's daughter who's a swimmer with a deep voice."

"I'm going back in there to wring her neck. Charge her with obstruction and Mac too."

"Pellner, she's a kid. You probably scared her. It's why you had me look into the death of that woman last winter. Because people tell me things." Usually way more than I wanted to hear.

"Fine. What did she tell you?"

I repeated our conversation.

"What connection do you have to Mac's daughter?"

"None that I know of."

"Think about it. There must be something."

"I have, and I can't think of anything. The only connection I have with Mac is that he was on the school board when the superintendent was killed. And I occasionally shop here."

Pellner frowned. "Thanks for the information."

"While I waited for you, I looked her up. Her first name

is Victoria. She's a sophomore at Boston University and is on their swim team."

"Okay. Thanks. Now go home."

"I will." Pellner watched me get in my car. I was going home, but only so Harriet could pick me up. I'd called her while I waited for Pellner. My plan was for us to get to Mac's daughter before Pellner did. I knew that if he talked to her first that she'd never talk to me.

Chapter Thirty-One

Riding in a Porsche was almost like flying, or it would have been if there hadn't been any traffic. Harriet wore a blue paisley dress that flowed around her like a robe. It must be hippie day in Harriet's wardrobe rotation. She'd told me when we first met that she was trying to figure out her new life after retirement. Her husband had died several years ago, and her children didn't live close by.

Forty-five minutes later we were parked in the visitor parking outside a classroom building. According to Victoria's social media accounts, she had a class ending in twenty minutes. We hoped to catch her on the way out.

"Any news on Emil?" I asked Harriet.

"I've been checking into Emil's background," Harriet admitted. We waited, sitting on a short brick wall for what would become a flower garden when it warmed up.

"I was afraid you wouldn't let that drop." I wasn't sure I wanted to hear what she had to say. But since we were here waiting to find out Victoria's story, it must not be terrible.

"I haven't heard back from the people I reach out to yet." Harriet glanced down at her feet.

"I hope no news is good news."

"He may just be very good at covering whatever he's up to."

"I just wish I could figure out who the kidnapper is. I want this to end."

"We'll get there. If not us, the police."

I hoped Harriet was right.

Twenty-five minutes later a group of students came out of the building. They separated and went in different directions.

"That looks like her." I pointed to a girl that fit Victoria's description as Harriet and I stood.

"Victoria," I yelled. Two girls turned, stopped, and waited for Harriet and me to walk over to them.

On the drive here, Harriet and I had once again talked strategics. Harriet was going to take the lead.

"Victoria Danucci?" Harriet asked.

One of the girls looked just like Victoria's photos on social media minus the fish lips. She looked a little like the sketch and, in her big hooded sweatshirt and baggy sweats, a little mannish. The other girl had dark braided hair and smaller features.

"Yes?"

I wanted to give her a speech about stranger danger, but that would have to wait until we finished talking to her. I'm a terrible person.

"We need to speak to you about something." Harriet looked pointedly at the other girl. Victoria exchanged a look with her.

"I'll catch up with you in a couple of minutes," Victoria said.

"You sure?" The girl eyed us suspiciously. As she should.

"Yes. It's fine," Victoria said.

Harriet and I did look respectable and trustworthy. I'd changed into a pencil skirt and sweater before we'd left. Harriet also had a way of carrying herself that exuded confidence and sent out "trust me" vibes. She'd make an excellent serial killer.

"I need some information about an Alice in Wonderland costume that you picked up," Harriet said.

Victoria's eyebrows met in the middle as she scrunched her face in concern. "What about it?"

"Do you still have it?" Harriet asked.

"It wasn't returned?" She frowned. "It was a beautiful costume."

"No, it hasn't been," I said. "Do you know where it is?" Oops. I forgot that Harriet was supposed to be doing the talking. I glanced at her, but she didn't look upset.

"I don't. I picked it up for a friend."

Aargh. A friend. "It seems like Chelmsford is a bit out of the way from here," I said. Boston University was about seventeen miles from Ellington, and add on another ten miles to Chelmsford. It didn't make sense to me. Harriet put a hand on my arm. I'm sure I sounded too aggressive, but I was feeling desperate. I wanted to grab Victoria by the neck and wring the information out of her.

"You must be a good friend to drive all that way for someone," Harriet said. Her voice calm, soothing.

"I was home working for my dad so I was in the area anyway," Victoria said. She looked back and forth between us. "But now I'm regretting it. Am I going to have to pay for that costume? It was expensive. I'm already up to my ears in student loan debt, and I'm only a sophomore."

"Who is the friend who asked you to pick up the costume?" Harriet asked. "It seems like they would have to pay."

Watch and learn, I told myself.

"Gabe Tuttle asked me to pick it up."

I didn't know anyone by that name. I gave a slight shrug to indicate that to Harriet.

"Does he live in Ellington?" Harriet asked.

"Yes. He still lives with his parents. We went to high school together," Victoria said. "Sometimes he works part time at my dad's grocery store." She reddened a bit.

Hmmm. Maybe they were in a relationship, or she wished they were. High school crushes could hold a lot of power over someone. However, the voice on the phone had sounded more mature than that of someone only a couple of years out of high school. And with the kidnapping, and knowledge of drug deals and auctions, it just didn't seem like it could be someone that young to me. But who knew? I wished I did.

"How did he get hold of you?" I asked. I glanced at Harriet, and she gave a small nod. It was a good question, because maybe it hadn't been Gabe but the kidnapper pretending to be Gabe.

"Gabe sent me a text," Victoria said. "Here, I'll show you." She swiped through a bunch of messages before turning the phone toward us.

"There's just a number. No name. He's not in your contacts," Harriet said.

"I guess he got a new number," Victoria said. Her phone rang, and she glanced at it. "My dad."

Oh, no.

"I'll call him back when we're done."

Whew.

"Would you mind sending me a screenshot of the text thread with Gabe?" Harriet asked.

"I'm not sure," Victoria said. She took a step back.

Oh, no. We were losing her.

"I get that you might hesitate," Harriet said, "but this is important. Beyond the costume going missing."

Victoria studied Harriet for a minute. Harriet kept her face friendly, interested. "Okay," Victoria said.

Harriet gave Victoria her number, and moments later had the screenshot. "Did you take the costume to Gabe?" Harriet asked. She'd picked up on my line of thinking.

"He asked me to leave it on his porch. Gabe said he was at class and then worked. He couldn't get to the shop before it closed."

"What time was that?" Harriet asked.

"Early Thursday evening. I don't remember an exact time."

Harriet and I exchanged a quick, concerned glance. "Thank you for the information," Harriet said.

"Sure."

"What did he want the costume for?" I asked. I kept my voice even like Harriet had hers.

"I didn't really ask." Victoria's face went up to a brighter shade of red. "I need to get going."

"Victoria, I'm glad you talked to us, but be careful who you give information to," I said. "There are a lot of creeps out there."

She frowned at me. "Whatever."

Harriet and I watched her walk away. "Do you think we should have told her the police will be looking for her?" I asked Harriet.

"No. She'll know soon enough."

"I feel sorry for her. They will tell her about the costume ending up on Crystal Olson."

Chapter Thirty-Two

As soon as we got in the car I turned to Harriet. "I'll look up Gabe Tuttle. It seems like we should talk to him."

"I agree, but I'm betting he's not going to know anything about an Alice in Wonderland costume."

"I hope that isn't true. If it is, it makes me worry about why the kidnapper picked Victoria to do his bidding. How would he know she'd go out of her way to do something for Gabe?"

Harriet lifted a shoulder and dropped it. "Can you think of any connection between you and Victoria?"

"Only that I know her dad because of what happened with the school board."

Harriet was silent for a couple of minutes, concentrating on the traffic. "It seems like a tenuous connection at best."

"I agree." I started searching for Gabe Tuttle. It didn't take too long to find a wealth of information on him. "Gabe lives in Patriots Ridge, not too far from where Alice Krandle lived." A shot of sadness swept over me. I hated thinking about Alice in the past tense. It made me all the more determined to pursue the kidnapper.

"Maybe there's some connection there."

"He's a cute guy." I showed Harriet his picture. He was leaning against a lifeguard stand with a whistle around his neck. Curly brown hair, brown eyes, a dimpled smile, and a confident stance that seemed to say "the world is mine."

"He's going to Ellington Community College and works as a lifeguard at the pool on Fitch. Victoria and Gabe have swimming in common."

"Good point."

"According to his most recent post, he's headed over to work at the pool right now. I can call someone to get us sponsored on base."

"Let's do it," Harriet said.

My friend Eleanor sponsored us on base. We arrived at the pool at two fifteen. It was an Olympic-size indoor pool. In the summer there were chairs to lounge on outside and a splash pad open for kids six and under. The pool and swim lessons were free to active-duty military, and a minimal fee was charged for their families, military retirees, and guests. It was a nice perk.

Fortunately, I knew the girl working at the desk. She let us in without paying and pointed out Gabe to us. It was easy to spot him, sitting in the lifeguard chair, watching alertly as a Mommy and Me swim class was taking place. Kids were screaming with joy, and moms were smiling as they helped their kids float. The instructor looked a bit harried as she tried to get everyone's attention.

Harriet and I walked up to the lifeguard stand. "Hi, Gabe," I said. "I wondered if we could ask you a few questions about Victoria Danucci."

Gabe frowned. "I guess I'll have time when this class is over. Is she okay?"

Gabe didn't sound anything like the kidnapper did. "She's fine. I just saw her. When's class over?" I asked.

Gabe blew his whistle and told a little boy not to run. "Another ten minutes. You can wait over by the office."

Fifteen minutes later Gabe came over to us. He'd thrown on a gray Ellington sweatshirt and sweatpants. "Who are you?" Gabe asked.

At least, unlike Victoria, he asked, but that complicated things. "I'm Sarah Winston. I used to live on Fitch, but I live in Ellington now. And this is my friend, Harriet Ballou." I hoped he didn't press us further. I hoped throwing out that I used to live on base would help.

"What do you want to know about Victoria?" he asked.

Apparently my strategy had worked. "Victoria told us you asked her to pick up an Alice in Wonderland costume at the Masquerade Costume Shop in Chelmsford and for her to drop it off at your house," Harriet said.

Gabe was shaking his head before Harriet finished the sentence. "I have no idea what she's talking about."

That wasn't too surprising given the different phone number that had been used and how different his voice sounded from the kidnapper's. But still I was disappointed. I wanted to be able to call Pellner and tell him to come pick this guy up. To wrap this up and to be able to go on with my life without looking over my shoulder, worrying about friends, and being afraid to answer my phone.

Harriet told Gabe about the costume being dropped off on his porch. "Is this your cell phone number?" Harriet rattled off the number.

Gabe shook his head again.

"You haven't used a burner phone?" Harriet asked.

"What's this all about?"

I'd been surprised he hadn't asked earlier.

"We're just trying to track down the Alice in Wonderland costume," Harriet said. "Thanks for answering our questions."

"Is there any chance your parents would have seen who delivered the package?" I asked.

"No. They go to Key West every year from December to May."

"Do you have a security camera at your house?" Harriet asked. "Or what about one of those doorbells that tells you who's at the door?"

"No. Ellington's a safe place to live," Gabe said.

If only he knew what was going on, he'd probably be installing cameras all around his house and putting bars on the windows. "Do you know if any of your neighbors have any security cameras?"

He nodded. "I think my neighbors across the street have one. Maybe that would help."

"What's your neighbor's name?" Harriet asked.

"Dean Daynard."

"Thanks, Gabe."

We didn't mention that the police might be coming by to Gabe either, and I didn't give him my mom speech about talking to strangers.

"Do you think he was telling the truth?" I asked Harriet as we walked away.

"Yes. I don't think he would have mentioned his neighbor to us if he wasn't."

"Or he's sending us on a wild-goose chase."

"It's possible. But let's check it out, and then we'll have a better idea. Does the name Dean Daynard sound familiar to you?"

I shook my head. "I wish it did, but I've never heard of him. I'm going to have to do the talking at the Daynards' house," I said to Harriet as we headed back to her car.

"Why?" Harriet asked.

"Because we're going to have to lie, and I don't want to make you do that."

"You have a very expressive face. The whole time we were talking to Gabe, your eyebrows were popping up or you were frowning. Do you think you can handle the lying part?"

"I've gotten better at it." I'm not exactly sure that was something to be proud of. Although apparently I was not that good if I hadn't even noticed I was reacting while Gabe talked. "If I concentrate, I'll be fine."

"Are you sure you don't want to just call Pellner and have him check Dean out?"

"This will be faster. If the police are involved, it will mean they go to the house, get any available video, take it to the station, and watch it themselves several times. Then if they don't know who the guy picking up the costume is, they may call me in to watch the video. In that amount of time we could have already identified the guy, called Pellner, and been done with this." In the past I'd been good about sharing information with the police. Not doing so created a lot of anxiety for me, but, since the first call from the kidnapper, I had believed what I was doing was the right thing to do. I stood by those decisions.

"And that's only if the guy is willing to let them without getting a warrant."

"That makes a crazy sort of sense."

"Harriet, I don't want you to do anything you think is unethical. I can go there alone."

"I'm not deserting you now."

Chapter Thirty-Three

I looked up the Daynards' address. We went out the back gate of Fitch, which meant we were in Concord. Harriet drove on narrow, windy backroads as we headed to the Daynards' house. Trees and low stone walls lined the roads. If your car broke down here, there was nowhere to pull off. We passed the Thoreau Farm where Henry David Thoreau had been born. Of all the famous authors who had lived in Concord, he was the only one born there. After a few turns we would end up back in Ellington.

"Why do you think the kidnapper would involve Victoria and Gabe in this? It seems risky," I asked Harriet.

"He must have been trying to create layers between himself and the crimes. It worries me."

"Why?"

"It shows a high level of planning. Exceptional organizational skills to pull all this off."

I nodded. "We keep talking about a 'him,' but almost everyone on the list I gave the troopers is female." I was so confused. "Stella said that it was a man who had burst into her apartment. But she also said he was masked so would she know for sure?"

Harriet shrugged. "Who is number one on your list?"

I thought for a couple of moments. "Damaris or Zoey, but I'm not sure how Damaris would know Gabe and Victoria."

"But Zoey could know Gabe from base and could then have learned about Victoria through him."

"Yes."

"We can't rule them out. I'm guessing the kidnapper also planned an exit strategy if he feels like he's going to be caught."

"That means we'll have to be extra careful when we find him or her." I said it with more confidence than I felt because part of me thought we'd never find him. "I hope the Daynards' security camera captures the street."

"Don't get your hopes up, Sarah. The man behind all this has been savvy enough to avoid being caught up to this point. It's likely he sent someone else to pick up the package or avoided looking at any cameras."

That was a disheartening thought. "You're right. But eventually you'd think we'd catch a break." My phone rang at three ten. Seth. I thought for a moment about not answering it, but if I didn't he'd probably worry.

"Mike wants the three of us to have a meeting."

What? That was unusual. I was always the one calling Mike, asking him to meet me because I needed his help with something. "Why?"

"I don't know. Mike just contacted me through a system we have set up and requested the meeting. Can you make it?"

That sounded mysterious. I started picturing spies leaving an *X* on a mailbox. "Sure. When and where?"

"In an hour and a half. Just the three of us, no one else. It's at a safe house I have access to."

"What about your guards?" I asked.

Seth didn't say anything for a minute. "I don't have them anymore. I didn't tell you because I didn't want you to worry."

We'd have to talk about that later. I glanced over at Harriet, who kept her eyes on the road. I wondered how much she could hear. "Okay."

"I'll text you an address."

I hung up after we said our "I love yous and good-byes."

"Everything okay?" Harriet asked.

"Yes." My phone binged with a text from Seth with the address. He said the door would be unlocked. I turned my attention back to the neighborhood. "These houses are spaced far enough apart that the two houses might not even face each other squarely."

Harriet pulled up to the Daynards' house. It did face Gabe's house. While both houses sat on large lots, they weren't set back far from the street. Both had massive side yards and probably huge back yards too.

We walked to the door even though I'd told Harriet again that she didn't have to go with me. I rang the doorbell as I studied what security cameras I could spot. The doorbell was obvious. No other cameras were. That was disappointing.

A short man with broad shoulders and bulked-up arms opened the towering door. He looked like he spent a lot of time at the gym. The door was at least ten-feet high, which made Mr. Daynard look even shorter. From the looks of the door, if it were any bigger, he'd need a hydraulic system to open it. His bright blue eyes weren't welcoming. I was surprised he had opened the door instead of just talking to me through the doorbell.

"Hi," I said. "I'm with the Masquerade Costume Shop in Chelmsford."

"I'm not interested." He started to close the door.

I wasn't about to stick my foot in it because it looked to be three inches thick of solid wood. And I preferred not to have my foot crushed. "Wait. Mr. Daynard. It's about a crime."

He hesitated, but stopped. "What crime?"

"We recently found out a costume we'd had delivered to the Tuttles had been stolen off their porch. Gabe told us you might have security cameras that would have captured the thief's face."

Mr. Daynard's face lit up, which surprised me. He held the door open wider. "My son went to high school with Gabe. He's a good kid. Come in. Let's see if we can catch the rat who did it."

We settled in his office. His desk was almost as wide as his front door was tall. Mr. Daynard had three large monitors and an expensive desk chair with all kinds of ergonomic features on it. Maybe he was a gamer, or maybe he worked from home. Whichever it was, I was impressed.

He set two smaller chairs on either side of his desk chair for Harriet and me. After we were all seated, he typed in a few things, and an extensive set of camera views popped up. The photos covered every inch of outdoor space in his yard and were in full color. One camera looked out on the street, and we could see the Tuttles' front door. I gave him the date of last Thursday and told him early evening. Mr. Daynard typed in a few more commands.

He scrolled forward quickly, but slowed down when a car came in to view. We watched it pull up to the curb and Victoria bound up the driveway. She tucked the package to the side of the door, walked back to her car, and took off. The next three minutes of video seemed like an hour. Another car pulled up to the house. Green, slightly rusted on one of the back panels, with four doors.

"Any chance you can see the license plate?" I asked. It probably didn't matter because chances were high that the car was stolen. But maybe the kidnapper had screwed up this time.

Mr. Daynard scrolled back. Stopped the video as the car approached. He zoomed in. The license plate was as clear as if I'd typed it on my phone.

"Ha. Got him. I'll print that out for you." A minute later we heard the quiet whir of a printer. Mr. Daynard reached over and passed me the license plate number.

"Thank you," I said.

"Let's keep watching," Mr. Daynard said.

A figure got out of the car, in baggy jeans and a black hoodie that blocked his face. The person looked like a similar size as the person who'd stolen Gregory Kiah's car. He trotted up to the door, grabbed the package, and headed back to the car, looking down the whole way.

"This is disappointing," Mr. Daynard said. "He must have done this a lot."

At the bottom of the drive, the man looked up for just a second, as if something had startled him.

"There!" Mr. Daynard said. He scrolled back, stopped, and zoomed in. "We've got him."

I stared in horror, wishing I didn't recognize him.

Chapter Thirty-Four

"Would you please print that out?" I asked. "And I'll take it to the police. Maybe they'll recognize him." My voice sounded so calm that I was beginning to wonder if I was having some kind of psychotic break. Inside, my body seemed to have alarms going off all over the place. Everything seemed jiggly, and my vision had dark edges around it. I fought it off.

After quick good-byes and thanks for the help, Harriet and I sat in her car.

"Who is he?" she asked. "You know him, right?"

I continued to stare down at the photo. "Mike Titone's brother Diego. He's been staying with Mike in the apartment next to mine." I shook my head. "He's one of the men who sit out in the hall guarding Mike's door. He was watching me the whole time." That thought scared me the most.

"Mike's in on this?"

I hadn't thought of that, but now I knew why Mike wanted to meet. Maybe he'd figured out that Diego was involved. "No. He couldn't be. I can't imagine any world in which he'd do that to me. But someone had to help

Diego." Who? Francesco? I didn't want to believe that any more than I wanted to believe Mike had helped.

"Why would Diego do this?"

"I don't know." Had someone forced him to do this? I thought back over my interactions with him. There hadn't been that many. Diego had even told me Alice's death wasn't my fault. And he should know, because it was his. Mike, on the other hand, had helped me out more often than I cared to admit. But last winter I'd helped him out too, which had kind of evened the score.

"Is there any chance Diego is being used by the kidnapper too?" Harriet asked. Her voice concerned but calm.

"I thought the same thing. But Mike and his brothers aren't the kind of men to bend to someone else's will. They are benders not bendees."

Harriet nodded. "Are we going to the police?"

"No."

"Somehow I didn't think we were. Are you sure?"

"I need to think this through for a moment. I'm worried Mr. Daynard could be at risk. If Diego figures out that Mr. Daynard has a security system, he could try to do something about it to protect himself."

"Then we need to go to the police."

"Not yet. The kidnapper said he'd know if I got hold of the police." I stared straight ahead, mind whirling. "I have to go back and warn Mr. Daynard." I also had to decide if I should tell Harriet about the meeting with Seth and Mike.

"Good idea. I'll wait here."

"I think I have an idea that will keep Diego from finding out we're on to him. I need to think this through. Please don't call anyone."

Harriet nodded. "I promise. I mean it."

I jumped out of the car, ran up to Mr. Daynard's house, and rang the bell again. He answered quickly.

"I'm worried that, if the thief figures out you have a security camera, you could be at risk," I said. "While the man in the picture is a thief, I'm also concerned he's been involved in other crimes." I took a deep breath. "I'm not exactly who I told you I was."

Mr. Daynard frowned. "What kind of crimes, Sarah?"

"I can't tell you. I can't risk it." Then it hit me. He'd called me Sarah. I hadn't introduced myself. I took a step back. "How do you know who I am?"

"You've been in the paper enough. Ellington's local hero."

I had thought all that kind of thinking had died down after I'd been able to keep out of the press for the past few months.

"I don't let strangers in my house or help them. I figured if you showed up here, there was a good reason."

"Thank you for trusting me."

"Go get him. Whoever he is."

Harriet drove to the Dunkin's, pulled through the drive-thru and we both ordered coffee medium regulars or "regulahs" as the natives would say. Medium regular coffees came with three sugars and three creams. I wasn't sure caffeine was the best idea because I was already on edge. But ordering and drinking coffee would take up some time while I waited to meet with Seth and Mike. After we got our coffees Harriet parked in the Dunkin's lot.

It didn't take me long to decide to tell Harriet about the planned secret meeting with Mike and Seth. "I'll show

them the picture and let Seth figure out the next steps."
I felt so relieved. This would be over soon.

"Why do you think Mike wants to meet?" Harriet asked.

"I wondered the same thing. Maybe he figured it out?
And he wants to let Seth and me know. And he'll know I'll
be somewhere safe."

"Could be," Harriet said. "Unless he's involved."

My mind was racing back through everything that had
happened. "At the auction the record showed Lew Carrol
put lot five in the auction. My address was on the paperwork. I was shocked at the time and mad to see my address.
I never thought that the kidnapper was also living at my
address. That he was thumbing his nose at me. Daring me
to figure out it was him."

"There's no way you could have figured it out."

"It was right in front of my face." I put my head in my
hands for a moment. "If I'd been smart enough, Alice
Krandle would be alive."

"Don't blame yourself for this. It's all on Diego, not you."

Harriet could say that until she was blue in the face, but
it would take some time before I would believe her.

"I'm afraid, Harriet. What if Mike's brother follows him?"

"What if Mike's in on it with him?"

"He's not." I hoped I was right. "I just want to make
sure the three of us are safe."

"Let's call for some backup then." Harriet paused. "I
have a gun in the car."

My eyebrows shot up. "I don't want to put you in
danger."

"I can handle it."

"I think I'll call Emil and Pellner. Now that we know
it's Diego, I trust Emil. Let's drive to Pellner's house. Even
though he gave me that burner phone, I'd rather talk to him

face-to-face." I didn't really trust phones anymore. Who knew what app was there? Who was watching?

We left Dunkin's, and I gave Harriet instructions on how to get to Pellner's house. "We have plenty of time to do that and for me to get to the meeting place." I was meeting Seth and Mike at a house near Spring Lake in Bedford.

While we drove to Pellner's house, I called Emil. "Are you free right now?"

"No. But I'm cheap." He laughed.

"I need your help." I filled him in on what was going on. I knew he was good with a gun because of the night in the cemetery.

"I'll be there," he said. I made arrangements for him to meet Harriet.

There was a police SUV parked in front of Pellner's house so I assumed he was home. I hoped he wasn't sleeping. With shift work you never knew. I knocked on the door while Harriet waited in the car. Pellner's wife opened it.

"Hi, Sarah."

"Is Scott here?" I asked.

"Sure. Let me get him. But first, thank you for finding that beautiful cobalt vase and the vintage valentine for me."

"You're welcome." Last Valentine's Day, Pellner had asked for help finding his wife something unique and had told me about her collection of blue glass. I'd quickly figured out he was talking about cobalt glass from the Depression era. I'd found an Art Deco cobalt vase and the valentine. I was glad they had made her happy. Pellner showed up, looking over his wife's shoulder. "I need to ask you something."

His dimple deepened, a sure sign he wasn't happy to

see me. But he'd probably been a step behind me all day. "I'll talk to Sarah on the porch, honey." He kissed his wife's cheek, stepped out on the porch, and closed the door behind him. He crossed his arms. "What?"

"I need you to trust me. We used to trust each other. Just a few months ago you asked me to help with an investigation."

"That was a few months ago when I did trust you."

I nodded. "Okay then. I understand. Never mind." I started to turn to go.

Pellner pinched the bridge of his nose. "I must be an idiot. What's going on?"

I handed him the picture of Mike's brother. "He's the kidnapper."

"Who is it?"

"Diego Titone. Mike's brother."

"Why do you think he's the kidnapper?"

I walked Pellner through everything I knew and told him about the meeting with Seth and Mike. Pellner didn't look happy to learn I'd tracked down Victoria, Gabe, and Gabe's neighbor. But he also didn't look surprised. "Emil and Harriet are going to keep an eye on the house from a safe distance just in case Diego or anyone else show up. I just wanted to tell you what was going on."

"I'm coming too."

I was relieved. We'd be safe. "Thank you." My voice choked up. I needed to hold it together for just a little bit longer. I told Pellner where Harriet and Emil were going to meet.

Thirty minutes later Harriet dropped me a half block away from the house where I was supposed to meet Seth and Mike. I was ten minutes early. I hadn't wanted to go back home for my car and risk running into Diego.

"Good luck," she said.

"Thanks. I feel bad for Mike."

"I hope your instinct is right."

"It is."

"Okay, I'm off to meet up with Emil and Pellner."

Houses on the street were modest Cape-styles, but the lots were fairly large. All of them on one side backed up to a creek. On the other side they backed up to more houses. A few had been torn down and replaced with ugly McMansions.

The street was a dead end, and the house we were meeting in was the last one on the block. It was painted pale green, the curtains were drawn, and no cars were parked in the drive or carport. I spotted Seth's car across the street, but not Mike's car as I walked down the block. The air was brisk, I was cold, and clouds gathered in the distance. I rubbed my hands together as I hurried along. I tried to look casual, but kept glancing about on the lookout for trouble. Fortunately, there were no signs of any.

I walked up the well-maintained brick sidewalk. And tried the door. It was unlocked, as Seth had said it would be. I stepped into the narrow hallway that was all too reminiscent of the house where I'd found Crystal Olson. Fortunately, I didn't see any feet sticking out into the hall. A staircase was to the left. The walls were wallpapered with a blue flower and ivy pattern. The colors were faded. The floors linoleum. I closed the door.

"Seth?" I called. "Mike?"

"In the kitchen." It was Mike. Whew.

I hurried down the hall, peeking in the rooms I passed. Living room to the right. Sparsely furnished with a faded rose-colored couch and two mismatched club chairs. More wallpaper. A closed door under the steps—probably a closet to the left, across from the closet there was a green-tiled full bath to the right. An odd quirk of houses in this area was to have a full bath on a floor with no bedrooms. I turned right into the kitchen and stopped. Mike and Seth were tied to metal folding chairs. Their mouths duct-taped shut. Diego stood there with a gun in his hand.

Chapter Thirty-Five

Mike and Seth both looked at me for a moment, then glared at Diego. Mike's eyes narrowed. Seth's large with rage. Both jerked on their bindings, but Diego had done a good job of tying them up. They must have arrived separately because I couldn't imagine Diego getting the jump on both of them at once.

The kitchen was small. No island or fancy appliances. Nothing out on the countertops. Two doors. One must be a pantry or lead to a basement and the other to the carport. I never realized how much Mike's brother sounded like Mike. Or maybe Diego was just adept at imitating voices. He'd sounded like Jack Nicholson on the phone calls. I kept glancing at Seth and Mike, but it was hard not to stare at the gun. Diego stood there, enjoying my reaction. Enjoying. How sick was that?

I hadn't imagined a scenario in which Diego would show up first. Emil, Harriet, and Pellner would have no way of knowing what kind of trouble we were in. They were supposed to watch the house just in case someone arrived. We'd all be dead before they realized something was wrong or saw Diego walk out the door. Here I was a hostage and the only one who could also be the negotiator.

"You tied up your own brother?"

"That was my brother until you two"—he gestured at Seth and me with the gun—"ruined him."

Mike made a growling noise and shook his head.

"You two turned him into some kind of sissy who dropped everything whenever either of you called." Diego shook his head like he regretted what he had to do.

Okay, that question had only made him angrier. I thought back to when Awesome had been angry at one of our meetings. About Harriet's calm, even voice that had diffused the situation. I would try to do the same thing. I summoned my inner Harriet, because my inner Sarah was terrified. "If you are mad at Mike, why put me through all of this?"

"To watch him squirm like a worm on a hook. Hurting you hurt him more than just killing him would have." Diego looked at Mike and shook his head.

It was almost exactly what I had told Harriet just the other day. I just had it wrong, I thought someone was going after Stella. I never dreamed Diego would betray Mike in this way.

"You should have seen him pacing around the apartment. 'Something's wrong with Sarah. I'm so worried about Sarah.' It was nauseating."

"Who was Crystal Olson to you?" I asked.

"My girlfriend until she decided to dump me."

I was horrified, but tried not to show it. However, the gleam of a smile on Diego's face as he watched me said otherwise. Had he really killed her because she dumped him? The memory of Mike's asking me to fix Diego up flashed through my head. "So you killed her?" There was no hope for the three of us if Diego would kill someone who broke up with him.

"She overdosed. I took that as a sign it was time to move forward with my plan."

That was what had set off this chain of events—a breakup and an overdose? It took a sick mind to be inspired by that. Maybe Diego had helped with Crystal's overdose. "Why Alice in Wonderland?"

"It was always my favorite story as a kid. I love all the layers to that story. Like I told you on the phone. It's an adventure story, and you gotta admit this has been one heck of an adventure for you."

"Who helped you? You couldn't have done everything by yourself. You don't know me or Ellington well enough."

"You know how many times Mike has dragged us out here? It isn't hard to get to know a little town and its goings on. Just go to the coffee shop, or the barber's or DiNapoli's. People in this town love to talk. And a kid I met at Danucci's didn't mind following you around."

The kid with the old eyes. Yeah, I'd seen him around. But it was a small town, and it hadn't ever struck me as unusual. That explained how Diego had ended up using Victoria and Gabe, since they both worked at Danucci's too.

"You are damned hard to kill," he said to me.

My dying easier wasn't exactly what I was hoping for Diego to say. "What are you talking about?"

"I thought Elmer would take you out at the auction in a fit of temper, but, in case he didn't, I had a backup plan or two in place. You evaded the drug dealers in the cemetery. I was really hoping you'd be with Alice Krandle in her house." He shook his head again. "Even when God sent me the fortuitous gas leak. You escaped."

Since we were talking about God all of the sudden I'd

go with that angle. "Maybe God doesn't want me dead. Maybe you should just put the gun down and walk away." Walk right out into Pellner's arms. "Maybe if you try to shoot me the gun's going to jam or explode and kill you." Maybe I should shut up. Maybe I should be begging and trying to appease Diego. But I didn't think that would work. In fact, I thought he'd enjoy it.

Diego glanced at the gun. "Naw. God wants you dead, and, even if he doesn't, I do. But actually, watching you suffer was almost as much fun as watching you die is going to be. All those times you dragged yourself up the stairs after I sent you on an adventure gave me joy. And not only that, but just look at Mike right now."

I did. His face was almost purple. He fought against his restraints.

"Mike made me suffer for years," Diego said. "It's great for him to get a little taste of what it's like."

I flicked my head toward Mike. "He's still your brother. Are you going to kill all of us? Kill him?" There was nothing in the kitchen I could grab to use as a weapon. I didn't have the hairspray in my pocket or the wine bottle in my purse. I had thought I'd be safe.

"He's going to watch you die. If he's learned his lesson, then we'll talk." Diego raised his gun. Pointed it at me.

I didn't want to die. I looked at Seth. "I love you."

The door to the right of Diego burst open. Pellner charged in wearing full SWAT gear. Diego swung the gun around and shot. Pellner fired too and fell back. Diego looked shocked. Blood spread across his chest. But he somehow lifted the gun again. Mike dove at his brother, chair and all, knocking him down.

The room filled with cops and noise. I glanced back

and forth between Seth and Pellner, not knowing which one to check on first. Seth jerked his head toward Pellner. I ran over to where Pellner lay on the floor. Pushed past one of the other officers leaning over him and dropped to my knees.

Pellner moaned and opened his eyes. "Son of a bitch, that hurts."

I could see the bullet imbedded dead center in his Kevlar vest. "Oh, thank heavens you're okay." Another cop helped Pellner up. I'd known Pellner was part of the Northeastern Massachusetts Law Enforcement Council's SWAT team, but I'd never seen them in action. I hoped I never did again.

I stood and turned back to see someone helping untie Mike. Tears streamed down his face. His brother. Mike leaned against a kitchen counter, pale and somehow looking smaller than normal. I couldn't begin to imagine what he was going through. I could barely stand to look. Diego had had no Kevlar vest to protect him from Pellner's shot. And Pellner's shot had been just as dead center as Diego's had been. Another cop was untying Seth. I ran to him, and we wrapped our arms around each other. I shook so hard I was surprised the dishes weren't rattling in the cupboards. Mike joined us.

"I'm sorry. I never thought he'd get here first. I didn't think he'd show up," Mike said. "I thought he'd headed out of town. To somewhere people couldn't be extradited from."

"Did you call the cops?" I asked Mike. Diego had found out somehow that we were going to be here.

"I didn't. But I'm sure glad they showed up."

"Me too." I couldn't think about what the outcome

would have been if not for Pellner. I turned to survey the room.

"Diego must have heard me on the phone with Seth," Mike said. "I can't imagine another way he would have found out we'd be here."

"What made you think he was involved?" I asked.

"Several things. I found out about the Alice in Wonderland costume this afternoon through a contact I have." Seth and I glanced at each other. Who would have told Mike that? "Diego always loved that story as a kid. It creeped me out. I started to think through things. Remember that day I said Diego had terrible taste in women and asked you to set him up?" I nodded. "I knew he was mad because he turned bright red."

"I thought he was blushing."

Mike shook his head. "He stormed out a few minutes later. He's been on edge lately, but I chalked it up to the breakup. Then he was so nice to you the day your client's house blew up. I loved my brother, but that just seemed out of character for him. Of course, I was hoping he was changing. Couldn't have been more wrong."

I didn't know Diego well enough to know what he was really like.

"But the final thing was seeing a picture of his ex and seeing how much she looked like you, Sarah. I wanted to meet with both you and Seth to talk this out. I held out some hope I was wrong. But if you both thought I was right, I was hoping to find a way to capture Diego without bloodshed."

We all glanced toward Diego. I wished there'd been a different outcome too. Sometimes it seemed like death was the easy way out.

I walked back over to Pellner. He was talking into his shoulder mic.

"You can release Harriet and Emil now," he said, then he clicked off the mic and looked at me.

"Release them?" I asked.

"I had them taken in for questioning about the kidnapper. I wanted to keep them safe and out of the middle of this." His dimple was deep, deep, deep.

"Thank you." I gestured at everyone. "Thank them for me. How did you know Diego was in here?"

"A tree. A man. Binoculars and a crack in the curtain. Basic police work."

"You called in the cops." I didn't add "after I asked you not to," because if he hadn't there would be three people dead right now.

He lifted his chin, looked down at me. "Them, I trust." He walked away, rubbing the spot where the bullet had hit.

He didn't have to add the "you, I don't." I got it. And it broke my heart a little.

When Troopers Kilgard and Rodriquez showed up, I knew we were in for a long night. For once I thought I detected a modicum of sympathy as Kilgard looked over the scene and at me. Two hours later, Seth, Mike, and I had been questioned and given permission to leave. Diego had been put in a body bag and taken away. We walked out to the street. A black SUV was idling at the curb, presumably to pick up Mike, because that was what he always rode in. We all looked at one another.

"I'm sorry." We said it in unison.

"You two have nothing to be sorry about," Mike said.

"I convinced you to work with me," Seth told Mike.

"I'm the one always asking you for help," I said.

"I was in the minute you asked, Seth. You know that. And Sarah"—he gave a small chuckle—"my world can be a dangerous place, and you provided a way to help someone who's a good person." Mike shook his head. "My brother used all that as an excuse. I should have seen his bad side, but I ignored any warning signs, and it almost got us all killed. I'm the one who's sorry." He shook his head again and walked to the SUV. He climbed in without looking back.

"My car's across the street," Seth said. "Let's go." He grabbed my hand. His hand was warm and reassuring. "I can't believe I asked Mike and his brothers to stay next door to you. To protect you."

"How could you know? I saw Diego every day and didn't figure it out." My heart hurt for Mike. But Seth's hand reminded me that, even in the dark, there was always some light.

I showered quickly Friday morning, hoping Mike was still next door. Seth had left at five and I'd gone back to sleep. Things still felt a little off between us. After he'd left he sent me a text saying an investigation determined that there was a faulty pipeline to Alice's house, but that it also showed signs of having been tampered with. Diego had lied yesterday when he tried to blame Alice's death on God. Instead it was an opportunity he'd latched on to. He somehow found out about the gas leak and I'd always wonder if he really had something to do with Alice passing out. What he hadn't said, and what I believed, was that if that hadn't worked, he would have killed Alice another way, if he had thought it would get to me. Get to Mike.

I had realized that Diego had been laying out a trail of clues for me to follow. Like leaving my address on the form at the auction house. If only I'd figured it out sooner. Alice might be alive.

I went out my door. A man I recognized from prior interactions sat on the folding chair in the hall. He was one of Mike's trusted men. His nickname was Two Toes. I still didn't want to know why. He wore an old T-shirt that pulled tight across his paunch. Sweatpants and running shoes with no socks, like he'd gotten dressed hastily. His gray hair was in disarray. His arms tattooed. He stood as I walked toward him. Eyes red, skin blotchy like he'd been crying.

"I need to see Mike," I told him. "How's he doing?"

"Not good."

I tried to prepare myself for a Mike I wasn't used to seeing.

Two Toes knocked on the door and opened it. "She's here."

I guess Mike was expecting me. I went into the living room. Francesco was slumped on the couch. Mike stood by the window. Dressed in slacks and a sweater. Clear eyed. Now that I was here, I wasn't sure what I wanted to say. "I'm sorry" or "are you okay?" seemed inadequate. "You're still here." Was that the best I could do? I knew how it felt to think your brother had turned against you. What Diego had done was way worse than anything mine had done to me.

"We will be for a few more days while we clean house in Boston and figure out who was helping Diego."

I nodded. "I'm glad you're staying." It would be nice to have someone next door.

"I found out that Diego killed Jimmy and dumped him in the harbor."

From what Mike had told me about him last January, Jimmy had been easily manipulated. And the Titones were all expert manipulators when they wanted to be.

"Why would Diego do that?"

"Because Jimmy knew that Diego was hatching a plot to take over."

"How sad. I'm sorry."

"Do you know what the name Diego means?"

I shook my head no.

"Supplanter. One who replaces. I should have seen it coming."

Mike must be carrying a lot of guilt around because of his brother's actions. "You're a victim here too."

"Yeah. And I don't even know how to be one."

"No one does. It will take time to learn how to live with it."

Chapter Thirty-Six

Saturday morning the sun was warm on the town common. It was the perfect day for a garage sale. Yesterday had been a blur of finishing pricing and organizing for today. Harriet had come over to help and let me know that Emil hadn't been involved in any of this. But Harriet still thought his obsession with *The Phantom of the Opera* was creepy. I'd been sure it wasn't him. Relieved that no one had to tell Rosalie that her nephew wasn't the man she thought he was.

I'd also had to go to the police department to give another statement. I'd found out through Seth that Diego had not only been dating Crystal, but also a woman in Seth's office and blackmailing someone in the police department.

Towns like Ellington have such small police departments that Diego really would have known if I'd contacted anyone there. I shuddered at the thought. Maybe he had hoped I would. It bugged me that I wouldn't ever know for sure if I'd saved Stella on my own or if Diego had led me to her. In the end I guess it didn't matter since she was safe.

I had some guilt to deal with. I'd thought back wondering why Diego would go after Alice. But the morning of her sale I'd invited all of the Titones to attend. They hadn't shown up, but it was probably why of all the people I knew, Diego had picked Alice. It would take a long time to get over that.

It turned out the kid from Danucci's with the old eyes was the son of the realtor who had the listing for the Ghannams' house and the empty store where Diego had left the Alice in Wonderland doll. It was how Diego had known the properties were empty. The kid claimed he'd only made calls. That he had thought it was all a joke and didn't realize Diego was actually kidnapping and killing people.

However, the kid's phone records showed he had known about the drug deal going down. The police had also found out that he worked part time at the auction, so he had helped set that up. And he'd been the one to follow me after the auction to try to scare me. He'd never know how well it had worked.

Damaris had gotten hold of me and told me that the anti-Sarah group had disbanded and that she was confident she'd convinced them to make sure they didn't blame the wrong person for the actions of their loved ones. It confirmed what Louisa had said. I just hoped they were both right. Damaris had also told me I was a lucky woman to be dating Seth. I had gotten the impression that if we ever broke up she'd move in faster than Freud could analyze someone.

I redirected my thoughts to the sale. Tables were loaded with goods to be sold. It was exactly two years since I'd organized a garage sale for Carol. Two years since I'd started a new life. The women from the base stood at the ready. All we needed were customers. It was oddly quiet. I'd never done a sale before where there weren't a few annoying early birds trying to get the jump on everyone. Harriet was talking to one couple when there should be twenty. A few people had stopped by, but I was worried this fundraiser wasn't going to raise any funds.

"Rebecca, I'm sorry," I said a few minutes later. "I can't imagine why more people haven't stopped by yet." I'd checked my calendar when I had first started planning this event to make sure there weren't any conflicting events that would keep people from coming.

"It's okay," Rebecca said.

Zoey had wanted to have the event on base, but I'd convinced the group that more people would come if we did it on the town common. I couldn't have been more wrong. I was wrong about Zoey being involved in Stella's kidnapping too. That was a relief, but I hoped she hadn't somehow sabotaged this event. Rebecca looked over my shoulder. Her eyes got wide, and her mouth opened. I whirled around, wondering what now.

People were pouring out of the old town hall, led by the DiNapolis. It wasn't an angry mob coming to boot me out of town. The people carried signs that said "Congratulations on two years of business" and "We love you, Sarah." I clapped my hands to my mouth. Rebecca tapped my shoulder and pointed to the Congregational church. Its doors were flung open. People were carrying tables out and putting them up. A band set up, and an upbeat tune soon blasted across the common. Other people brought food out of the church.

"Did you know about this?" I asked Rebecca.

She smiled. "I did."

"Here I was having a panic attack, and you knew all along."

"Yep. I just love a good surprise."

The DiNapolis reached me and pulled me in for hugs. We were surrounded by people I loved.

"Thank you," I managed to choke out. My throat had a lump the size of a serving of Bedford Farms ice cream.

"I'm sorry I tried to set you up with Emil earlier. You'll always be part of our family, no matter what," Rosalie said. She looked at Angelo. "He gave me a little talking to about that."

"We love you, kiddo," Angelo said. He hadn't called me that in a long time.

A happy tear rolled down my face. "I love you both too. Thank you for doing all this." I swept my hand around until it struck a hard chest. Seth. I hadn't seen him in the crowd.

"It was Seth's idea," Angelo said. "He knew what a rough time you've had." Angelo stood looking back and forth between us.

"Let's give them a moment," Rosalie said.

"I have a story I want to tell Sarah," Angelo protested.

"Come on, Angelo. Let's go make sure the lasagna is hot." Rosalie winked at me.

"They'd better be hot, or they're going to find out they messed with the bull." Angelo put his hands on either side of his head and pointed his index fingers like they were horns. He'd done that one of the first times I had met him. "They don't want to get the horns," he said as they walked off.

I turned to Seth. We hadn't seen each other since yesterday morning. And I'd been worried about how things were between us. While this was a lovely gesture, I realized it might take Seth a while to completely trust me again. "Thank you. I'm almost speechless, and you know that doesn't happen often."

Seth kissed me. "You're welcome. You deserve it. Since

I met you, you've helped raise Ellington's profile, brought tourists into town, solved some murders. I thought it was time we thanked you."

We looked over the town common. People were buying things. Kids were running around. People were eating and laughing. Carol waved to me from a table where she sat with her husband and three kids. It was almost perfect. If only Stella were here. I'd had a message from her that she'd been offered a small part in a movie based on an audition the director of Phantom had recommended her for. She was considering taking the part. I wondered if she'd ever come back.

"What?" Seth asked. "You looked sad for a moment."

I smiled up at him. "I'm fine."

"I'm sorry for what I said about you trusting Harriet more than me. Turns out you were right about that, since Diego was using an employee in my office."

I shook my head. "It wasn't you I didn't trust. It was the possibility of someone in your office finding something out. I'm sorry that I made you feel that way."

"Forgive me?" he asked.

"If you forgive me," I said.

He kissed me instead of answering.

"I love you." Once upon a time it had been so hard for me to say that to him. Not anymore.

We heard car doors slam over by my apartment. I turned to see Stella climbing out of Awesome's car. Seconds later she was running across the grass and flinging her arms around me. It was as if I'd conjured her by thinking about her. I hugged Stella tight.

"I'm back," she said as we pulled apart.

"Thank heavens. I've missed you so much. But what about the movie?"

"I'm going to go back in a few weeks for filming. It's a small independent film backed by some big names. Can you imagine me in a movie?"

"I can," I said. "You'll be wonderful."

Stella's green eyes sparkled; her hair shone. Happiness oozed out of her pores—if such a thing could happen. I looked over her shoulder to see Awesome and Pellner standing there.

"Go on, you two," Stella said, looking at Awesome and Pellner.

"I trust you, Sarah," Pellner said. His dimple not so deep as to scare me.

"I'd depend on you to find anyone," Awesome said. "Even if it meant bending some rules." He glanced down at his shoes for a moment. "I get it. I understand what you did and probably would have done the same thing."

I nodded slowly. Stella must have done a lot of convincing. "It wasn't easy. I hope I never have to put anyone in that position again. But thank you." Even though they had said the right things, I knew it would take some time for them to actually believe it.

"We have a surprise for you," Awesome said.

"A surprise?" I couldn't imagine what he was talking about.

Awesome and Pellner looked back at the car and made a "come here" motion with their hands. The back passenger door opened. A foot came out, and then Alice Krandle stood up.

For the second time today I clapped my hands to my mouth for a moment. "How?" I looked at Pellner and Awesome as Alice strode over to us. I turned to Seth. "Did you know?"

He shook his head. "I didn't."

"Alice was out for a walk when her house exploded," Pellner said. "After you and almost everyone else had left the scene, Alice came walking up the sidewalk. I hustled her into the back of my police SUV so no one would see her. I made a snap decision to hide her for a couple of days."

"Two supposed attempts on her life made the decision for Pellner," Awesome added. "And he didn't tell anyone else what he was up to."

I gave Alice a big hug when she arrived by my side. She stood stiffly accepting the hug and didn't push me away. She gave me an awkward pat on the shoulder as I breathed in her spearmint chewing gum scent.

"I agreed because I didn't want the third time to be a charm," Alice said.

"Where have you been?" I asked.

"I've been at the Parker House Hotel in Boston, spoiled rotten with room service and enjoying Parker House rolls and Boston cream pie."

The Parker House had originated both.

"So Diego tampered with Alice's medications and that's why she passed out?"

"We don't think so," Awesome said. "He either heard it on the police scanner or through his source at the police station. We talked to Alice's doctor and looked over the tests he ran that day. Nothing seemed out of the ordinary. But Diego letting you think he'd done it worked into his whole scheme."

"I might just go back to the Parker House," Alice said, "since I don't have a house to live in. A woman of my age deserves Boston cream pie on a regular basis."

We all laughed at that.

"Come on," Stella said to the three of them. "Let's go get some food."

Seth and I watched as they walked off. He slung an arm around my shoulders and squeezed me to him. The rest of the morning passed in a blur of friends and strangers stopping to congratulate me. Miss Belle donated a hefty sum of money to the fund. Charlie auctioned off a beautiful diamond necklace. James, Eleanor, and other base friends stopped by. Frida Chida auctioned off a month of cleaning, and my former client Kitty auctioned off a chance for someone to have his or her pet painted by her. The event was successful beyond my wildest dreams, and my heart was full.

By two we were cleaning up. I watched as Seth rolled up his sleeves and carried tables back into the church. I was lucky to have him in my life. Lucky to have so many friends and this wonderful place to live. In the past people had questioned why I stayed here instead of going back to California after my divorce. There I would have returned as a failure. Here, I'd become a success. I looked over the town common again at all the people pitching in. This was why I stayed.

Acknowledgments

To John Talbot and Gary Goldstein—it doesn't seem that long ago that a garage sale mystery series was just an idea we were tossing around, and here we are at book nine! Thank you both for all you've done for me.

Thanks to Mark Bergin, a retired police lieutenant from Alexandria, Virginia, and the author of the fabulous book *Apprehension*. Also to Bruce Coffin, a retired detective sergeant from Portland, Maine, who writes the bestselling Detective John Byron Mystery series. All errors are mine!

Fabulous independent editor Barb Goffman, this was barely a story when I gave you my manuscript to edit; with your guidance you helped me turn it into a novel. Barb continued to give advice and support up until the moment I hit send.

To Jason Allen-Forrest, Christy Nichols, and Mary Titone—thank you for your friendship and for being my beta readers. Your eagle eyes caught many mistakes I didn't even notice.

To Ashley Harris, beloved former neighbor—thank you for talking me through the struggles military families face when they have a family member who has special needs. And thank you for talking to me about rare diseases.

Thanks to Lou and Marilyn DiNapoli, our wonderful neighbors in Massachusetts, for sharing your amazing stories with me.

Jennifer McGee, you are virtually wonderful, and I don't know what I'd do without you.

Julie Hennrikus, who knew a car ride from Lake Winnipesaukee to Logan Airport could be so productive. The time we spent plotting was invaluable. What would I have done without you?!!!

To The Wickeds—Jessie Crockett, Julie Hennrikus, Edith Maxwell, Liz Mugavero, and Barbara Ross—by the time this book comes out we will have been blogging together for seven and a half years. To all who wish to write, find your people—the five of you are mine.

To my family who supports me through the ups and downs of the creative process—I wouldn't be here without you. Thank you for being smart enough to stay out of my way when my deadline is near. As my daughter said, "We avoid her around her deadline because all she has on her mind is murder."

Keep reading for a special excerpt of the first book in an all-new series by Sherry Harris!

FROM BEER TO ETERNITY
A Chloe Jackson, Sea Glass Saloon Mystery

A whip-smart librarian's fresh start comes with a tart twist in this perfect cocktail of murder and mystery—with a romance chaser.

With Chicago winters in the rearview mirror, Chloe Jackson is making good on a promise: help her late friend's grandmother run the Sea Glass Saloon in the Florida Panhandle. To Chloe's surprise, feisty Vivi Slidell isn't the frail retiree Chloe expects. Nor is Emerald Cove. It's less a sleepy fishing village than a panhandle hotspot overrun with land developers and tourists. But it's a Sea Glass regular who has mysteriously crossed the cranky Vivi. When their bitter argument comes to a head and he's found dead behind the bar, guess who's the number one suspect?

In trying to clear Vivi's name, Chloe discovers the old woman isn't the only one in Emerald Cove with secrets. Under the laid-back attitude, sparkling white beaches, and small town ways, something terrible is brewing. And the sure way a killer can keep those secrets bottled up is to finish off one murder with a double shot: aimed at Chloe and Vivi.

Look for FROM BEER TO ETERNITY, on sale now.

Chapter One

Remember the big moment in *The Wizard of Oz* movie when Dorothy says, "Toto, I've a feeling we're not in Kansas anymore?" Boy, could I relate. Only a twister hadn't brought me here; a promise had. This wasn't the Emerald City, but the Emerald Coast of Florida. Ruby slippers wouldn't get me home to Chicago. And neither would my red, vintage Volkswagen Beetle, if anyone believed the story I'd spread around. Nothing like lying to people you'd just met. But it couldn't be helped. Really, it couldn't.

The truth was, as a twenty-eight-year-old children's librarian, I never imagined I'd end up working in a beach bar in Emerald Cove, Florida. In the week I'd been here I'd already learned toddlers and drunk people weren't that different. Both were unsteady on their feet, prone to temper tantrums one minute and sloppy hugs the next, and they liked to take naps wherever they happened to be. Go figure. But knowing that wasn't helping me right now. I was currently giving the side-eye to one of the regulars.

"Joaquín, why the heck is Elwell wearing that armadillo on his head?" I asked in a low voice. Elwell Pugh sat at the end of the bar, his back to the beach, nursing a beer in his wrinkled hands. I had known life would be different in the Panhandle of Florida, but armadillo shells on people's heads?—that was a real conversation starter.

"It's not like it's alive, Chloe," Joaquín Diaz answered, as if that made sense of a man wearing a hollowed-out armadillo shell as a hat. Joaquín raised two perfectly manicured eyebrows at me.

What? Maybe it was some kind of lodge thing down here. My uncle had been a member of a lodge in Chicago complete with funny fez hats, parades, and clowns riding miniature motorcycles. But he usually didn't sit in bars in his hat—at least not alone.

Elwell sported the deep tan of a Florida native. A few faded tattoos sprinkled his arms. His gray hair, cropped short, and grizzled face made him look unhappy—maybe he was. I'd met Elwell when I started working at the Sea Glass. I already knew that Elwell was a great tipper, didn't make off-color comments, and kept his hands to himself. That alone made him a saint among men to me, because all three were rare when waitressing in a bar. At least in this one, the only bar I'd ever worked in.

It hadn't taken me long to figure out Elwell's good points. But I'd seen more than one tourist start to walk in off the beach, spot him, and leave. There were other bars farther down the beach, plenty of places to drink. So, Elwell and his armadillo hat seemed like a problem to me.

"Elwell started wearing it a few weeks back," Joaquín said with a shrug that indicated *what are you going to do about it*. Joaquín's eyes were almost the same color as the aquamarine waters of the Gulf of Mexico, which sparkled across the wide expanse of beach in front of the Sea Glass. With his tousled dark hair, Joaquín looked way more like a Hollywood heartthrob than a fisherman by morning, bartender by afternoon. That combination had the women who stopped in here swooning. He looked like he was a few years older than me.

"It keeps the gub'ment from tracking me," Elwell said in a drawl that dragged "guh-buh-men-t" into four syllables.

Apparently, Elwell had exceptional hearing, or the armadillo shell was some kind of echo chamber.

"Some fools," Elwell continued, "believe tinfoil will stop the gub'ment, but they don't understand radio waves."

Great, a science lesson from a man with an armadillo on his head. I nodded, keeping a straight face because I didn't want to anger a man who seemed a tad crazy. He watched me for a moment and went back to staring at his beer. I grinned at Joaquín and he smiled at me. Joaquín didn't seem concerned, so maybe I shouldn't be either. I glanced at Elwell again. His eyes always had a calculating look that made me think there was a purpose for the armadillo shell that had nothing to do with the "gub'ment," but what did I know?

Chapter Two

"Whatta ya gotta do to get a drink round here?" a man yelled from the front of the bar. He was one of two men playing a game of rummy at a high top. They were in here almost every day.

"Not shout for a drink, Buford," Joaquín yelled back. "Or get your lazy as—" he caught himself as he glanced at Vivi, the owner and our boss, who frowned at him from across the room, "asteroid up here."

Vivi's face relaxed into a smile. She would have made a good children's librarian considering how she tried to keep things PG around here. Joaquín tilted his head toward me. I took a pad out of the little black apron wrapped around my waist and trotted over to Buford.

"Would you like another Bud?" I asked Buford. "Or something else?"

"Sure would," Buford said. There was a "duh" note in his voice suggesting why else would he be yelling to Joaquín.

"Another Maker's Mark whiskey?" I looked at Buford's card playing partner as I wrote his beer order on my pad.

"You have a good memory," he said, looking at his half empty glass. "But I'm good."

Good grief, I'd been serving him the same drink all week, I'd hoped I could remember his order. I made the rounds of the other tables. By each drink I wrote a brief description of who ordered it: beer, black hair rummy player; martini, dirty, yellow Hawaiian shirt; gin and tonic, needs a bigger bikini. I'd seen way more oiled-up, sweaty, sandy body parts than I cared to in the week I'd been here. Not even my dad, a retired plumber, had seen this many cracks at a meeting of the Chicago plumbers union.

Those images kept haunting my dreams, along with giant beach balls knocking me down, talking dolphins, and tidal waves. I'd yet to figure out what any of them meant— well, maybe I'd figured out one of them. But I wasn't going to think about that now.

Nope, I preferred to focus on the scenery, because, boy, this place had atmosphere—and that didn't even include Elwell and his armadillo shell hat. The Sea Glass Saloon I'd pictured before I'd arrived had swinging, saloon-style doors, bawdy dancing girls, and wagon-wheel chandeliers. This was more like a tiki hut than an old western saloon, though thankfully I didn't have to wear a sarong and co-conut bra top. I could fill one out, but I preferred comfortable tank tops. Besides, the Gulf of Mexico was the real star of the show. The whole front of the bar was open to it, with retractable glass doors leading to a covered deck.

The Sea Glass catered to locals who needed a break from the masses of tourists who descended on Emerald Cove and Destin, the bigger town next door, every summer. Not that Vivi would turn down tourists' money. She needed their money to stay open, as far as I could tell.

Like Dorothy, I was up for a new adventure and finding

my way in a place that was so totally different from my life in Chicago. I only hoped that I'd find my own versions of Dorothy's Scarecrow, Tin Man, and Cowardly Lion to help me on the way. So far, the only friend I'd made—and I wasn't too sure about that—was Joaquín. He, and everybody, seemed nice enough, but I was still trying to adjust to the relaxed Southern attitude that prevailed among the locals in the Panhandle of Florida. It was also called the Emerald Coast, LA—lower Alabama, and get this—the Redneck Riviera.

You could have knocked me over with a palm frond when I heard that nickname. The chamber of commerce never used it, nor would you see the name in a TV ad. But the locals used it with a mixture of pride and disdain. Some wanted to brush it under the proverbial rug, while others embraced it in its modern-day form—people who were proud of their local roots.

The Emerald Coast stretched from Panama City, Florida, fifty miles east of here, to Pensacola, Florida, fifty miles to the west. The rhythm and flow was such a contrast from the go, go, go lifestyle in Chicago, where I'd lived my entire life. The local attitude matched the blue-green waves of the Gulf of Mexico, which lapped gently on sand so white you'd think Mr. Clean came by every night to tidy up.

As I walked back to the bar Joaquín's hips swayed to the island music playing over an old speaker system. He was in perpetual motion, with his hips moving like some suave combination of Elvis and Ricky Martin. My hips didn't move like that even on my best day—even if I'd had a couple of drinks. Joaquín glanced at me as he added gin, tonic, and lime to a rocks glass. I'd learned that term a couple of days ago. Bars had names for everything, and "the short glasses" didn't cut it in the eyes of my boss, Vivi Jo Slidell. And yeah, she was as Southern as her name sounded. I watched with interest as Joaquín grabbed a cocktail shaker, adding gin, dry vermouth, and olive brine.

"Want to do the honors?" Joaquín asked, holding up the cocktail shaker.

I glanced at the row of women sitting at the bar, one almost drooling over Joaquín. One had winked at him so much it looked like she had an eye twitch, and one was now looking at me with an openly hostile expression. Far be it from me to deprive anyone from watching Joaquín's hips while he shook the cocktail.

"You go ahead," I said with a grin and a small tilt of my head toward his audience. The hostile woman started smiling again. "Have you ever thought about dancing professionally?"

"Been there, danced that," Joaquín answered.

"Really?" the winker asked.

"Oh, honey, I shook my bootie with Beyoncé, Ricky Martin, and Justin Timberlake among others when I was a backup dancer."

"What are you doing here, then?" I was astonished.

"My husband and I didn't like being apart." Joaquín started shaking the cocktail, but threw in some extra moves, finishing with a twirl. "Besides, I get to be outside way more than I did when I was living out in LA. There, I was always stuck under hot lights on a soundstage. Here, it's a hot sun out on the ocean. Much better." He winked at the winker, and she blushed.

The women had looked disappointed when he mentioned his husband, but that explained Joaquín's immunity to the women who threw themselves at him. He didn't wear a ring, but maybe as a fisherman it was a danger. My father didn't wear one because of his plumbing, but he couldn't be more devoted to my mom.

"Put three olives on a pick, please," Joaquín asked. While he finished his thing with the shaker, I grabbed one of the picks—not the kind for guitars; these were little sticks with sharp points on one end—fancy plastic toothpicks really. Ours were pink, topped with a little flamingo, and I strung the olives on as Joaquín strained the drink into a martini glass. "One dirty martini," Joaquín said with a hand flourish.

I popped open a beer and poured it into a glass, holding the glass at an angle so the beer had only a skiff of foam on the top. It was a skill I was proud of because my father had taught me when I was fourteen. Other fathers taught their daughters how to play chess. My friends knew the difference between a king and a rook. Mine made sure I knew the importance of low foam. You can guess which skill was more popular at frat parties in college.

As I distributed the drinks, I thought about Boone Slidell, my best friend since my first day of college. The promise that brought me here? I'd made it to him one night at the Italian Village's bar in downtown Chicago. We'd had so much fun that night, acting silly before his deployment to Afghanistan with the National Guard. But later that night he'd asked me, should anything happen to him on his deployment, would I come help his grandmother, Vivi. He had a caveat. I couldn't tell her he'd asked me to.

"Yes," I'd said. "Of course." We'd toasted with shots of tequila and laughter, never dreaming nine months later that my best friend in the world would be gone. Twenty-eight years old and gone. I'd gotten a leave of absence from my job as a children's librarian and had come for the memorial service, planning to stay for as long as Boone's grandmother needed me. But Vivi wasn't the bent-over, pathetic figure I'd been expecting to save. In fact, she was glaring at me now from across the room, making it perfectly clear that she neither needed nor wanted my help. I smiled at her as I went back behind the bar.

Vivi was a beautiful woman with thick silver hair and a gym-perfect body. Seventy had never looked so good. She wore gold, strappy wedge sandals that made my feet ache just looking at them, cropped white skinny jeans, and an off-the-shoulder, gauzy aqua top. I always felt a little messy when I was with her.

"A promise made is a promise kept." I could hear my dad's voice in my head as clear as if he were standing next to me. It was what kept me rooted here, even with Vivi's dismissive attitude. I'd win her over sooner or later. Few hadn't eventually succumbed to my winning personality or my big brown eyes. Eyes that various men had described as liquid chocolate, doelike, and one jerk who said they looked like mud pies after I turned him down for a date.

In my dreams, everyone succumbed to my personality. Reality was such a different story. Some people apparently thought I was an acquired taste. Kind of like ouzo, an anise-flavored aperitif from Greece, that Boone used to drink sometimes. I smiled at the memory.

"What are you grinning about?" Joaquín asked. Today he wore a neon-green Hawaiian shirt with a hot-pink hibiscus print.

"Nothing." I couldn't admit it was the thought of people succumbing to me. "Am I supposed to be wearing Hawaiian shirts to work?" I asked. He wore one every day. I'd been wearing T-shirts and shorts. No one had mentioned a dress code.

"You can wear whatever your little heart desires, as long as you don't flash too much skin. Vivi wouldn't like that." He glanced over my blue tank top and shorts.

"But you wear Hawaiian shirts every day," I said.

"Honey, you can't put a peacock in beige."

I laughed and started cutting the lemons and limes we used as garnishes. The juice from both managed to find the tiniest cut and burn in my fingers. But Vivi—don't dare put a "Miss" in front of "Vivi," despite the tradition here in the South—wasn't going to chase me away by assigning me all the menial tasks, including cleaning the toilets, mopping the floors, and cutting the fruit. I was made of tougher stuff than that and had been since I was ten. To paraphrase the Blues Brothers movie, I was "on a mission from" Boone.

"What'd those poor little limes ever do to you?"

I looked up. Joaquín stood next to me with a garbage bag in his hand and a devilish grin on his face. He'd been a bright spot in a somber time. He smiled at me and headed out the back door of the bar.

"You're cheating," Buford yelled from his table near the retractable doors. He leaped up, knocking over his chair just as Vivi passed behind him. The chair bounced into Vivi, she teetered on her heels and then slammed to the ground, her head barely missing the concrete floor. The Sea Glass wasn't exactly fancy.

Oh, no. Maybe incidents like this were why Boone thought I needed to be here. Why Vivi needed help. The man didn't notice Vivi, still on the floor. Probably didn't even realize he'd done it. Everyone else froze, while Buford grabbed the man across from him by the collar and dragged him out of his chair knocking cards off the table as he did.

I put down the knife and hustled around the bar. "Buford. You stop that right now." I used the firm voice I occasionally had to use at the library. Vivi wouldn't allow any gambling in here. Up to this point there hadn't been any trouble.

Buford let go of his friend. I kept steaming toward him. "You knocked over Vivi." I lowered my voice, a technique I'd learned as a librarian to diffuse situations. "Now, help her up and apologize."

He looked down at me, his face red. I jammed my hands on my hips and lifted my chin. He was a good foot taller than me and outweighed me by at least one hundred pounds. I stood my ground. That would teach him to mess with a children's librarian, even one on a leave of absence. I'd dealt with tougher guys than him. Okay, they had been five years old, but it still counted.

He turned to Vivi and helped her up. "I'm sorry, Vivi. How about I buy a round for the house?"

Oh, thank heavens. For a minute there, I thought he was going to punch me. Vivi looked down at her palms, red from where they'd broken her fall. "Okay. But you pull something like that again and you're banned for life."

Connect with U(s)

Visit us online at
KensingtonBooks.com
to read more from your favorite authors, see books
by series, view reading group guides, and more.

Join us on social media

for sneak peeks, chances to win books and prize packs,
and to share your thoughts with other readers.

facebook.com/kensingtonpublishing
twitter.com/kensingtonbooks

Tell us what you think!

To share your thoughts, submit a review,
or sign up for our eNewsletters, please visit:
KensingtonBooks.com/TellUs.